A guy darted across the street—tall, broad, muscular—and leaped into action. He threw a powerful arm up and into the thief's chest, stopping the perpetrator in his tracks.

Her mugger went down in a hard sprawl, dropping the knife.

The thief scrambled away from the bigger man as if terrified, grabbed his knife and bolted across traffic. Horns blared and cars screeched to a halt.

Immediate relief flooded her, and her body released the fear and anger that held her muscles tight. She had never seen anything so heroic except in movies and TV shows.

The do-gooder picked up her purse and jogged down the block to her.

Up close, he was more of everything.

"Care for a little assistance?" he asked, gesturing to the glass and her bare feet.

"Uh, yes. Please. Thank you."

Although she couldn't imagine how he'd be of any more assistance. Then he swept her up from the sidewalk and into his arms like she weighed nothing.

HIGH-PRIORITY ASSET

JUNO RUSHDAN

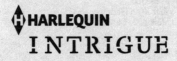

HARLEQUIN
INTRIGUE

Thank you to my very own Brenda C. I can always count on you to drag me out of my writing cave and to be a cheerleader in my corner since the beginning of my writing career.

ISBN-13: 978-1-335-13686-2

High-Priority Asset

Copyright © 2020 by Juno Rushdan

Recycling programs for this product may not exist in your area.

This edition published by arrangement with Harlequin Books S.A.

For questions and comments about the quality of this book, please contact us at CustomerService@Harlequin.com.

Harlequin Enterprises ULC
22 Adelaide St. West, 40th Floor
Toronto, Ontario M5H 4E3, Canada
www.Harlequin.com

Printed in U.S.A.

Juno Rushdan is the award-winning author of steamy, action-packed romantic thrillers that keep you on the edge of your seat. She writes about kick-ass heroes and strong heroines fighting for their lives as well as their happily-ever-afters. As a veteran air force intelligence officer, she uses her background supporting Special Forces to craft realistic stories that make you sweat and swoon. Juno currently lives in the DC area with her patient husband, two rambunctious kids and a spoiled rescue dog. To receive a FREE book from Juno, sign up for her newsletter at junorushdan.com/mailing-list. Also be sure to follow Juno on BookBub for the latest on sales at bit.ly/BookBubJuno.

Books by Juno Rushdan

Harlequin Intrigue

A Hard Core Justice Thriller

Hostile Pursuit
Witness Security Breach
High-Priority Asset

Visit the Author Profile page at Harlequin.com.

CAST OF CHARACTERS

Horatio "Dutch" Haas—A former Delta Force operator, he's part of the US Marshals' Fugitive Apprehension Response Team in Louisiana. He fits the right profile for an undercover assignment to recruit a high-priority asset. If he fails, sensitive WITSEC data and the personal information of the marshals based in San Diego will be auctioned on the black market.

Isabel Vargas—Owner of Kismet, an upscale art gallery. She is independently wealthy thanks to the inheritance her father left her. She's desperate to move on after a bad breakup that still haunts her.

Brenda Reaver—Best friends with Isabel for many years and assistant at Kismet, she is loyal and supportive.

Dante Emilio Vargas—Isabel's uncle, whom she loves dearly. Most know him as an upstanding pillar of the community, but is he really the head of a powerful drug cartel?

Chad Ellis—A prominent businessman and Isabel's ex-boyfriend.

Will Draper—US marshal in charge of the San Diego office who is running Dutch's assignment in LA.

Allison Chen-Boyd—A deputy marshal from San Diego sent to LA to support Dutch.

Chapter One

No matter where she went or what she did, Isabel Vargas couldn't escape *him*.

Some days were better than others, but Thursdays were the worst. The one night of the week she closed her art gallery alone so her best friend and assistant, Brenda, could take a yoga class across town with the hottest instructor in Santa Monica.

The one night she relived the traumatic encounter with her ex. Remembered the bruises, his breath on the back of her neck, his angry hands on her skin. His body holding hers captive. The malevolent rasp of his voice, his vile words pouring into her ears, punctuated by one delusional phrase he kept repeating. *I love you.*

The doorbell rang. She jumped at the buzzing sound, her heart racing. Drawing in a deep breath, Isabel calmed herself. She powered down her laptop, grabbed her quilted-leather purse and turned off the lights on the upper level of the gallery. Going as slowly as possible, she hoped whoever was at the locked front door would go away.

Please, don't be him. Please.

The doorbell buzzed again, pitching her nerves higher. She rummaged in her handbag and pulled out the tan bottle. Tiny white pills rattled inside. Her therapist had prescribed Ativan after her last incident with *him*, which had necessitated a restraining order. Isabel refused to think or speak his name. Doing so only gave him power when she needed to reclaim it.

She'd started jogging three miles every other morning, taken up boxing, Krav Maga and city-safety classes for women. She even got a dog. A ferocious Doberman named McQueen that she'd had trained as a guard dog. Keeping him in the office had proven too confined a space and customers got antsy around him in the gallery, so he was at doggie day care on Montana Avenue.

From the railing that overlooked the ground floor, she couldn't see who was at the front door. The bell rang in frantic succession. The irritating buzzer reverberated inside her.

Isabel popped the lid, put a pill in her mouth and swallowed it dry. Twice a day, every day. It kept the benzodiazepine in her system and her on an even keel.

She took her time down the stairs, her Jimmy Choos clacking against the dark hardwood of the steps. At the bottom, she saw a man wearing a suit and tie standing out front.

Spotting her, he banged on the glass door. "Hi! I was hoping someone was still here."

She edged closer. "What do you want?"

"I know you just closed ten minutes ago."

Every Thursday, at seven on the dot, she locked the door and finished wrapping up until she was ready to leave.

"You're usually open until eight," he said, glancing at the sign. "Except Thursdays, apparently. It's my anniversary and my wife has been dying to get that painting, the waterfall by Kush." He pointed to the far-left wall behind her, but she didn't turn and look at it.

Isabel kept her eyes on the man.

He was clean-cut and appeared pleasant enough, but the same had been said about Ted Bundy. The United States had more serial killers than any other country and Isabel knew firsthand what kind of twisted soul could hide behind a dazzling smile and a good suit.

"Sorry." She lifted the flap of her purse and stuck her hand inside, fumbling over her EpiPen and grabbing hold of her pepper spray. "You'll have to come back tomorrow." No one ever died from too much paranoia.

"Oh, please. I'm only ten minutes late. Don't make my wife suffer for my poor planning." He looked exasperated and distraught.

If he was being genuine, Isabel felt for him and his wife, but it wasn't her problem. "No purchases after closing, but tomorrow, I'll give you a ten percent discount." She'd take the money out of her forty percent commission. "I'll even write a note apologizing to your wife on your behalf, telling her it was my fault the gift was a day late."

"If I don't come home with the Kush, she might finally divorce me." His voice grew more insistent. "I'd hate to lose the best woman in the world because I ran ten minutes behind. Please. Can you help me?"

Isabel pulled out her pepper spray with her left hand and pointed it in his direction—a show of force that she meant business despite the door separating them—and took out her cell phone with her right. "Leave. Now. Or I call the cops."

"Whoa, lady." He put up both hands. "I'll buy her jewelry instead." With a scowl, he backed up to the curb, then he ran across the street, hopped in his Lexus and sped off.

"Good luck," she muttered under her breath. All the jewelry stores in the area were closed too by now. She dialed the valet at the parking garage she used two blocks down. "Hi, Jim, it's Isabel."

"Ready for your car?" he asked in an always cheery voice.

"Yes."

"It'll be waiting for you by the time you get here."

"Thank you." She hung up.

Smiling, Isabel tossed the mace and phone back in her purse. She turned off the rest of the lights and grabbed the Patrón Añejo tequila from behind the front counter.

The bottle was for Jim. He didn't have to go out of his way to accommodate her, sparing her the curbside wait while he went to fetch the vehicle. She showed her appreciation with a bottle of his favorite spirit once a month. It was easier to hand him a fiver when she picked up her car, but the personal touch of getting to know someone and making them feel special was important.

Her gallery was on the one block within a quarter mile that had a red curb, prohibiting parking, thanks to the fire hydrant and bus stop. She'd kill to have a parking meter out front she could feed all day. Proprietors had authorized spots around the back of the shops, but the rear door was steel, and anyone could be waiting on the other side. Anyone of course being *him*.

The back-side parking was also isolated, away from public view and passersby who might be able to save her life by calling the cops. Lord knew she certainly couldn't depend on any help beyond someone dialing 911.

She peered through the large display window, to the left and right, cursing the angle of the alcove in front. It was a great spot to hang a backdrop and photograph people as they arrived for special events, but it also limited her view. She scanned across the street.

Nothing. All clear as far as she could tell.

But unease slithered through her, making her shoulder blades hitch together. She had that familiar feeling again that she was being watched. Maybe it was her pervasive paranoia, which had become her new normal. Maybe it was just another Thursday when the memories surfaced, putting her on edge. Or maybe someone was out there, watching her.

Once she got to her car, she'd be all right, she told herself.

After grabbing her keys, Isabel set the alarm, unlocked the door and stepped outside. A creepy-crawly prickle shot down her spine, but she tried to shake it off.

She turned to lock up. First, the bottom latch on the handle and then the dead bolt at the top, but the key wouldn't go in.

She summoned her patience with a deep breath that did little to relieve her tension. Trying to tamp down the hopped-up energy zipping along her nerves, she double-checked that she had the right key and tried sliding it in the slot again.

Darn it. For the third time, it wouldn't go in. Was the problem the key or the lock?

Bending over for a closer look, she saw what was wrong.

The keyhole was jammed with something. *What the hell?*

A shadow lunged up behind her.

The hot burn of alarm flared through her chest. Isabel whirled around, sucking in a fearful breath. A man she'd never seen before had her blocked in. Five-o'clock shadow. Dark, hateful eyes. The hood of his zip-up jacket was pulled over his head.

Steel glinted in the dying sunlight. A cold knife pressed against her throat as panic slammed into her.

He shoved her backward. "Scream and I'll cut you," he said in a low, harsh voice.

Her throat constricted. Her mouth went dry. She shut her eyes against a shattering sense of chaos and the stark threat of violence.

"Give me your weekly bank deposit," he demanded.

Brenda made the deposit on Wednesdays. Sometimes Fridays. She found her voice, the words like gravel in her throat. "We never make deposits on Thursdays." Her heart thundered in her ears. She pressed her lips together as if the small gesture would keep the rest of her from falling apart.

She hadn't learned how to defend against weapons yet in her Krav Maga class. There was nothing she could do with the knife to her throat.

Stay calm. Cooperate.

"Don't lie to me. I want the bank deposit."

Tears stung her eyes. Something brittle inside her cracked. "I'm not lying." Her voice was steady, but she trembled with terror.

"Don't think I won't slit your throat," he said, with the blade still to her jugular.

Her whole life flashed before her eyes along with all the things she'd never done, but that she wanted to live long enough to experience.

What am I supposed do?

Think, Isabel.

"Give me your wallet," he snarled.

His caustic words brought everything into sudden clarity. It was the same phrase her Krav Maga instructor used in practice.

She pulled herself together. More or less. Her body tensed. The breath stalled in her lungs. Muscle memory from training firing up, she found her center.

"Take it." She dropped the keys and opened the flap of her purse, coiling in readiness.

As he looked down, going for her wallet, the knife lowered, easing away from her throat.

With a quick, powerful thrust, she struck his face with the heel of her right palm. A distinctive crunch and the flow of blood from his nostrils told her she'd broken his nose.

"Ah!" He cupped his face as a gurgling noise came from him. Furious eyes flashed up at her.

Isabel prepared to throw an elbow strike, to kick and claw.

But then he lunged at her like a rocket.

Oh, God!

Chapter Two

He swung a backhanded punch to her face.

Absorbing the stinging blow across her cheek, anger came faster than the pain, burning acid in her belly. She struggled to regain her bearings and move into a defensive stance.

With a brutal yank on her purse strap, he snatched her bag from her shoulder and took off running.

Utter shock stilled her for a nanosecond, then white-hot rage consumed her.

That was vintage Chanel! From her father!

Isabel kicked off her heels and bolted after him barefoot. "Hey!" She sprinted down the sidewalk. "Give it back!" Noticing pedestrians across the road, she said, "He's stealing my bag!" Then she remembered what she'd been told in her self-defense classes. "Fire! Fire!" She kept chasing him, grateful she'd worn the dress with a flowing accordion bottom rather than a restricting pencil skirt. "Call 911!"

The robber picked up speed, nearing the corner, and she worried she'd lose him and the purse that her father had given her before he died.

Digging deep, Isabel pushed harder, ran faster, pumping her arms while still carrying the stupid Patrón.

She switched hands with the bottle, moving it from

left to right, her high school days of softball springing to mind. Slowing for a beat, she cocked back her arm and lined up her aim. She launched the hefty glass container at him.

The Patrón bottle soared through the air and struck him in the back of the head, throwing off his step. The bottle crashed to the ground, shattering.

Her mugger didn't stop and neither did Isabel. She kept sprinting after him, determined to get back what was hers until fire bit into the sole of her foot. Gasping, she froze and looked down at the smashed bottle. She was standing in the middle of the shards.

Glass had cut her, and the spilled alcohol made the wound sting.

Isabel thought for certain her assailant would get away, flee around the corner and disappear forever.

But a guy darted across the street—tall, broad, muscular—and leaped into action. He threw a powerful tattooed arm up and into the thief's chest, stopping the perpetrator in his tracks.

Her mugger went down in a hard sprawl, dropping the knife. The Good Samaritan grabbed him by the back of his sweatshirt and hauled him up as he flailed. Somehow the mugger slipped out of his hoodie, disentangling himself, and threw her purse like he no longer wanted it.

The thief scrambled away from the bigger man as if terrified, grabbed his knife and bolted across traffic. Horns blared and cars screeched to a halt.

Isabel dragged in a ragged breath. Immediate relief flooded her, and her body released the fear and anger that held her muscles tight. She had never seen anything so heroic except in movies and TV shows.

The do-gooder picked up her purse and jogged down the block to her.

Up close, he was more of everything.

Larger. Taller. Maybe six-three. His light brown hair was cropped close. A dark T-shirt stretched over defined shoulders, sliding down a muscular torso. Jeans hung low on his tapered waist.

He wasn't attractive, not the least bit pretty. He was gorgeous in a rough-and-tumble, almost scary way, but instead of sensing danger from him, his proximity made her mouth water.

"Hey, there." The stranger handed Isabel her irreplaceable purse. "Are you all right?"

Yes. No. Maybe. She settled for nodding and taking a deep breath.

"Care for a little assistance?" He gestured to the glass and her bare feet.

"Uh, yes. Please." She clutched the bag to her chest. "Thank you."

He swept her up from the sidewalk and into his arms like she weighed nothing. But Isabel wasn't a skin-and-bones type of woman. She loved carbs. Jogging only burned off so much and her curvy figure showed it.

"Where to?" he asked. His mesmerizing brown eyes bored into hers, and an entirely new feeling enveloped her.

"The Kismet art gallery down the block."

Tucking her close against his body, he took long strides toward her shop. He smelled powerful and sensual and safe all at once—an arresting mix that had her relaxing in degrees. She wrapped her arm over his shoulder.

"I can't believe that jerk tried to mug you."

"Me either."

"You've got a great arm. You threw that bottle like an ace," he said, and she picked up his accent. Not West Coast. Something distinctive. She'd guess Boston, New

York or Chicago. "You clocked him good. That'll teach him a lesson."

"Thanks." She smiled and pain bloomed in her cheek. "Ouch." Holding her purse, she pressed the back of her hand to her face.

"Did he hit you?"

"Yeah."

"If I'd known, I would've kicked his butt up and down Santa Monica Boulevard."

To that she wasn't sure what to say. White knights weren't her thing and she never wanted to be treated like a damsel in distress. But she had needed help and appreciated his.

"Better yet, I could've held him for you while you did. The way you were chasing him down, man, that was something. You strike me as a fierce woman who can take care of herself."

Fierce? Nobody had ever described her that way, especially not her overbearing uncle, who was determined to coddle her like a child. She would've smiled at the compliment if it wouldn't have hurt. "I'm just glad you intervened. Thanks, again."

At the door, he set her down gently, and she winced. He bent, grabbed her keys and shoes from the ground and gave them to her.

Isabel unlocked the door and when she opened it, the alarm sounded.

The stranger whisked her inside. "Where's your security panel?"

She pointed to the wall behind the front desk.

He carried her to it and shifted so she could access the keypad. "Go on. I won't look."

Turning his head away, he didn't glance back.

A guy with physical prowess *and* sex appeal *and* integrity. He was a mythical creature lost in California.

Still, she held her purse at a strategic angle, shielding the keypad while she punched in the code, shutting off the alarm. One could never have too much paranoia.

He set her down in the chair at the front desk. "Do you have a medical kit?"

"Um, I think Brenda, my assistant, keeps one there." She pointed to the bottom drawer closest to him.

He opened it, pulled out the kit and took a knee in front of her.

Serious, intricate ink was tattooed on his arms, adding to his already hard-and-gritty edge.

Not so long ago, men such as him, quintessential bad boys, had been her catnip. It was always exciting and fun in the beginning, and inevitably short-lived and a major disappointment. Every bad boy had been a bad decision, but none had ever made her fear for her life.

The one time she decided to give a corporate guy a try, a respectable businessman, he ended up being her worst nightmare.

The stranger lifted her left leg and glanced at her foot.

Instinctively, Isabel adjusted her skirt, making sure she didn't flash him.

"Have no fear and don't let my appearance fool you. My mom raised me better than to look up any woman's dress. Unless I've been invited to first." His voice was suggestive, his lips twisting in a teasing grin.

Brushing off the sole of her foot, he inspected the skin, using the utmost care and a gentle touch. His tenderness caught her off guard. She wondered what other surprises this man had hidden beneath his devastating exterior.

"What's wrong with your appearance?" she asked.

"Nothing. In my humble opinion."

"I bet you're many things, but I doubt humble is one of them."

A laugh slipped past his full lips. The sound was rough and masculine, almost musical. "There are plenty who'd agree with you." His eyes flicked up, meeting hers. "I thought with the fancy gallery, you might draw certain assumptions about my tattoos, my boots."

Her gaze dropped to his worn-in riding boots. He was a biker.

Where was his helmet?

Only fools didn't wear one and there wasn't anything foolish about this man.

"I like the tattoos." She liked the whole package. "You have a certain je ne sais quoi that outshines what you're wearing."

His grin spread.

Stop flirting. She'd sworn off men for a year after messing with…him.

Six months to go.

"Or maybe stopping that guy and getting my purse back earned you a free pass in the judgment department," she added.

Another laugh, richer, deeper as their gazes locked. Warmth spread through her, tickling her ribs.

"Well, losing money and having to cancel your credit cards is always a bummer."

"It wasn't about that. My father gave me this." Memories washed over her as she clutched the bag in her lap. "The last present from him before he died when I was fourteen."

"Sorry. About your dad. Never easy losing a parent. And teenage girls need their dads a lot. My younger sister Wendy turned into a hellion after our dad passed away. Heart attack. I tried to fill in for him where I could, but…" He shrugged.

"My uncle and I are very close, and he tries to do the same. Play dad." She loved her uncle dearly for his efforts and didn't know what she'd do without him. "But it isn't the same."

He nodded; the understanding in his eyes was comforting. "You told me your assistant's name, but not yours."

"Isabel. Vargas."

"Dutch Haas."

"Is Dutch your real name?"

"No." He lowered his eyes for a beat. "It's Horatio." He cocked a brow as if waiting for her to judge.

"Don't worry. I told you that you earned a free pass." With her joke, his features lightened. "Were you named after Horatio Hornblower, or the character from *Hamlet*, or a relative?"

He waved a finger at her. "Fierce, beautiful and well-read. I think you might be the perfect woman."

Blushing uncontrollably, she hoped her toes didn't turn red.

"The only thing that'd seal the deal is if you enjoy pizza and motorcycle rides," he said.

"I have Pizzarama on speed dial and I've been on the back of one or two bikes."

"Yep," he said, with a smile that'd melt any woman into a puddle of hormones. "Perfect."

Clearing her throat, she broke the eye contact. "You never answered my question. Hornblower, Hamlet or relative?"

Lifting her other leg, he checked her right foot. "Hornblower. My mother was an English teacher."

"Why did she name your sister Wendy?"

"Believe it or not, from *Peter Pan*. My sister lucked out, right? She should've been named Titania, Desdemona or Goneril."

Isabel laughed. Instantly she regretted it as agony flared in her cheek and she winced.

"You've got some glass in your foot. Once I get it out, we need to put ice on your face." He took a closer look at her sole. "You don't happen to have a pair of tweezers, do you?"

"Other side of the desk in the manicure set."

He moved around the back of her chair and dug out the tweezers from the other drawer. Lowering down on his knee, he looked up at her. "This might hurt a little."

"Not as much as a punch to the face. I'll be okay."

His features pinched in a scowl, one hand tightening into a fist as if he wanted to beat that mugger senseless. "Do you want to call the police and file a report?"

"What's the point? I'm sure that guy is long gone, and I'd rather not waste the time." She'd prefer to get her dog and her car and go home to her condo in Malibu.

"Karma will get that dude. Trust me."

She hoped so, but she didn't want to think about the mugger anymore. "How did you get the nickname Dutch?"

"When I was little, kids in school bullied me and made fun of my name. One day I watched this old movie *Predator*, and Arnold Schwarzenegger's character was this butt-kicking tough guy named Dutch. I wanted to be like him. After I started working out, bulked up and called myself Dutch, nobody picked on me anymore." Turning his attention back to her foot, he squinted and carefully plucked out a shard of glass with the tweezers.

He had the skill of a surgeon.

"I barely felt that," she said.

"Good. The last thing I want is to cause you pain." Something in his tone rang sincere. He grabbed the antiseptic and cleaned the area. "Will you be able to walk in your shoes?"

"Yes."

"Sure? I can carry you."

Was he for real? "I can handle it." She slipped on her heels and stood. Not letting the soreness that she felt show, she schooled her expression. "Thank you. I appreciate it."

"How about we go across the street? Let me buy you a drink and we can get ice for you."

Holy crap. Her pulse started racing again. Was he asking her out?

Even more surprising, she wanted to go with him. Dutch was mysterious, a contradiction of the best kind. On top of that he'd saved her purse, carried her back to the gallery, tended to her foot and had been charming and vulnerable rather than creepy or aggressive.

But she was done rushing into dates and adding guys to her long list of regrets.

"Thanks, but I don't drink." She loved red wine and missed sipping a fine Brunello, but alcohol didn't mix well with her meds.

"What about dinner?" he asked, his honeyed, husky tone making heat rise in her face. "Or we can just get you some ice and keep chatting."

The offer was more tempting than she dared admit, but she had to learn from her mistakes. If she kept doing the same thing repeatedly, expecting different results, then she was more deranged than he who shalt not be named.

"The valet is waiting for me to pick up my car at the garage two blocks down." She hiked her thumb in the opposite direction from which the mugger had run. "And I've got to pick up my dog from day care."

"Okay. Just hang on." He held up both palms. "Give me two minutes. Please." Dutch backed up, darted out of the gallery and dashed across the street.

For such a big guy, he was fast. Agile.

Isabel put away the med kit and reset the alarm. Gathering her courage, she forced herself to lock up again, ignoring the hairs that rose on the back of her neck.

It was a natural response after what had occurred. She'd been through the routine of working past the residual fear of an attack before.

Getting to the dead bolt, she cursed under her breath and made a mental note to call a locksmith in the morning.

She spun around, throwing her keys in her purse and grabbing her pepper spray. Dutch was already pushing through the doors of a restaurant and hustling across the boulevard to her.

"Here you go." He handed her a plastic bag filled with ice. "Put that on your face. You'll thank me tomorrow."

His thoughtfulness warmed her from the inside out. The wall she hadn't realized she'd built around her heart softened, but it didn't crumble.

"Thank you." She took the bag from the sweetest man she'd ever met. "You didn't have do that."

"Can I walk you to your car?"

"No. I…I…" She didn't know how to explain it. "I have to go on my own." The way she would any other day. No crutches, metaphorically speaking.

"All right. But you've got no objections to me standing here and watching you walk two blocks, do you?"

Why did he have to be so irresistible? "No objections. Thanks again. For everything."

"How about we continue this conversation tomorrow over lunch? Or on your day off?"

She felt a flutter in her stomach and she shoved it away, replacing it with common sense. He was a hard man to refuse. A chivalrous bad boy. Or was that an oxymoron?

Maybe she was the moron for even considering it.

Six months. Then she'd take it super slow, with someone.

"Good night." Isabel tightened her grip on the pepper spray, put the ice to her cheek and walked away at a fast clip.

Dutch was a beautiful risk, but too dangerous to take with her track record.

Chapter Three

"Is she all right?" *he* asked the private investigator he'd hired to watch Isabel when he was at work and unable to keep a close eye on her himself.

"Yes. I think so," Olga Olsen said, no doubt from her perch in the coffee shop that sat diagonal to the gallery, where Brenda picked up Isabel's morning latte—coconut milk, double shot of espresso, a sprinkle of cinnamon. "I wasn't sure if I should've interceded since you gave explicit instructions never to engage with her, but then that guy came out of nowhere and helped her."

"What are they doing inside the gallery? Is she flirting with him?" He clenched his jaw, his temperature rising.

Isabel could be such a horny minx. Batting those long dark lashes, flipping her thick, curly hair over her shoulder, throwing more sway in her walk than necessary, drawing male attention like moths to a flame.

Gritting his teeth, he couldn't wait to climb on top of her again and lose himself in her.

"It looked like she hurt her foot and he put a bandage on it or something," Olga said. "She's walking to her car now."

"Alone?" His chest tightened and he squeezed the cell phone in his hand, imagining that man carrying her to the art gallery, fawning over her. Disgust soured his stomach.

Isabel was the most beautiful creature he'd ever seen. And she was *his*.

No one could touch his property. Not a mugger and especially not riffraff who wasn't fit to lick her shoes, even if he had intervened on her behalf.

"Yes." The background noise on Olga's end changed as if she had moved outside. "She's alone."

He released a breath of relief.

It had better stay that way.

Good girl, Isabel, for not letting him escort you to your car. Such foolishness would demand punishment.

Remind her who she belonged to.

So far, he'd played along with the restraining order, the long *tease*. As if a slip of paper would keep him away from her. Every woman loved the chase, but none more than Isabel.

Deep down she knew that he'd never stop pursuing her. This game was fun, *foreplay*, building the anticipation until they were reunited. She needed time to miss him, appreciate him, to realize no one could ever love her the way he did. When she came crawling back home to him things would be different, better than they'd been in the beginning.

Only he was good enough for her, understood her standards, how to take care of her, what she really needed.

"But the man is still in front of the gallery, watching her head to the valet," Olga said.

"Stay on Isabel. If that man comes sniffing around her again, call me immediately." He'd handle it personally.

After he hung up, he checked the lunar calendar app on his phone and smiled, satisfaction seeping through him. In the meantime, he'd pay Isabel a visit later tonight.

STANDING IN FRONT of the Kismet art gallery, Dutch watched Isabel limp away and thought about Karma.

How he was going to be its instrument and make sure that jerk got what he deserved.

Anger washed through him in a cold fury, the burn hard.

He stormed across the street, hurried around to the back side of the empty building that was up for rent, past his parked motorcycle, and entered from the rear rather than using the main entrance off Santa Monica Boulevard. Flying up the stairs, he took them three at a time. He threw open the door and charged into the surveillance hub the US Marshals Service had set up.

Dutch had reached his limit. He'd been yanked from the Fugitive Apprehension Response Team out at Camp Beauregard in Louisiana and given this undercover assignment only two days ago. Apparently, he was at the top of a short list of potential candidates fitting the *right profile*—whatever the hell that was supposed to mean—to accomplish the job.

But he was unprepared. Exposed.

With an eleventh-hour assignment, there hadn't been time to create fake credentials. The best they could do was alter the dates for his actual prior service military record and his type of discharge, from *honorable* to *general*, which meant he'd done a good job until he engaged in misconduct or received nonjudicial punishment under Article 15 of the Uniform Code of Military Justice. After that, it was easy enough to make it appear as if he'd never been a marshal.

Not only was he forced to use his real name, but his support team were marshals he'd never worked with before.

So far, the operation was off to a shaky start.

"Where is he?" Dutch asked Allison Chen, a slim

Asian deputy marshal from the San Diego office, supporting this operation.

Alarm widening Allison's dark eyes, she tipped her head toward the left.

Dutch marched across the wide space past tables with surveillance equipment and his gear—riding jacket and helmet. In the adjoining open space, he found Deputy Marshal Jake Prindle, assigned to the LA office. The blockhead who decided to hit a woman.

Prindle was seated in a chair, his head hung over his lap with a compress to his nose, forearm resting on his leg. His eyes flashed up at Dutch and he straightened.

Dutch seized him by his T-shirt and yanked him up from the chair, ripping the cotton. "What in the hell were you thinking? You used a knife! You punched her!"

"Hey, dude."

"You call me deputy or Haas." Dutch's voice dropped low, turning menacing. "Not dude."

"The knife was authorized. It was a dull blade no sharper than a butter knife and I only held the spine to her throat. She wasn't in any real danger."

"Why'd you hit her?" Dutch wanted nothing more than to pound his fist into Prindle. Pulverize his face, finishing the job that Isabel had started. "What kind of man does that?"

What kind of well-trained marshal?

"It was a reflex. An accident." Prindle tried to wrestle free of Dutch's grasp. "She was kicking my butt. Broke my nose. Or did you miss how I'm profusely bleeding?"

A toilet flushed and water ran in the bathroom, then Will Draper joined the party. He was the US marshal in charge of the San Diego field office and acting liaison with their LA counterparts.

"Haas," Draper said, hurrying up to them. "Let the man go. Now!"

Dutch was barely able to keep it together, but he shoved Prindle against the wall and released him.

"That wasn't the plan we discussed." Dutch stalked away and paced. The floor of the makeshift command center was spacious and open, but he felt contained, crowded. Caged.

Prindle dropped into a chair and put the compress back to his nose.

"Listen," Draper said, "the LA office is in charge of their own guys and made some last-minute changes that I approved of."

"You thought it was a good idea for this idiot to put a knife to her throat and hit her?"

Dutch had watched the fake attack transpire from the window in the command center. When Prindle had pulled the knife and pressed it to her jugular, Dutch shot out of there like a bullet, hightailing it across the street.

After reading the file on Isabel and staring at her picture for hours, he'd expected her to be a spoiled princess, too pampered to handle a broken nail. But beneath her refined beauty was a solid core of pure strength.

She had serious grit and impressive self-defense skills. He had genuine admiration for her that had turned to something more as he carried her back to the gallery and took care of the cut on her foot.

Attraction, sure, but something else, too, something intangible.

Draper shoved his hands in his pockets. "Hitting the asset was an accident."

"I want him written up for inappropriate and excessive use of force. It needs to be documented in his file."

Dutch wanted it taken into consideration on Prindle's next review.

"Okay." Draper raised his palms. "Calm down."

Prindle got up, kicking back the chair and flounced out into the front room.

"Was a knife necessary?" Dutch asked.

"The knife increased the intimidation factor and the perceived threat to a necessary level. It helped you initiate contact in an impactful way."

"I didn't agree to this," Dutch snapped, shaking his head.

"You don't have to agree with or like any of this. Just do your job and follow orders. Understand, Haas? Don't forget the gravity of this situation."

How could he? The WITSEC database for the Pacific Coast region had been compromised. A crooked marshal out of the San Diego office was responsible for the breach, but sensitive data—the new identities of all the witnesses and the personal information of the marshals and their families throughout California—had fallen into the hands of Dante Emilio Vargas. The ruthless leader of the West Coast branch of the *Los Chacales* cartel. The Jackals.

As powerful and brutal as *Los Chacales* had become in recent years, they were considered the largest-growing threat to national security. To make matters worse, Vargas planned to auction the information to the highest bidder.

Now, here was Dutch, brought in to cozy up to Isabel in order to get close to her uncle and retrieve the compromised data before it was sold.

"I know what's at stake," Dutch said. "But I'm questioning the means by which we get it done."

The use of violence against her, heck, simply *using* her to get in with her uncle, struck him as wrong.

"The asset is our only way in." Draper threw his hands up in exasperation. "The one connection we have to exploit."

"She has a name," Dutch said through gritted teeth, hating how they kept throwing around the word *asset* like she wasn't a person.

His temporary boss sighed. "Do you have a better plan? One that's foolproof? And will work in the short amount of time we have?"

No, he didn't.

"Think of all the men, women and children counting on us," Draper said. "On *you*."

A lot of lives were on the line if Dutch failed. Those of witnesses, good marshals and their families. He despised the method of achieving the goal, but he'd handled more challenging assignments in Special Forces, and he'd toed the mission line.

So why did it leave a bitter taste in his mouth and have his stomach turning?

Isabel. She had money and the unfortunate luck of being related to Dante Emilio Vargas, but there was nothing in the file to indicate whether she knew about her uncle's illicit affairs and turned a blind eye or if she was an innocent, ignorant that he was the leader of *Los Chacales*.

Face-to-face, she was vivacious and witty and kindhearted.

Damn it, he liked her. He'd been genuinely worried about her and the emotional state that attack might've left her in. Any other woman would've taken up his offer to at least walk her to the parking garage to make sure she got in her car safely.

Not Isabel. Independent. Strong. *Fierce.*

Yeah, he really liked her.

"The FBI has much more experience with undercover

work than we do," Draper said, "and that's the reason we consulted them on how to proceed. It was one of their behavioral analysts who picked you for this, decided the best avenue of approach you should take with her was a romantic one and created the threat scenario that played out with Prindle and the *asset*."

Figures it was some profiler, a person with extensive experience assessing victims and diving into the twisted minds of murderers who'd decided this was the right course of action.

Exactly what made him top choice for this assignment?

Maybe it was better if he didn't know, but there was a glimmer of something real between him and Isabel. He hadn't planned to tell her about his father and sister, to share intimate information. It'd flowed out of him naturally. No thought, no deception, no steering the conversation. One tiny connection sparked another and another, a flame in dry underbrush kindling unexpectedly on its own.

"Any updates from our contact on the inside?" Dutch asked.

A deep-cover FBI agent who'd infiltrated the organization learned about the plans for the auction set to happen at some unspecified time and got word to the Marshals. Though, this ticking time bomb wasn't the FBI's problem and they refused to get further involved, choosing instead to protect their agent's cover and pursue their own mission objectives.

"No." Draper shook his head. "As soon as I hear something, I'll pass it along."

Allison walked up to the doorway, her long black ponytail swaying behind her. "Did it work? Did Isabel agree to go out with you?"

Dutch folded his arms across his chest. "Not quite."

"Either you're in with her or not," Allison said. "Which is it?"

"I'm in, she just hasn't agreed to a date yet."

"What is that supposed to mean? Did you meet the objective?" Allison's eyebrows drew together, and she stepped deeper into the room. "She has to trust you. According to the profiler's report, it starts with you helping her in some life-threatening situation. Then there needs to be chemistry. We followed the recommendation by picking you. The only question is, are you the right guy for the job? Is she interested or not?"

Dutch drew in a deep breath. "She is, but cautious. If I push too hard, I'll lose her. She needed space, so I gave it."

"How can you be sure that she's interested and not blowing you off?" Allison asked.

He'd set out to do this assignment with cold detachment and unwavering objectivity, and after spending twenty minutes with Isabel, raw magnetism had punched a hole in his intentions.

That degree of attraction, which was scorching, wasn't one-sided. Of that, he was sure.

"Trust me—I've got her attention."

"Good." Allison's eyes were deadly serious, her composure so calm it was a little irksome. "You better keep it because there are families at risk. My family. I'm the one deputy marshal linked in the database to every witness who has gone into WITSEC as a result of testifying against the *Los Chacales* cartel."

"How is that possible?" Dutch asked.

"There have only been three and they were all women in fragile emotional states when the FBI brought them in. During the handover to us, they requested a female marshal to escort them to the safe houses and be on the protection detail until they testified. It was only me and Charlie Killinger in the San Diego office and her bedside manner left much to be desired."

Dutch had met Charlie out at Camp Beauregard. She ended up being his replacement on the Fugitive Apprehension Response Team. Kickass and fiery, Charlie wasn't the babysitting, hand-holding type.

"The only one I didn't protect every day was the last," Allison said. "Lori Carpenter. She was put in a safe house out in Big Bear for a year waiting for the trial to start. I've got a small kid and couldn't do something long-term like that, but I made the initial drive up and helped get her settled. My name is tied to all three women. Vargas is dangerous and vengeful. You mess this up and the deaths that follow will be on you."

Burdened with such an immense responsibility, Dutch compartmentalized his feelings. He never mistreated women, never used them, didn't even have one-night stands. His parents, the army, Delta Force, had taught him how to be a man with honor. If Isabel knew the truth about her uncle, then she was complicit, and Dutch need not feel an iota of guilt. If she were unaware, he'd do everything in his power to safeguard her heart in the process.

But this had to be done.

He pushed aside the doubt gnawing at his resolve to see this through. There was too much on the line not to give it his all.

Chapter Four

Nightfall couldn't come fast enough. It was a new moon. The sky was pitch-black perfection, the ocean roiling darkness.

An ideal time to pay his doll a visit. To keep their one-of-a-kind connection alive. To stoke the passion between them.

Wearing dark clothes and ball cap pulled low, he strolled down the private beach off the north end of Malibu Road, cloaked in the night. Found his prime spot to tuck himself in among the boulders of the rocky outcrop, where he had a bird's eye view of her third-floor condo.

The corner one-bedroom in the small, exclusive building faced the water. There were no other balconies adjacent to hers, only above and below. Two-story houses on either side of the building sat lower than her place, giving her a false sense of security. Privacy. Large, expansive windows nearly surrounded the apartment, putting her on display in her glass cage.

Isabel, his doll. A thing of beauty and grace.

His lingering rage over her mugging and that man fondling her was a wild beast inside him, but the longer he stood there, watching her, the more the turmoil faded.

She was healthy and safe, with him now. Even if he was at a distance.

He could reach out and touch her whenever he liked and do as he pleased, caress her with care, or damage her a little. Dolls with flaws were the prettiest because they were unique.

Sometimes love had to hurt. A crazy-beautiful pain.

Not so hard it made her black-and-blue.

Just enough to bring her back to you.

He liked this game. It turned him on, whetted his appetite for her. One day soon he'd have another taste of her.

Isabel poured a glass of sparkling water and squeezed a wedge of lime in it. Six months ago, she stopped drinking wine. Probably her attempt to become her best self... for him, right along with getting fit. She'd started jogging.

So did he, even knew her favorite trails.

She took boxing once a week and Krav Maga on Tuesdays and Thursdays, always in the afternoons. He couldn't have them growing apart. To stay in sync with her, he signed up at the exact same places. Learned what she learned, but at an accelerated rate going twice as often as she did. He stayed two steps ahead.

Nothing like the element of surprise to fan the flames.

She strutted across the room in her skimpy nightgown, parading around, wanting to be seen, to be coveted. A lace chemise clung to her breasts, a generous 38F cup, and skimmed her thighs, showing off her curvy legs.

Tease. She knew that was his favorite one. Could she feel him watching now?

Of course she did. That's why she chose to wear it. For him. Their bond was special. Unbreakable.

She curled up on the sofa and turned on the TV with that stupid dog at her feet. Some reality show that she'd DVR'd was most likely on the screen.

Staring at her, he remembered the scent of her shampoo in her hair, the feel of her skin, the taste of her mouth.

Isabel. I'll love you forever.
The same way he'd loved Patricia.
Until the day she died.

Chapter Five

Once Isabel had finished spilling her guts to her bestie, Brenda, about what had happened yesterday, she took a sip of her coconut-milk latte and set the cup on the front desk of the gallery.

"Oh. My. God." Brenda sat wide-eyed. "That's why we have the new electronic dead bolt on the door. Are you all right?" Her friend jumped up, blond curls bouncing around her shoulders as she enveloped Isabel in a tight hug.

The warm embrace was nice. A comfort she wished she didn't need.

"Yeah." Isabel pulled back. "I'm fine." Her face was still a little sore, but the slight bruise was easily concealed with makeup thanks to Dutch getting her an ice pack as soon as possible.

The whole incident had rattled her to the point that she'd imagined someone was watching her from the beach last night. That the crazy nameless one had been out there, hidden in the darkness, spying on her.

But she refused to close her windows and draw her blinds like she was living in a prison.

She had a waterfront condo in Malibu for goodness sakes. While she was in her home, she'd enjoy the temperate breezes and the relaxing sound of the waves rolling in.

The beach was private, and he stopped stalking her after the restraining order. The almost mugging yesterday had dredged old feelings to the surface, triggering delusions and nightmares. That's all. Nothing more, she told herself.

She'd barely slept and had brought McQueen up on the bed with her, but she'd gone for a jog this morning on her sore foot, even though she didn't have to.

No one was going to mess up her life and take away her sanity. She'd worked too hard to get to this mental place where she wasn't a trembling wreck.

One setback wasn't going to derail her.

"I'll cancel my Thursday yoga classes." Brenda sat down. "You're not locking up alone again."

"You're not canceling anything." She put her hand on her friend's. "We stick to our routine." The only way for things to feel normal was to pretend that they were until it became reality. "Nothing changes."

Brenda shook her head, familiar pity filling her eyes that made Isabel cringe inside. "At least take your uncle up on his offer to hire a bodyguard for you."

Her uncle Emilio would love nothing more than to hear that he was right and coddle her. "Absolutely not. I live in Malibu to get breathing room from him. It's like he didn't get the memo I'm a grown woman." The last thing she'd do was bolster his overprotective instincts.

Someone pounded on the back door. Isabel's hand flew to her chest as her gaze snapped to the rear of the gallery.

"It must be the delivery. The stuff we're renting for the party." Brenda stared at her.

Tomorrow night they were hosting their annual charity event at the gallery. Cocktails and canapés would be served as people mingled and purchased art. Fifty percent of the proceeds went to the local children's hospital. There'd be a huge turnout. It was their biggest event of the year.

"I forgot," Isabel said, her heart still racing.

"Are you sure you're okay?" Brenda stood and they walked toward the door in the back.

"Yes. Just a little jumpy." Isabel fluffed out her long hair to hide how her hands were shaking. "One good thing came out of what happened yesterday."

"The hunky hero who got your purse back?" Waggling her eyebrows, Brenda smiled.

Dutch had definitely been a welcome surprise, the best part of yesterday in fact. Isabel wondered if she'd see him again after rejecting not one but two offers to go out.

Brenda opened the door and waved the delivery guy in who was carrying a tray of glasses. "Put it upstairs on the table we have set out."

The short guy nodded and walked past them.

"No, I'm not talking about the Good Samaritan," Isabel said as they stepped outside. "I made a bucket list."

"Really?" Brenda looked over the items they'd ordered in the van. "Let's hear it."

"Well, I only have five things on my list so far. I hope it doesn't sound pathetic. I want to fall in love. Get married. Have kids. Learn to surf. Have earth-shattering sex," she said, and Brenda chuckled. "And I want to see the northern lights, something magical and wondrous."

"That's six things." Brenda stepped away from the van and turned toward Isabel. Her eyes went wide as her mouth dropped open.

"Doesn't sound pathetic at all," a deep male voice said, and Isabel spun around to face Dutch. "I can help with at least two of those things on your list."

Isabel gulped, her heart fluttering and thighs tingling at the gorgeous sight of him.

Oh, goodness. How much of her list had he heard?

Well, if he thought it wasn't *pathetic*, then he'd heard everything. Including the part about sex. She couldn't have been more mortified if she'd been standing there naked.

"Hi," she said. Her cheeks were on fire.

"Hi." Dutch smiled, and the heated sensation in her face spread lower throughout her body.

"I didn't think I'd see you again."

"Hope that doesn't mean you're disappointed I swung by." Dutch flashed a sexy half grin. "When I invited you to lunch, you didn't say no. Only *good night*. I didn't take it as a definitive refusal."

"Hi, I'm Brenda." Her best friend shook his hand. "You're exactly as she described. Big and strong and... *mmm*." Brenda acted like she wanted to eat him. "She raved about you all morning."

Isabel threw a warning look at Brenda. "I briefly mentioned how grateful I am that you'd been there."

"Nice to meet you." Dutch lowered his eyes like the comment embarrassed him and he shoved his hands in his pockets.

The young delivery guy zipped past them and grabbed more glasses.

"You need help with that?" Dutch asked.

"Sure, man. Thanks." The kid pointed out some racks and Dutch took them inside.

Once the guys were out of earshot, Brenda turned to her and clutched her arm. "He is so yummy. Why didn't you agree to lunch?"

"One-year moratorium on dating. Remember?"

With an eye roll, Brenda waved a dismissive hand.

"You're always talking about how you want your life to be normal after what—"

Isabel lifted a cautionary finger.

"After what CNO did," Brenda finished, using the acronym for the crazy nameless one. "Every time you turn down a date or think about why you shouldn't get back out there, you're really thinking about *him* and giving CNO power. It's great that you got a dog, but you need a man. Someone hot and sweet to put a little sizzle in your life. Someone like that." Brenda pointed to Dutch, who was walking toward them through the gallery, chatting with the delivery guy. "His chakras are off the charts and when he was standing next to you your aura got brighter and turned fuchsia."

Before Isabel could ask what any of that meant, the men came back outside.

"Okay. The only thing left is the fridge." The kid pointed to the large glorified cooler that was a single-section unit with a glass door strapped to a wheeled hand truck.

"Use the elevator," Brenda said.

Isabel winced. "You can't. I forgot to tell you the repair guy had a personal emergency and canceled yesterday, but he'll be out tomorrow afternoon in time for the event."

"I can't come back tomorrow," the delivery guy said, rubbing the nape of his neck. "I'm going to be slammed with back-to-back drop-offs all day. Saturdays are always crazy."

Dutch patted the kid's shoulder. "You grab one end, I'll take the other, and we'll carry it up the stairs."

"No can do, buddy. I'm not covered for that kind of thing. If I slip and get hurt, I won't get worker's comp. I'm sorry. I'll have to leave it on the ground floor."

"We need to get the beverages in today, so nobody

has a warm drink tomorrow," Brenda said. "Everyone will expect cold bubbly with the amount we hope people will spend. Maybe we have to set the bar up downstairs."

Isabel pressed a palm to her forehead. "The whole point of having it upstairs is to encourage everyone to see the paintings on the second floor."

"I can take it up for you," Dutch said.

Isabel turned to him. "How? You can't carry that up on your own."

He was strong and it was a single unit, but everyone had limits. The fridge had to be a good two hundred pounds.

"Do you have an extra strap in the van?" Dutch asked.

The kid nodded. "Yeah."

Dutch directed the delivery guy to wheel the fridge out of the van. Then he adjusted the two straps, removing them from the hand truck and retightening them around the cooling unit. He slipped his arms through the straps like someone would with a backpack and he had the delivery guy wrap the third one horizontally around the center of the fridge and Dutch's torso, fastening it tight.

Bending at the knees, Dutch shifted the weight of the unit around before he stood and leaned over with the fridge balanced on his back and headed inside.

Isabel, Brenda and the delivery guy followed. They stood at the stairwell, marveling at Dutch carrying the fridge upstairs as though it were a death-defying circus act.

"Whoa," the kid said low, amazement ringing in his voice.

Okay, Dutch was really strong. And smart.

"To hell with your moratorium. Are you seriously not going to give him a chance?" Brenda pointed at Dutch while staring at Isabel like she was crazy. "If you don't want him, can I have him?"

"Hell, I'd date him," the delivery guy chimed in.

Isabel sighed. "Maybe we can hang out. Baby steps. Get to know each other better without all the physical stuff."

Brenda threw her an unmistakable are-you-kidding-me look. "The physical stuff is the best part."

Isabel had jumped into bed with CNO and look where that had gotten her. "But it shouldn't be the best part. It should be the icing on a fantastic cake, the cherry on a sundae."

"I'd eat his cake with a spoon," Brenda said, staring at Dutch as he came back downstairs.

Isabel shook her head. Brenda could wrap men around her little finger like twine. Except for the yoga instructor she'd set her sights on. The limber yogi was proving to be the ultimate challenge.

Then there was Dutch. He hadn't given Brenda the once or twice-over most men did with her sunny curls and sparkling smile and swimsuit-model physique. All his attention had been focused on Isabel.

"Here you go." Dutch handed the straps to the delivery guy who gave him a two-finger salute and left.

"Thank you so much," Isabel said. "How can I repay you for everything?"

"The only payment I'd accept is the pleasure of your company over lunch."

"She says yes." Brenda shoved Isabel forward. "You two should leave right now."

"I can't," Isabel said, not enjoying the sudden on-slaught of pressure. "There's too much to do before to-morrow." The charity event was highly publicized. Who's who of LA would be there, including the mayor. It had to go off without a hitch. Not to mention, she hated being put on the spot.

Hadn't Brenda been listening?

Chatting over coffee was a baby step. Not lunch.

Brenda's doe eyes shifted to her, a sad kind of pleading in their depths. "Please go," she mouthed.

Her best friend wasn't reckless, or impulsive, and tended to be more protective than her uncle Emilio at times. She also had great instincts.

The first time Brenda had met CNO she'd said, *His aura is so dark. He skeeves me out. Doesn't something about him give you the heebie-jeebies?*

No. He'd been the sort everyone wanted her to go out with. Wealthy, owner of several businesses, wore a suit and tie, held open doors for her, spoke three languages.

He'll show you his true colors sooner or later and when he does, run like the wind and don't look back, Brenda had said.

In hindsight, Isabel should've pulled the rip cord right then.

Her internal creep-radar might be broken, but Brenda's wasn't. Maybe one meal with Dutch would be okay, if he got Brenda's endorsement.

"I know you're busy, but you've got to eat," Dutch said. "As soon as we order, I'll explain to the waiter that we're in a rush and ask for the check, so you're not stuck with me for too long. What do you say?"

"She's starving and would love to," Brenda said to him, then turned and whispered in Isabel's ear. "Go, start living again."

The past six months, she hadn't been living. Only surviving.

Something about Dutch made her feel safe. Made her want to toss her rule book into the trash and move forward, not worrying about the past or shadows or mistakes. To be her old self.

Baby steps. For now, she'd hang on to the rule book. "Okay. A quick, casual lunch between new friends?"

Disappointment flashed in his eyes, but he nodded. "Where to?"

"There's a grill. Ten-minute walk. They have a variety of fantastic burgers."

Dutch held the door open for her.

Isabel grabbed her purse and they headed out.

"I should've asked yesterday," he said as they strolled down the street. "Do you have a boyfriend?"

She flinched. "No. I don't."

"To be benched in the friend zone is a tough place to ever move out of."

"I'm sorry—it's just that I'm not dating right now. I haven't had the best luck in the men department."

"Ah, I see. You don't want to rush into anything?"

"Exactly," she said, brightly, relieved he understood. "I want to get to know a guy before I jump into something hot and heavy." No more sleeping with the enemy.

"I have to admit I have one technical concern."

Technical? He was a standard-issue guy. Of course there was a catch. "What's that?"

"It's the kiss of death for a guy to be labeled *friend*," he said as if the word stung his tongue. "Before you know it, you'll start looking at me as a big brother."

She swallowed a chuckle. The only way that'd happen was if she had a frontal lobotomy.

"It's all about the way we frame things in our heads," he said. "How about you think of me as a potential? A possibility. Just a prospect. And we take things as slowly as you'd like. I won't even kiss you unless you ask me to. Absolutely no pressure."

Stopping in front of the grill, she frowned at him, weighing whether he was serious or not. "Really?" What would it be like to have to *ask* this hot hunk to kiss her?

"You're gorgeous, Isabel, and I'm attracted to you on multiple levels, but I swear on my father's grave that I'm more interested in earning your trust, in getting to know you, than I am in sleeping with you." The way he spoke, holding her gaze, held no hint of deception. He meant the words and she believed him.

"You're attracted to me on multiple levels, huh?"

"I'm even having a hard time picking which feature of yours is my favorite."

Unease rippled through her, making her stiffen. She braced for the routine, where a guy looked her over from head to toe, cataloging her *features* like she was an object instead of a person.

"Your eyes," Dutch continued, "or…" He ran the pad of his finger from the bridge of her nose to the tip with the lightest, most intimate touch. "Your pert nose."

Oh, she was an idiot for assuming the worst. She wanted to crush the presumptions that had built over the years, but sometimes they flared to the surface with no warning. "If I put you on the spot and made you choose?"

"Then hands-down it'd have to be the freckles on your cheeks and nose. I love that you don't use heavy makeup and let those beauties shine through."

This man sure did know how to give a woman a compliment. She'd gone out with boob men, butt men, leg men and none were bashful about telling her which they found most attractive. But he was the only one to call a feature she'd hated growing up *beautiful*.

"Okay. Let's give the whole 'prospect' thing a try." Not dating, just entertaining the possibility. She liked it.

The smile that spread across his face was a ray of

sunshine breaking through a cloud bank. Any lingering reservations she had dissolved.

For the first time in a long time, she was hopeful.

He opened the door to the restaurant and let her go inside ahead of him.

The grill was a large place that stayed busy from open to close. The hostess escorted them to a table near the front, handing them poster-sized menus. They were lucky to get a table without a wait. Sometimes eating at the bar was the only option for a quick bite.

She sat where she could see the entire bar and all the tables while Dutch faced the door.

A server came to them straightaway and took their order. What were the odds? Sometimes you had to flag one down. The universe seemed to be conspiring to get her through lunch as quickly as possible and Isabel wasn't sure that was what she truly wanted anymore.

"I'll have the salmon burger with garlic truffle fries," Isabel said, as Dutch looked over the menu. "And can I get the veggie burger wrapped in lettuce, no fries, to go." She glanced at Dutch. "It's for Brenda. She'd kill me if I didn't bring one back for her."

"That's considerate of you. I'm sure she'll appreciate it." He turned to the waitress. "The monster burger for me, medium well, with everything on it. Thanks. And one check."

"No, separate bills," Isabel said, then leaned over toward Dutch, dropping her voice. "This isn't a date. Remember?"

"If you could bring the one check as soon as you can, that'd be great." He gave the waitress a wheedling smile that was downright irresistible. "We're in a bit of a rush."

"No problem." The waitress flashed a pleasant grin and left, ignoring Isabel's request.

"Before you say anything, please let me explain." His tone was soft and unassuming.

She bobbed her head once for him to go ahead.

"I invited you to lunch and I was raised that the person extending the invitation pays. If not for Brenda's help, I'm not so sure you would've agreed to come with me to begin with. As far as I can tell, I owe you both."

Not wanting to make a thing out of it after she saw the logic of his rationale, she said, "Your accent. Where are you from?"

"New York and Chicago are both sort of home to me."

"What do you do?"

"I was in the military. Special Forces," he said, casually like it was no big deal. "I'm on terminal leave, using up the last of my vacation days. Before you ask, the answer is no, I have nothing specific lined up. And I'm okay with that."

She'd never gone out with someone on the verge of unemployment and once again he was easy-breezy about it. Leaning toward him again, she put her hand on the table between them. "Let me pick up the tab for lunch. You should conserve your resources. And you did save my purse."

He laughed and covered her hand with his large palm. Her skin danced beneath the warm weight of it, the solidity. "I don't know what kind of fellas you're used to, but that's not how I operate. Financially, I'm good, not destitute."

The down-to-earth air about him, devoid of pretenses, wasn't what she was used to. It was refreshing.

"I'm renting an apartment in Ocean Park."

Nice area. Close to her gallery. "Why did you pick California to call home?"

Moving his hand from hers, he sat back and held her

gaze. "I've been stationed and deployed to some hell-holes. I wanted sunshine. Perfect weather. The ocean. But continental US. What about you? Why do you own an art gallery? More specifically, how does one come to own one?"

The waitress brought them two ice waters and a basket of bread.

"I was an art history major. In college, I did internships at museums. I wanted to be a docent, giving tours and talking about my passion." She took a warm roll and slathered butter on a piece. "But my uncle told me to set my sights higher, to own a gallery instead, where I could control my own destiny. When I decided to buy one, he didn't want me to use my inheritance from my father and bought it for me."

"So, he owns the gallery?" Dutch asked.

"On paper yes, but it's mine. Other than using his accountants, I run it freely."

"Who's your uncle?"

"Dante Emilio Vargas." Her uncle was a bit of a celebrity on the West Coast, and she waited for the usual reaction of awe, but Dutch's eyes didn't so much as light up. For once, someone who didn't know him. "To me, he's just Uncle Emilio. Dante was my grandfather and my uncle has never appreciated the title *junior* and doesn't use it."

Dutch sipped his water. "I think I might've heard the name."

"He's a huge venture capitalist. What Elon Musk is to the car industry and space exploration, my uncle is to advancements in farming organically and education. Building a better world is so important to him." Her uncle was driven, shrewd and tough, but he had the biggest heart and would do anything for her.

"Are you some kind of socialite who comes from old money?"

Isabel laughed. "Oh gosh, no. I come from humble beginnings. When I was little my father and uncle started investing their money in technology and buying farms. I guess they got in at the right time. My uncle compares it to buying stock in Microsoft or Apple when those companies were just getting started. I don't know." She shrugged. "I guess they got lucky."

His brows knit as he seemed to study her closely in a way that made her self-conscious. "Does he live here?"

"Thank heavens, no. San Diego. He's such an important man he's surrounded by bodyguards. You'd think he was the president or something. If I lived down there, he'd insulate me with bodyguards, too." Trading one personal hell for another. "I need my freedom. To breathe." She was finally starting to get to a place where she could once again.

Maybe this lunch with Dutch was the first step in the right direction.

"What has your uncle thought of your previous paramours?"

Sighing, Isabel dropped her gaze to her lap. "I haven't introduced any to him. He'd never approve of someone he didn't pick and who didn't check every box on his list, which is different than mine."

He perked up at that with a bright smile and something in the conversation shifted from investigative to inquisitive. "What's on your list? What kind of guys are you into?"

Someone like you. Isabel blushed. "Excuse me a minute. I have to use the restroom."

She stood, grabbing her purse, and crossed the length of the restaurant down to the other side. All the tables were now taken and there were only a few open spots left at the bar. They'd arrived at the perfect time.

Inside the restroom, she checked her makeup, fluffed her hair, running her fingers through her brown curls, and washed her hands.

She threw away the paper towel and left the bathroom.

In the few short minutes that she'd been in there, every seat at the bar had been taken. Passing the row of customers parked on bar stools, she homed in on Dutch. Even from behind, he drew attention with his brawny build and the wink of tattoos she glimpsed through the crowd.

The food was already on the table, but it looked as if he'd waited for her. *Another good sign.* As she sat down, she spotted three to-go containers on the side of the table.

"It really picked up in here," he said. "I figured if you couldn't finish your meal, you'd want a to-go box. It might take the waitress a good ten minutes to grab one later."

"You're a planner. I like that." Isabel picked up a fry, took the first delicious, hot bite and glanced up toward the bar.

Her heart nearly stopped, the blood in her veins turning to slush as she locked gazes with *him*.

Chapter Six

A thousand thoughts rushed through Isabel's head like a high-speed train derailing. She couldn't think. She couldn't move. Couldn't speak.

At the far end of the bar, *he* was seated in the very spot that she had passed on the way back from the restroom. He must've arrived while she was inside.

Well-groomed as always, wearing a tailored suit, he resembled a thirtysomething Hugh Jackman. Looking at him, no one would suspect what he really was. Isabel hadn't the first time they met. He'd lured her in with his good looks, smooth charm and sophistication, his ability to talk to anyone about anything. She'd been flattered when he'd asked her out.

He sat there in the restaurant, staring at her. Unblinking. His eyes rabid, excited. His body rigid. With his elbows propped on the bar, he brushed one index finger across the other and mouthed, "Shame on you."

Isabel choked on the French fry going down her throat. She coughed, patting her chest, struggling to breathe, to gain her bearings.

Why was he here?

But deep down she knew. He was here because of her.

"Are you all right?" Dutch asked, handing her a glass of water. "You look like you've seen a ghost."

More like a living, breathing nightmare.

Her nerves stretched tight as bowstrings as she tried to gauge how far away he sat. At least seventy-five feet in the large restaurant. The restraining order only stipulated fifty.

He was within legal bounds.

The last time he'd pulled a stunt like this, he had shown up at LACMA, Los Angeles County Museum of Art, when she'd been enjoying her time off with Brenda. For days she and Brenda had planned the excursion, texting back and forth about shopping on Rodeo Drive afterward and having a late lunch at the best Peruvian restaurant in town. Isabel had stood her ground and called the police.

And they had done absolutely nothing.

If the petitioner was aware the respondent was in the vicinity and wasn't violating the provisions of the restraining order, then it was the petitioner's responsibility to leave.

Not the other way around.

She had argued that it hadn't been a coincidence and the police had countered that LACMA was the largest art museum in the western United States with a new exhibit that'd just started. Could she prove that it wasn't a coincidence?

Of course not.

It didn't help the situation that *he* was well-known by the cops, well liked and respected.

Trepidation weighted every muscle in Isabel's body and her stomach clenched hard as a fist. "I have to go."

"What?" Dutch froze with the burger in his hand midair before taking a single bite. "What's wrong?"

Dropping her gaze, she said, "There's an urgent call I have to make. I need to leave."

"All right. Let's box up the food."

"No." Grabbing her purse, she stood. "I'm not hungry anymore. I lost my appetite."

"Isabel, what's happening right now?"

"I told you." Her gaze flickered up to the far end of the bar.

He was still staring at her. An ominous smile full of evil spread on his face. Like some demon sent from hell to torment her. That's what he wanted—to possess her, body, mind and soul.

A chill spilled down her entire body, and she had an almost uncontrollable urge to make the sign of the cross over her chest.

Dutch turned as if to see what she was looking at, and that sicko glanced away almost immediately and called to a bartender.

Isabel could barely swallow, her throat growing dry as sandpaper. She spun on her heel and dashed out the door.

Heavy footsteps thudded after her. A warm, strong hand took her wrist, callused fingertips pressed against her skin, bringing her to a gentle stop on the sidewalk in front of the restaurant.

"I know something is wrong," Dutch said, facing her. "You just did a one-eighty on me for a reason. Please, tell me what it is."

Shame burned a hole in her heart. There was no clear way to explain—her lack of judgment and poor instincts, every twisted thing that man had done to her, the degrees of sickness she had tolerated, how she'd allowed him to steal her dignity. The ways he'd terrorized her after she'd ended the relationship.

How did she let any of it happen?

A sob rattled her chest.

If she told Dutch, once she finished spewing out the whole sordid story, he would no doubt see her as a victim.

It was bad enough her best friend looked at her with *poor you* in her eyes. She wasn't inviting another person to the pity party.

"I'm sorry. Today wasn't a good day for lunch. I have to go." Isabel turned and fled at a pace just short of running.

No wasting precious seconds glancing back over her shoulder. No waiting at the light to cross—she held out her hand to cars and dashed across traffic. No aching lungs or quivering thighs holding her back. No letting her three-inch heels slow her down. She'd scurry down the street on stilts if she had to.

Hot tears blurred her eyes, and she thumbed them away.

Shoving through the gallery door, she almost bumped into Brenda.

"Why are you back so soon?" her friend asked. "Did you have time to eat?"

She hurried up the stairs. "He was there."

Brenda stopped dead in her tracks and recoiled. "Not...*him*."

On the mad dash back to the gallery, the fear that had been bubbling inside Isabel had turned to boiling anger. Just when she thought she could pick up the pieces of her life and move on, that bastard came back. Taunting her. Admonishing her.

How dare he invade her life again. Who did he think he was?

"Yes. Chad Ellis." The sound of his name grated on Isabel's ears.

For months, she'd told herself that if she didn't say the name of that twisted man, refused to see his face in her mind's eye, started training, got stronger, that somehow it would take away his power.

But all it had done was make her hypersensitive to him. Left her weakened and unprepared for a face-to-face encounter.

That was a mistake she wasn't going to repeat.

Brenda's heels clacked up the stairs after her. "What are you going to do?"

"Stop pretending that he's going to disappear." Isabel sat behind her desk and picked up the phone. She dialed the One Stop Home Security Superstore that had installed the alarm system in her condo and where she'd also purchased the pepper spray.

"Hello, Douglas speaking. How can I help you?"

Good, it was the owner. "Hi, Doug, this is Isabel Vargas from—"

"I remember you. How is everything working out?"

"The last time we spoke about tools I could use for personal safety, other than a gun, you made a recommendation that I thought wasn't necessary, but I've reconsidered."

"Oh, you're talking about the *Pacifier*." A fourteen-inch stun gun baton that delivered 10,000 volts. "Yeah, that'll make someone trying to attack you regret it. Guaranteed."

"Yes. That's it. I'd like to purchase five."

"Five? That's a lot. You sure you need that many?"

"You heard me correctly." Two for the gallery, one for her purse and two for her home. She'd never be caught without one. Ever. "Can you have them delivered to the gallery?"

"Sure can. They'll be there within the hour. Would you like me to use the credit card we have on file?"

"Yes. Thank you." She disconnected, raised a finger

to Brenda, asking her to wait, and called her Krav Maga instructor at the self-defense school. "Hi, John. It's Isabel. I was wondering if you had room for me in your evening class tonight."

"Sure. No problem. Everything all right?"

"No. It isn't."

"I can have Abraham take the class later and we can work one-on-one, if you'd like."

She let out a deep breath, her muscles slowly beginning to loosen. "I'd appreciate that very much. Thank you." She hung up. Already the panic was receding, and she felt grounded.

"Did you tell Dutch?" Brenda asked.

"No," Isabel snapped. The answer to every problem wasn't a man.

"Why not?"

The only person she could depend on to always be there for her was herself. She'd relied on her father for everything from support, reassurance, comfort, to unconditional love. And one day, he was gone.

Killed in a drive-by shooting.

The pain, the hole his death left seemed never ending. The only way to get through it was to be the person her father had always wanted her to be.

Strong and capable and happy.

Two out of three wasn't bad, so that's what she'd focus on.

"I can take care of myself."

Dutch set the to-go containers of food on the front desk of Kismet and wrote his cell phone number on the top of the carton. Something had spooked Isabel, but no sense in her or Brenda starving, especially since lunch was paid for.

Voices came from the office upstairs, but he didn't want to intrude. He'd followed Isabel back to the gallery, giving her plenty of space while making sure that she was okay. She'd almost gotten hit by a car crossing one street, but she seemed more concerned about whatever she'd been running from.

"Why do you have to be so stubborn?" Brenda asked, her voice heavy with concern. "You don't have to do this alone. I'm sure Dutch would help you, but you have to tell him what you're up against."

"I want him to see *me*," Isabel said, "not Chad Ellis's victim!" A hand slammed against a wooden surface and a chair scraped against the floor. "I have to help myself. Do you understand? I'm not going to accept my uncle's bodyguards who'd only spy on me and report every move I make back to him and I'm certainly not going to start leaning on a man I just met, expecting him to protect me from that maniac!"

Dutch stiffened as he eavesdropped on their conversation.

Maniac? Chad Ellis?

The name hadn't been in Isabel's file.

"I like Dutch, okay! He's a solid prospect for once. I won't let Chad ruin that, too. He's taken enough away from me."

Dutch crept out of the gallery as quietly as he'd entered. His thoughts spun around Isabel's reaction in the restaurant and everything he'd overheard.

Not a lick of it added up with the information he'd been given, troubling him a little and angering him quite a lot.

Going around the back way, he went to the command center across the street, where he found Allison and Draper. Jake Prindle hadn't come back.

"How did it go?" Allison asked.

"Not well, but it had nothing to do with me." He looked at Draper. "Who is Chad Ellis?"

A stupefied expression crossed his boss's face. "Never heard the name."

"Cut the crap and stop playing me," Dutch said. "I can't do my job if I don't have all the information."

Draper put his hands on his hips. "You have the same file the FBI gave me."

"It's true," Allison said, as though she sensed Draper's word couldn't be trusted. "I saw it myself. The same behavioral analyst who recommended you put the file together on Isabel Vargas for us."

"I want a name," Dutch demanded.

"Sheila Rogers," Allison said. "Out of the LA office on Wilshire Boulevard."

Dutch turned for the door.

"Hold on, Haas. I can't have you stirring up trouble with the FBI."

"I'm going over there to get answers and there's nothing you can do to stop me."

"Fine." Draper yanked on his suit coat. "But I'm coming with you."

LESS THAN THIRTY minutes later, Dutch and Draper were seated in Special Agent Rogers's office that was the size of a broom closet. They were so close to her desk that Dutch's knees practically touched the hardwood.

"Thank you for seeing us on such short notice, Agent Rogers," Draper said. "We appreciate you taking the time from your busy schedule."

Agent Rogers responded with similar professional chitchat.

They didn't have time for pleasantries. The inconsistencies surrounding Isabel had been rolling around in Dutch's head like a pinball, ringing warning bells and raising red flags. He needed answers. To hell with the rest.

"The file we were given on Isabel Vargas was incomplete," Dutch said. "Why?"

Frowning, Draper threw him an irritated glance. "You have to excuse Deputy Marshal Haas. He can be overly direct."

Agent Rogers was a petite woman with long, straight dark hair framing her narrow face and elfin features. She looked between them, finally setting her gaze on Dutch. "Based on your mission objectives, the limited amount of time you had to prepare and your lack of undercover experience, I gave you the relevant information you needed to be successful."

Leaning forward, Dutch put his forearms on his thighs. "There's some maniac she's terrified of who's making her life hell."

"Chad Ellis," Agent Rogers said matter-of-factly. "She has a restraining order against him."

"What?" His elevated tone drew Draper's gaze and a reproving head shake. Dutch took a breath, trying to calm down. "I'd call that relevant."

"First, Ellis hasn't been in the picture for months."

"He showed up today in a restaurant where we went for lunch."

Agent Rogers straightened, a glimmer of concern passing over her face. "That's not good."

"You don't say. Isabel hightailed it out of there and I had no clue why. If I'd known, I could've confronted him. Warned him to stay away from her."

Agent Rogers folded her arms across her chest and studied him. "Did Isabel tell you about Ellis?"

Dutch sat back. "No. I overheard her talking about him afterward in her gallery."

Agent Rogers nodded slowly. "So, if you saw Ellis, a man you're not supposed to know, sitting in a place that he's not supposed to be, intimidating Isabel from afar, you would've done what? Went over, jerked him out of his chair by his shirt and threatened him?"

"Sounds about right," Draper said. "That's precisely what you did with Prindle when things didn't go the way you'd expected."

"And you would have blown your cover," Agent Rogers said in a soft, firm voice. "Believe it or not, I'm trying to help you. According to your profile, if you had known about Chad Ellis, your initial response to Isabel would've been overly protective and caused her to withdraw from you rather than endearing her."

"Speaking of my profile, why did you pick me?"

"*How* would be a better question," she said. "After discussing the situation with Marshal Draper, I did some research on Isabel Vargas with the help of our cyber unit. We issued a warrant and requisitioned her dating profile from a top-tier online matchmaking site and discovered she has a type. Not only physically." Agent Rogers gestured to Dutch. "But she's also attracted to men who are highly intelligent, but have a middle-class background, energetic, passionate, socially dominant and who exhibit appetitive-aggressive traits. Three out of the four she dated from the site also rode motorcycles and expressed an interest in extreme sports. In short, they were adrenaline junkies. Does this sound familiar?"

Dutch restrained the sigh building in his throat and refused to concede that she had just described him, although he wasn't certain about the appetitive-aggressive bit. "*How* me and not someone else?" He couldn't be the only guy in the USMS fitting that profile.

"The situation presented discriminating factors. No one from California could be used because of the data breach. We needed a single male, late twenties to early thirties, who wasn't on an active assignment, had been with the USMS less than three years and had a background we could tinker with, filling in your work history. The fact that you both lost your fathers in your early teens was a bonus. You were perfect. No one else came close to your numbers. Algorithms don't make mistakes."

That explained the easy, natural connection he formed with Isabel, but it also raised an important question. "This Ellis guy, are you saying he and I are alike?"

"Not quite. With Ellis, she deviated from her usual type. She met him at a function, not online. From what I can tell, Ellis exhibits psychopathic traits, which is quite common in the corporate world. Charming, arrogant, risk taker, no remorse, a master manipulator. Whereas you're honest, noble, and during your US Marshals assessment displayed a high degree of empathy. All strengths that could also be a weakness in this situation. The emotional handling required here is a delicate balance and having all the facts from her file would've hurt your ability to forge a bond with the asset."

Asset again. Dutch gritted his teeth. "I want to see the complete file."

"I have to advise against that. In this case, less is more where the asset is concerned. If you want to see more on her uncle, that's fine. But you need to trust that I've given you everything you need to succeed."

"I don't know you. I don't trust you. I need all the facts or I can't do my job effectively."

Agent Rogers turned to her computer and typed away

on her keyboard. "I just emailed it to Marshal Draper and cc'd Deputy Chen-Boyd."

The hyphenated name wasn't a surprise to Dutch. Allison had never used Boyd around him, but some days she wore a wedding ring and some days she didn't, like someone with unresolved feelings going through a separation.

"But I must warn you," Agent Rogers said. "Give serious consideration to how you've interacted with the asset so far and what's elicited a positive response. Don't deviate from that. Above all, don't let details that you're not supposed to know slip."

Dutch stood and shook Agent Rogers's hand. "Duly noted."

Chapter Seven

"Thank you for squeezing me in. I need this emergency session," Isabel said, grateful for John's help and happy that she kept extra workout gear in her trunk.

"No problem. We're here to help." John clasped her shoulder. Tall and built, he carried himself with the same confident awareness as Dutch. "What's up?"

"The guy I told you about popped up today out of the blue."

Concern tightened across his features. "Did he threaten you?"

This was where it sometimes got tricky with Chad. He hadn't violated the restraining order and he hadn't spoken to her. If she told anyone that he wagged his fingers at her as one might do a child, they'd blow her off. Tell her she was overreacting and to ignore the taunt.

But to dismiss the slightest action on Chad's part would be a mistake that could cost her life. Of that, she was certain.

"He intimidated me on purpose, but not in a way that I have a legal recourse." Not this time. Not yet. But she worried things might escalate. "And I froze when I saw him. The terror and panic came rushing back and I felt helpless."

"I understand." John tightened his hand on her in

a reassuring way. "I want to be clear—it's not okay for someone to make you fear for your safety or cause you emotional distress. When you have the option to call the cops and not engage, take it. That's best."

"What if that's not an option?"

"Then you need to fight until you can get away from him and get help. I think we need to work on some extreme scenarios where you feel legitimately threatened. Get you to the point where you don't hesitate. Freezing, even for a few seconds, can mean the difference between living and dying."

She was in favor of living. "Sounds good."

"But it'll take time for practice to become habit and habit to become a reflex. It's not going to happen in one or two sessions."

If only she knew how much time she had until Chad finally snapped. "I can come in more often."

John nodded. "What's your parking situation like at the gallery and your house?"

She explained about the valet garage two blocks down and told him about the gated garage with security cameras at her condo.

"There's a luxury valet service I know of. They'll pick your car up for you in front of the art gallery, fuel it, wash it and deliver it right at your door. It's a little pricey, but you might want to consider it. Save yourself the two-block walk."

Jim, the valet at the garage, wouldn't be happy to see her go, but the premium service was exactly what she needed. "I think I'll try it."

"You can grab a card at the desk on your way out. Now, let's go work on your self-defense skills."

Her phone rang. She glanced at the caller ID. It was her uncle. "I need to take this, but I'll only be a minute." After John nodded and stepped away, giving her privacy, she answered. *"Hola, tío."*

"Hola, mi hija." Since her dad had died, her uncle started calling her his daughter.

His love for her was undeniable. She felt deeply for him, treasured their bond, appreciated his attempt to fill the void left by her dad. He was almost a second father to her. Almost.

"I won't be able to make it to your fund-raiser this year. *Lo siento*," he said, apologizing in Spanish. "I know how much the event means to you."

"It's okay." She hid the disappointment in her voice. "I know you're a busy man."

"But I still want to see you." His deep voice and thick Mexican accent sounded so much like her father's sometimes it made her heart ache. "I have something to discuss. Next Wednesday, I'll come up to LA and we'll have dinner. Clear your evening for me."

He didn't make requests. He made demands. Not just of her, but everyone around him. He'd been that way for as long as she could remember, and she'd learned it was easier to go along with him than refuse.

"Okay. What time?" she asked.

"Let's say seven. I'll send a car for you."

"*Gracias, tío. Te amo.*" *Thank you, uncle. I love you.* "See you soon."

"*Te amo.* Adios."

Isabel hung up with a fresh wave of tension rising inside her. She dismissed it, not wanting the tightness in her chest to be related to her uncle's call and whatever he wanted to discuss. Instead, she focused on not letting that psycho Chad catch her off guard again. "John, I'm ready."

CHAD PUSHED THROUGH the men's locker-room door into the hallway and stopped short at the sound of a melodic voice that made his pulse race. *Isabel.* He peeked around

the corner, catching sight of her going into one of the
empty workout rooms with John.

*What are you doing here in the evening? Not like you
to deviate from your schedule.*

Had their encounter earlier stimulated her as it had
him?

From the gleam in her eye at the restaurant and the
way she ran out, she'd been aroused. Still was, and she'd
come here to work it out physically since she couldn't
have the type of release that he'd give her.

Fire sang in his blood even now. Growing hotter, burning brighter as he watched her.

Isabel's caramel-brown hair was pulled into a high
ponytail, her luscious hips swaying as she walked. He
saw how other men took notice of her, lusted after her
with their eyes. She liked it and so did he. As long as no
one else touched her.

John talked her through a movement, something basic
and easy. She got into position and then John lunged at
her. Without a second of hesitation, she responded the
way he'd shown her.

*Are you thinking of me? Imagining us together, tus-
sling, our limbs entangled, with me finally on top of you,
holding you down?*

He smiled, sensing their connection getting stronger.

"Hey, Chad," Abraham said, coming out of the locker
room.

Chad pivoted, facing him, and flashed a bright, easy
grin.

Abraham glanced over Chad's shoulder at the room
where Isabel and John were practicing, then looked back
at him. "Ready for class?"

"Actually, I got an emergency call from the office.
I need to go, but I'll be back tomorrow."

Part of him was tempted to stay, hoped she'd see him, giving her another spike of endorphins, making her skin flush only the way he could.

But that would spoil the foreplay.

He was eager to see what she'd do next and he had a few moves that she'd never anticipate.

"BEFORE YOU LOOK at the file, did Agent Rogers say why she withheld it?" Allison asked, sitting in front of the laptop in the makeshift command center.

Dutch set his motorcycle helmet on the table. "Something about not wanting me to treat Isabel in an overprotective manner because it'd push her away. And, uh, the more I knew, the easier it'd be to slip up."

"I'm going to make a coffee run. Anyone want anything?" Draper asked.

"Skinny cappuccino," Allison said. "Thanks, sir."

Dutch shook his head and Draper left.

"I've got to warn you," Allison said, her voice grim. "The redacted information made my skin crawl and it will definitely make your protective alpha instincts flare, so if you read it, don't go all caveman on the asset. Okay?"

Give him some credit. As an elite operator on the Fugitive Apprehension Response Team, restraint and patience were prerequisites. "Sure."

Allison got up and gestured for him to sit at the computer.

"Where should I start?" he asked.

"The restraining order." She clicked on the document and brought it up on the screen.

Dutch skimmed over it, trying to pinpoint the essential elements of information through the superfluity of legal jargon.

"You want to look at her allegations," Allison said, as if reading his mind. "She claims that over the course of their one-month relationship, Chad Ellis grew increasingly possessive, controlling and aggressive. She felt intimidated and scared and broke up with him."

"Any abuse?"

"Not physically, at least not while they were together. In her statement, Ellis comes across as charming and persuasive, like a cult leader. Isabel struck me as a bit inexperienced and too trusting."

"It's good she broke up with him before things got violent."

Allison grimaced. "But there's more. The night she ended it he tore up her apartment. After the breakup, the harassment started with him following her. She alleged that he called her at all hours, forcing her to change her cell number, but she still received calls at the gallery. Unfortunately, it was never proven. Ellis voluntarily handed over the records for his cell phone and all the landlines of businesses."

"It would've been easy enough for him to use a burner."

Allison nodded. "My thoughts exactly."

"What does the guy do for a living?" Dutch asked.

"Here's the creepy part," Allison said, bringing up other documents on the screen. "He owns a few car washes, several biohazard remediation cleaning businesses from Malibu to Laguna, and a couple of funeral homes with crematoriums."

Ice slid through Dutch's blood. "What is he, a serial killer in the making?"

"Maybe. With those resources at his disposal and his past behavior, he may have already killed someone and made the entire crime scene disappear. We may never know."

Dutch clenched his hand into a fist, thinking about how Ellis had shown up in the restaurant, intimidating and frightening Isabel to the point that she ran out. It made Dutch want to rip his head off.

"Isabel was never able to prove that he followed her or made the strange phone calls, but there was a witness who caught him accosting her. She was leaving the art gallery. Her car had been parked in a proprietor's spot around back, when he came up behind her, put his arm around her throat and allegedly told her that they'd always be together. The owner of the bookstore two doors down happened to be leaving around the same time. He testified that Ellis was shoving his hand up her skirt and Isabel stated that he tried to get her inside the car."

Dutch's fist tightened, the joints popping, his fingers beginning to ache.

Why would Agent Rogers recommend a mugging scenario with Isabel after what she went through?

Even though it had worked, the tactic was despicable, especially considering Isabel's history. Dutch hadn't known her long, but he had an overwhelming urge to shield her from violence and pain.

"Ellis claimed it was a misunderstanding," Allison said. "Isabel had called him earlier that day. She stated it was to demand that he stop sending her gifts, but he alleged she asked him to come to the gallery and that in the past Isabel liked him to be rough. Several police officers testified on Ellis's behalf, making him look like citizen of the year. He had a good lawyer who characterized Isabel as a scorned woman with a grudge, trying to defame Ellis. The judge issued a harassment restraining order for one year, where Ellis has to remain fifty feet away from her."

Dutch scowled, keeping a tight lid on the rage brewing inside him. "That's it. Only fifty?" He ran both his hands over his head.

Blood pounded behind his ears in a thunderous rush as his brain turned over the information, round and round, thinking of all the places where that freak could legally show up and still harass Isabel as he'd done earlier.

"It sucks. I know." Allison splayed her hands. "I'm sure the police testimonials were a factor, along with how careful Ellis had been. Thank heavens the bookstore owner came out when he did. I hate to think what could've happened to her if Ellis had gotten her into the car."

Biohazard remediation was another way of saying crime-scene cleanup. That would explain why Ellis had a good relationship with the police.

Allison pulled out the cell phone buzzing in her pocket. "It's my son—I've got to take it. My soon-to-be-former husband is already giving me enough hell over this short-term assignment. Like he doesn't get to jet off for his job whenever he wants. Damn double standards." She thumbed the accept button and strolled away. "Hey, munchkin." Her tone turned warm and cheerful. "How was school?"

Agent Rogers had had a legitimate concern. It was going to take every shred of Dutch's willpower to contain his protective impulses where Isabel was concerned. He wanted nothing more than to keep her safe from Ellis. Because he did care. Whether or not she was aware of her uncle's status as leader of a powerful and brutal cartel had nothing to do with this. In fact, it made him believe that she was completely unaware. Anyone familiar with the cartel and their vicious reputation could've had Chad Ellis disappear with one phone call to her uncle.

Isabel was innocent and suffering and needed help.

Dutch enlarged the picture of Chad Ellis. He wore an expensive suit and tie, clean-cut, with a practiced smile and Hollywood looks, but there was something cold and vacant about his eyes.

"So that's what a psychopath looks like," he muttered to himself.

Guys like Ellis didn't simply walk away on their own accord, or even when directed to by the law. Things would only build with him, getting worse until he struck out and physically hurt her. Did as much damage as possible.

Dutch had been right to push for the information. He had to know what Isabel was up against. The reason she'd been guarded, wary, fearful today.

Getting close to her without smothering Isabel in his red-hot need to protect her, to defend her against that violent creep wouldn't be a problem. His mother and sister had made him an expert in dealing with determined, independent women who could take care of themselves.

But he had to show Isabel that even the strong sometimes needed backup.

The next time Chad Ellis messed with Isabel, Dutch was going to see to it that he regretted it.

Chapter Eight

The annual fund-raiser was winding down but had gone better than Isabel had hoped. The elevator had been fixed earlier that afternoon. Canapés were being served and chilled champagne flowed all evening. Her uncle Emilio had purchased a painting over the phone, showing his support as always even though he couldn't attend. They'd exceeded their mark, raising twenty thousand over their goal, and still had two paintings left.

The one thing that'd make the night better was seeing Dutch.

Isabel checked the door again, hoping he might show. Not that he had any reason to. She'd run out on him at lunch yesterday without a legitimate explanation, hadn't called him to say thank you for dropping off the food despite his laid-back way of giving her his number and she'd neglected to extend him a formal invite to the event.

He must think she was a total basket case. Why would he come tonight unless he was a glutton for punishment?

"It's haunting," the mayor said about the abstract expressionist painting, yanking her from her thoughts. "This artist has the depth and passion of Jackson Pollock. I'll take it."

"Fantastic." She plastered on a hollow smile. Pulling off her biggest event of the year with such a resounding success should've made her happy. But there was a gaping hole in her life. If only she knew how to fill it. "Thank you so much for your support."

The mayor shook her hand and they held the pose for a photo op in front of the painting. With any luck, the picture would make the front of the Art and Entertainment section of the Sunday newspaper.

Isabel directed the mayor's assistant to Brenda to complete the purchase.

One painting left.

The phone rang. Isabel made her way through the milling crowd to the front desk and answered. "Kismet art gallery." She pressed her opposite ear closed so she could hear over the murmur of conversations in the background. "Isabel Vargas speaking. How may I help you?"

Heavy breathing rasped through the phone. Isabel's stomach plummeted, her muscles tightening. Long breaths in and out over the line in her ear, deep, slow grunting.

Her hand fluttered to her neck and she fiddled with the string of pearls she wore.

"I hate your lipstick," an altered male voice groaned, and the cold lump in her throat swelled to the size of a bowling ball. "That shade of red makes you look like a harlot. But I love the dress."

First, he'd shown up at the restaurant and now he was making harassing phone calls again. No matter how he disguised his voice, she knew it was him. Chad Ellis.

"Sophisticated, yet, enticing. A second skin against your body, showcasing your curves." He grunted, his breath growing heavier, deeper, viler. "You look beautiful tonight. Nice touch with the pearls. Such a *tease*."

Bile burned up the back of Isabel's throat as she dropped her hand from her neck and looked around out the front window. He wouldn't be easy to spot. That maniac was hiding in the darkness, where no one else would be able to see him.

No witnesses.

"I bet you smell even better," he said, dragging out each syllable in an eerie way that raised goose bumps on her skin, but she swallowed the bitter taste filling her mouth. "Maybe I'll come closer to take a whiff. I miss you. Can you feel my eyes on you? Like a physical touch you crave. Watching you makes me so hot—"

"Get a life, you sick pervert, and stay out of mine!" Isabel slammed the phone down and caught the shocked glances of those around her.

Embarrassment heated her face, her heart fluttering. "Sorry." She raised a trembling hand in apology. "Excuse me."

She was done. No more hanging up in silence. No more running away. No more living half a life because she thought there was something wrong with her. She wasn't the problem.

He was.

"Everything all right?"

Isabel turned around, freezing midspin. Dutch stood beside her, dressed in a slate-gray shirt buttoned almost all the way to the top and dark slacks. His face was tense, concern stamped across his features. The surprise was so pleasant and shocking she threw herself against his chest, hugging him.

An immediate spark of heat rushed over her skin at the contact, but she dismissed it as a histrionic reaction after the disturbing phone call from Chad. Still, Dutch's warmth and strength engulfing her took the chill away from her bones, nonetheless.

He held her, his arms banding tight around her in a comforting embrace.

"You came," she gasped.

Stroking her hair, he said, "All the work and worry you were putting into this event, how could I not come?"

She pulled back, regaining her composure, and looked up at him.

The relief in seeing his face and beaming smile was like a gift she'd prayed for but had given up hope on ever getting.

"When I walked in, you sounded upset on the phone. Who were you talking to?"

Isabel dropped her gaze to her peep-toed shoes. "No one worth discussing."

Brenda shimmied through the crowd and slid up next to her. "We just sold the last painting to that Hollywood producer."

"That's great," Isabel said, her voice flat and devoid of excitement.

"What's wrong?" Brenda asked.

"She just got an upsetting phone call from a *sick pervert*," Dutch said to Brenda while putting a comforting arm around Isabel.

Brenda's jaw unhinged and her eyes went wide. "The nerve of him."

"Him who?" Dutch asked.

"Chad Ellis," Brenda said. "Her ex."

"I don't want to talk about it." Isabel rolled her pearls through her fingers and remembered the disgusting things Chad had said to her. Was he still watching her? She lowered her hand, smoothing down the bottom of her Herve Leger crisscross bandage dress. "I think I need to get out of here. Would you mind if I cut out early?"

she asked Brenda, hating to abandon her friend, but she needed to leave the gallery, needed air.

"Not at all. This soiree is almost over. I've already roped the gorgeous party planner into helping me close and we're going to have drinks after. Go somewhere with Dutch." Brenda shifted her gaze to him. "Do you promise to take her somewhere fun and make sure she gets home safely?"

"I can handle that."

"You don't have to," Isabel said. "Really. I can just go home."

"It'd be my pleasure to take you out," he said.

"There. It's settled." Brenda kissed her cheek. "You deserve a break. You did awesome tonight, working the room and convincing people to open their wallets. Get out of here."

"Are you up for dancing?" Dutch asked.

"Sure." It might be a good distraction. "My uncle owns a nightclub in downtown LA. We could get a VIP table and a bottle of whatever you want."

He shrugged, not looking the least bit impressed. "Sounds like a lot of unnecessary fancy stuff if you ask me. All I need is you and some good music. You game?"

She was so accustomed to using the perks of her lifestyle to ingratiate herself with other people that she didn't know how to respond when Dutch shot down her offer.

He frowned. "If going to your uncle's club makes you more comfortable, then we—"

"No. It's just surprising. Most people jump at the chance to have VIP treatment."

"I'm not most people."

No, he wasn't. He was a beautiful anomaly.

"I'm game," she said. "Just give me a minute."

After saying a few quick goodbyes, she grabbed

her clutch from the bottom drawer of the desk. Since she hadn't realized the Pacifier required twelve hours to charge, all five were plugged in at home, juicing up. Rather than needing to lug a tote-size bag, she opted for something small and sparkly to match her shoes. It was only big enough to hold her driver's license, credit card, lipstick, pepper spray and EpiPen.

"Where are we going?" she asked.

"It's a surprise." Dutch took her hand in his, interlacing their fingers, and hauled her out of the gallery.

"Do I need to call for my car?"

"Nope."

Being led off into the unknown by a man she'd met two days ago should've felt reckless and risky, but it didn't. She didn't know Dutch well. His body was lethal, his face hard and rugged, but she was certain of two things. He was kind and considerate, and that made him exactly what she needed.

"Dutch, you're so right," she said, swallowing the words *almost perfect*, "that there must be something wrong with you. What is it? You don't have split-personality disorder or any other type of condition, do you?"

"I assure you, I'm as sane as you and Brenda."

Well, that wasn't saying much. Some days she was insane-asylum-batty, and Brenda was far from normal, in a wacky sort of way, but neither of them were psycho. Like Chad.

Something had been off about her ex, in his core makeup. He had probably tortured animals as a child. She'd sensed it in his eyes, in his touch, without being able to pinpoint what it was until he'd let his maniac flag fly.

Dutch was turning out to be everything she wanted

in a guy, her wish list made into flesh and bone. If she were looking for a perfect partner.

"And you've never stalked anyone, have you?" she asked.

"Never. But in freshman year of high school, I had a crush on a cheerleader and went to every football game. Fortunately, she was a senior and when she graduated, my obsession ended."

She chuckled.

"You're safe with me, Isabel." He leaned in and put their joined hands over his heart. "I promise, no harm will come to you while you're with me." He spoke the words like a vow.

She always picked the wrong guy, but Dutch was different and had given her plenty of reasons through his actions to take a chance on him.

They walked four blocks down Santa Monica Boulevard and over to the Third Street Promenade—a posh outdoor shopping center with luxury boutiques, restaurants and lively events. Between Wilshire and Arizona Avenue was a festive public party with a diverse crowd. Salsa dancing on the promenade, from the young to the old, beginners and talented dancers displaying expert footwork and head rolls and dips she could only dream of doing.

It was unpretentious. A stark contrast to the vibe at any club. No one cared about how they were dressed or was concerned with appearances only. Everyone simply wanted to have a good time.

Isabel had no idea that this was going on a short five-minute walk from her gallery.

Dutch whisked her into his arms. "Disappointed?"

"Not at all," she said, her feet already moving to the music.

Placing his hands in the right places, holding her in a firm yet gentle grip, he made it so damned easy with his *caliente* salsa moves. Their bodies pressed close, hips rolling in fluid sync.

She listened to the rhythm, surrendered to Dutch's lead and let go. He was a human live wire made of muscle.

Dancing. Who would've guessed it would feel so good?

Laughter, fun and romance were in the warm air as he held her closer, spinning away her worries to the energizing Latin beats.

Her blood heated. The provocative moves reminded her how sexual and carefree she used to be. Dutch's magnetism, the upbeat tempo, the sound of the trumpets in the music, the open-air environment, sparked life back in her veins and weaved a sort of magic around her.

She'd needed this. *Needed him.*

Dutch twirled her away from him. Smiling, she whirled with her arms extended. She did a two-count step, backing up to him, showing off a little.

Facing the large fountain topped with a dinosaur topiary, she spotted Chad watching her.

His jaw clenched hard. His eyes narrowed, his stare blistering. She could feel his fury like scalding lava on her skin.

If looks could kill, she would've been reduced to scorched earth.

Taking her wrist, Dutch spun her back into his arms. The unexpected touch made her catch her breath and sent her pulse hammering for good reasons. He smiled at her as if no one else in the world existed. Something in her chest lightened as fear evaporated.

God, she liked touching this delectable man, dancing with him, being near him. The way she felt safe with him. And nothing, absolutely nothing was going to spoil this moment.

Cupping his face in both her hands, Isabel rose on her toes and brought Dutch's mouth to hers. She didn't know if it was the adrenaline, her attraction to Dutch or her refusal to act as a victim that caused her to do it.

But he pulled her into the kiss, his lips hot and urgent, his tongue exploring deep.

And she didn't hold back. Nothing denied. Everything on public display for all to see.

Her body moved against his, sinuous and desperate for sweetness, for sanctuary.

Not that long ago, someone cruel had made her doubt herself and tried to convince her that love had to hurt.

But it didn't.

Dutch's hands were gentle and persuasive on her body. Each long, sensual stroke of his tongue stole her breath along with the ugly memories. Transcended her to the clouds, where she was floating. She moaned in his mouth and he held her tighter with those granite arms, flattening her against his rock-hard chest. They tasted one another again and again, sharing breath, fueling the mutual fire crackling between them.

In that moment, she was fearless and passionate, and had never felt more like her true self. A believer in happiness and romance. All from the most empowering kiss of her life with a man she was falling for. Against her self-imposed rules.

Dutch eased back and looked into her eyes. His hand came up to cradle her jaw. A smile spread across his face, brimming with heat that melted her. To heck with the rules.

"That's one hell of a way to ask a guy to kiss you."

She laughed, free and loud. The heartfelt sound emanating from deep inside her belly. Glancing over her shoulder, she looked at the fountain.

The demon was gone, banished back to hell.

For now.

DUTCH FOLLOWED ISABEL'S directions as he drove her home in her Maserati. A fine piece of machinery that handled tight curves with smooth precision.

Her dog was curled up on the back seat, asleep. A soft smile rested on Isabel's face, filling him with a sense of joy the likes of which he'd never known. With her tension gone, she looked younger than twenty-eight, vulnerable, adorable. He hadn't thought making someone else happy could bring him such gratification.

No one deserved a fun evening more than her. The dancing had done the trick. She came out of her shell and had blossomed in front of him. As soon as he'd read about the Third Street Promenade free salsa dancing in a local magazine, he'd thought of Isabel.

Not as a manipulative ploy. She'd popped into his head and he'd imagined her dancing and letting loose. And she had.

But that kiss had been unexpected. Instead of his reaction being one of professional restraint, it had been visceral, instinctual, taking the chemistry kindling between them from sparks to a brush fire.

Remembering it had adrenaline pumping in his veins akin to standing on the edge of a cliff preparing to jump into the deep blue below. He *was* into extreme sports. Cliff diving. Rock climbing. BASE jumping. Snowboarding. You name it, he'd tried it, but none of it compared to kissing Isabel.

A hunger for more was growing inside him. More kisses and salsa and smiles, like the one on her face now.

Dancing had led to dinner at an Italian place with good vibes, where they'd split a Neapolitan-style pizza while he kept one eye on the door. Waiting, hoping that cretin Chad dared set a foot inside, but he hadn't shown his face.

Isabel had eaten with a hearty appetite that he appreciated and laughed with no shadows in her eyes. They had chatted about their childhoods and the importance of family and their respective difficulties making friends when they were younger. About the places they'd both traveled to for fun and deployments. His time in the Sandbox and the mountains of Afghanistan. Even the gut-wrenching reality of what it had been like in spec ops.

He'd told her things he'd never shared with another soul, and she didn't diminish it with platitudes. She'd taken his hand in hers and showed her understanding through her eyes, through her touch.

Somewhere along the way he'd forgotten this was business and not pleasure, and the weight she carried seemed to lift from her shoulders, as well.

They'd only called it a night because she had to pick up her dog from day care before the place closed.

"Turn left here," she said. "That's my building." She pointed to a small modern complex with only six floors.

Dutch turned and she hit the remote, opening the gate to her garage. It was well lit and had plenty of security cameras, not leaving any blind spots.

Still, it was possible for someone on foot to slip in behind her car. Good thing she'd gotten the dog.

"Thanks for driving. I'll order an Uber for you," she said, as they had planned earlier, but he'd hoped to have a little more time with her.

They got out of the car and walked toward the door that led inside to the lobby. The well-trained dog stayed at her side without a leash.

"The app says it'll take twenty minutes." Her tone was disappointed, but he couldn't tell if it was because he wasn't staying longer or not leaving sooner.

"I can wait outside for it." The night had been the best date he'd had in a long time, but he didn't want to put any unnecessary pressure on her.

"No, please don't. I've got to take McQueen out one last time. Join us? The app will send an alert when the car gets here."

"Sure."

They strolled past the elevator and headed for the back deck.

"Since the gallery is closed tomorrow, if you don't have plans, I'd love to help you mark something off your bucket list."

"If you're talking about sex, I'm sure you're fantastic in bed, but—"

Dutch laughed. "I meant surfing. I'd love to teach you, but it's nice to know you have such confidence in my bedroom skills."

Cheeks turning berry red, she lowered her head and pursed her lips. "I'm sorry. I'd love to learn. Text me a time and a place and what I need to bring or wear."

He held the door open for her. Motion lights came on as they went outside. The dog ran past the swimming pool to a patch of fake grass on the far side of the large communal deck that had a locked gate.

"McQueen is such a kick-butt name," Dutch said, following Isabel to the railing, overlooking the beach. "I'm surprised you named him after the actor."

"Which actor?" She looked up at the stars.

"Steve McQueen. The king of cool. *The Thomas Crown Affair*, the original. *The Getaway*, once again the original. *The Magnificent Seven*."

Her gaze found his. "Let me guess. The original."

"Yes. And let's not forget *Bullitt*."

"Well, I named him after Alexander McQueen."

"Who?"

"The fashion designer."

After a beat of silence, they laughed in unison.

"Sounds like we'll have to have a movie marathon," she said. "I'll cook dinner and you'll…"

He brushed the hair from her face, caressing her cheek. Standing there, staring at her, he hid nothing, letting her see the cutting edge driving him, the genuine attraction drawing him closer to her. He was the kind of man who owned who he was and told the world to go take a flying leap if they didn't like it. But this was the best he could do, the most he could give in the moment. "Do the dishes and then rub your feet?"

She smiled, unguarded and bright. "You better stop, or I'll have to kiss you again."

"If that's your idea of a deterrent, you're going to have to work on that." He pulled her to him. But caught himself and lightened his grip, easing back.

"Do I still have to ask?" She tilted her head, wetting her lips.

"I want to respect your wishes and take this slowly." He had an important job to do and touching her was testing his willpower, but he had no intention of seducing her or using sex as a manipulation tactic. That was a line he wouldn't cross. "I want you to get to know me. To be comfortable around me. I want to understand what troubles you, keeps you up at night just like I know you want to see the northern lights." And he did, so damn badly. Not for his job, but for himself. "I get the sense this might scare you and I don't want to rush you."

"*You* don't scare me, Dutch. So stop talking and kiss me."

Lowering his lips to hers, he slipped an arm around her waist and gently touched her mouth, his tongue skating over hers. She leaned into the kiss, circling her arms around his neck. He threaded his fingers in her silky mass of loose curls cascading around her shoulders, breathing her in, molding her to him and savoring this.

He drank her in, the heady, delicate taste of her that was somehow wild and sweet at the same time. An enticing floral scent mixed with spice came from her hair and skin.

The soft heat of her, the way she smelled, how she tasted, the responding hunger in her touch, everything culminated in that moment of pure perfection.

No woman had felt better. So right.

Then her phone chimed, and he cursed the promptness of the Uber driver.

A PALL OF RED fell over the world as Chad seethed. Violent thoughts, gruesome cravings danced in his head the same way she had danced with that man.

Isabel.

He beat his fist against the boulder as he watched that man touching his woman. Kissing *his* precious doll, turning her into a wanton trollop.

Isabel!

The darkness around him on the beach seeped into his soul. His mouth tasted of ashes.

If that thug went up to her apartment, if she took him to her bed…

Chad squeezed his eyes shut, knowing what he'd have to do. Kill the interloper.

And cleanse Isabel of her sin.

On the deck, the two separated and Isabel pulled out her phone, then glanced at the screen. Her dog dashed out of the grass and ran around the pool, doing laps like it was racing around a track.

She snapped her fingers. The canine came to her and licked the man's hand. He bent down, rubbing its head. Even the damn dog liked him.

They traipsed back inside the building with her arm linked around his.

Chad's gaze slid to the third floor, to her apartment. He waited, growing still, the blood in his veins boiling, the leash slipping on the rage prowling inside him.

Finally, her lights came on and she entered her apartment. Alone. The inconvenient dog didn't count.

She'd come to her senses and sent that piece of garbage on his way for the night.

But she had put Chad in a difficult position. Now he had to save Isabel from herself before she violated the sanctity of their union.

He had no choice but to punish her.

Because I love you, Isabel.

Necessary preparations had been made. He'd anticipated this day might come, and he was ready to remind her who was in charge.

Chapter Nine

The wind was mild, the sun bright, the waves cool and steady with a long swell period. Perfection conditions for Isabel's first lesson, Dutch thought to himself.

He was in the water waist deep. Next to him, Isabel was on his board, wearing a provocative one-piece with a zipper down the front and cutouts on her waist. Her killer curves had been apparent from the formfitting clothes she wore, but in a swimsuit, her figure was jaw-dropping.

For an hour or so, they'd practiced on the sand, going over training footwork, teaching her how to pop up on the board and read the waves. Then they'd spent another hour in the water. Sitting on a surfboard seemed easy, but as Isabel discovered, it wasn't. Simply something you had to learn, feel. Right along with falling over—a crucial part and inevitable for all, especially beginners—and paddling, a key to good surfing.

"Remember," Dutch said, "when you're riding on the board, bend your knees, not your back."

She pushed her wet hair back from her face, focused on the water. "Okay."

As a wave rolled in, Dutch positioned the board. "Go. Now."

Isabel paddled like the devil to catch the wave, got up into a solid crouch, then stood and balanced.

Yes! She stood!

Even better, she rode that wave all the way to the shore.

Dutch marveled at how well she was doing on her first day. She had the potential to be good at it.

He whooped and cheered and encouraged her to try it again. They did a few more sets and took a break on the beach.

Isabel went to shower off and Dutch ran a towel over himself. He opened the cooler, took out the food he'd packed and set it on a blanket. Surfing always worked up his appetite. He figured it'd do the same for her.

She returned wearing sunglasses and a white cover-up over her bathing suit. Her skin was smooth and flawless. He loved her like this, carefree, no makeup besides a sheer lip gloss she'd applied. Not that she needed it with that natural rosy tint to her lips. She sat beside him, putting her tote bag down.

A breeze carried that divine scent of hers to him. Warm amber, floral and spice. "What perfume did you put on?"

"It's a perfume oil." She dug a delicate bottle out of the bag and showed it to him. "Marula Oil is the base, making it great for my hair and skin."

He leaned over and ran his nose up her neck, inhaling deeply. Vetiver struck him this time, the scent reminding him of Indonesia and wading through the tall, fragrant grass on an assignment. "I really love it on you."

"Then I'll have to stock up." As she was dropping the bottle back in her bag, the tote tipped over and a black baton rolled out.

Dutch picked it up, noting the wrist strap, rubberized armor coating and prongs on the end. "Stun baton?"

Turning her head away from him, she looked out at the water. "It's a deterrent."

"For whom? Chad Ellis?"

She went ramrod straight. "This has been such a lovely day." Reaching over, she took his hand in hers and looked at him. "I don't want to spoil it by talking about him. Please."

The vulnerability in her touch, her voice, tugged at his heart. Tied his gut into knots. He wanted to take away her pain, to mop up this problem of Ellis like a spill on the floor.

Isabel was an incredible woman, easy to fall for. Not at all the stuck-up princess he'd imagined her to be. If not for this assignment, their paths might never have crossed. He hated the circumstances and the necessary deception that had brought them together but spending time with her made him feel like the luckiest man on the planet.

Dutch put the baton back in her bag. "Okay." He rubbed her leg to reassure Isabel there was no need to discuss it, but his hand lingered longer than he'd intended. Her skin was so soft, supple as butter. "Hungry?" He started opening the containers of food he prepared.

"Starved." She flashed a bright smile. "You thought of everything."

AFTER CHAD PAID the parking fee, he pulled into a spot in the lot on the ridge above the beach. He double-checked that there were no CCTV cameras. Then he glanced down at the phone and read the text messages again.

Isabel: I'm excited, but nervous. Hope you're a good teacher, Dutch.

Dutch: You'll do great. Trust me, beautiful. Topanga Beach. 10 a.m.

Isabel: See you later.

ONE NIGHT SEVEN months ago, while Isabel had slept in his bed, Chad had taken her cell phone and the key fob to her car. He'd handed them off to his tech guy who did freelance work under the table. Two hours later, Chad had a clone of the RFID key fob and spyware had been downloaded on her phone. The malicious software gave Chad her GPS location, browser history, text messages, social media chats, emails and the ability to eavesdrop on her phone calls.

She'd been none the wiser. Still wasn't.

Despite the fact she'd changed her number, the mobile device itself and the SIM card were the same. Until she upgraded her cell, which wasn't going to be any time soon since he'd encouraged her to get the latest model shortly after they started dating, he was able to surveil her in ways even Olga couldn't. But the PI filled in the gaps.

If it hadn't been for Olga, it would've taken him days to find out about *Dutch*.

This was the first time Isabel had sent a message to another man.

Blood burned through his veins again, anger and adrenaline spurring him on.

Chad dialed Olga. She was somewhere down below on the beach. Like any good private investigator, she kept a variety of outfits in her car to blend in wherever she needed to and even had a bicycle in her trunk. "What are they doing?"

"Eating lunch."

"When they get ready to leave, I want you to film Isabel."

"I don't understand," Olga said.

"Record them saying goodbye and focus the video on Isabel getting into her car and driving off."

"Why?"

"Because I told you to," Chad snapped, letting his thinning patience resonate over the line. "No matter what happens, follow the man. Find out where he lives. Get me a full name."

"What's going to happen?"

Chad hung up, huffing his irritation. Olga was paid well not to ask questions and to do as she was instructed discreetly.

Before getting out of the car, he pressed down the fake mustache, ensuring it stayed in place, lowered the bill of his ball cap over his wig and slipped on gloves. He grabbed the robin's-egg-blue Tiffany box that he'd poked air holes in earlier, got out and walked quickly to Isabel's Maserati.

He hit the cloned key fob. Her lights flashed and the doors unlocked.

Grasping the handle, he opened the door and lowered to one knee. He slipped his little gift of *tough love* underneath the driver's seat, flicked off the lid—the faint sound of the box's inhabitants lifting his spirits enough for him to manage a smile—and slammed the door shut.

No fingerprints or any DNA traces of his left behind. His brother Brett, a reliable alibi, would swear that Chad had been at his house the entire day, where his car was still parked in the driveway.

He climbed back into the Chevrolet that belonged to Brett's gardener, an undocumented worker who enjoyed living in this country and understood the cardinal Ellis principle.

See no evil, speak no evil and no evil shall befall you.

Or as their crass thief of a mother would've said if she were alive and hadn't died in prison—*snitches get stitches.*

He turned the key in the ignition and the old engine rumbled to life.

Turning onto the Pacific Coast Highway, his one regret was that he wouldn't be able to see Isabel receive the punishment she deserved firsthand.

The video would have to suffice.

BEING WITH DUTCH was like finding a haven during a storm. Isabel imagined spending time with him every day for the foreseeable future and her smile deepened. He was laid-back and thoughtful. Made things easier in a way no one else she knew ever had.

The spread of food he'd brought was simple. Peeled hard-boiled eggs, hummus, baguettes, Manchego and cheddar cheeses, grapes, figs, carrot sticks and prosciutto. Even two prepackaged slices of chocolate cake with buttercream frosting. The simple meal hit the spot.

"The only thing missing is a glass of chilled chardonnay," she said.

"I would've brought wine or champagne, but you said you don't drink."

"Not for a while." At his curious expression, she said, "I'm not an alcoholic, but I'm on medication that doesn't mix well with alcohol."

Pressing her lips together, she considered whether to go on without opening the door that led to the freak show of Chad Ellis. Dutch had shared deeply personal things with her last night. About his call to serve in the army, losing battle brothers in dangerous military operations, how being in Delta Force took so much out of him that it'd scraped his soul bare and he needed a break.

She owed him the same transparency. In baby steps. "I'm on Ativan."

"I had a buddy who was on a cocktail of pills for his PTSD. Ativan was one of them. You don't have to tell me details, but I take it that you went through a rough breakup with Ellis."

"Yeah. You could say that." She was still going through it. Would it ever be over?

"I know you have Brenda, but with your uncle being down in San Diego, I'd like to be there for you."

Brenda was family. They'd been close since college, and she knew the ugly specifics of what Isabel had gone through. There were times she'd contemplated telling her uncle, since she shared everything else with him, but his support would've come with the strings of pity and bodyguards who'd spy on her. There had to be a happy medium.

Maybe Dutch was it. He was a good listener and didn't push.

"My uncle is coming up to have dinner with me on Wednesday," she said.

"Oh yeah. I'd love to meet him."

Lowering her shades down the bridge of her nose, she met his eyes. "Don't you think it's a little premature? We haven't even slept together. Why would you want to put yourself through such scrutiny?"

"You don't realize how special you are." He slung his arm around her, gripping her shoulder. "Maybe you should make all the men you date run that gauntlet. Trial by fire to see if they're worthy of your affection." His fingers moved along her arm, massaging, caressing. "Let me be the first. When I told you that I wanted to know you, I was serious. That includes meeting your uncle."

She enjoyed the possibility of endless tomorrows with Dutch and wasn't ready to lose him. "I don't think you understand what you're asking for. Once my uncle puts his stamp of disapproval on you…" That was it. There'd be no future.

Grasping her chin between his thumb and forefinger, he angled her face toward his. "I'm not a foregone conclusion, Isabel. *If* he doesn't approve of me, we cross that bridge when we come to it. But the way I see it, you're grown and financially independent. You date who you damn well please."

"He'll scare you off. He's very powerful, judgmental and can be a bit of a bully." A snobbish bully and that was putting it mildly.

"Do I seem like a man who's easily intimidated?"

No. He didn't.

"The only way I'll walk away from you is if you ask me to." Smoothing hair off her cheek, his fingers lingered, caressing her jaw, then gliding down her neck and back up again, sending tingles shooting through her. "I've gone up against my fair share of bullies. I can handle your uncle."

He drew closer, his hand tangling in her hair, bringing her mouth toward his. But he stopped short of giving her what she wanted, what she craved. Another taste of him.

So, she took it.

She kissed him and hummed her approval at the wet heat of his mouth as their breaths tangled. His eager tongue met hers, velvety stroke for stroke. Need drove urgency, bringing their bodies together into a hard squeeze of a hug that ended with him sucking on her tongue until her belly twisted with arousal.

"Isabel," he murmured against her lips, something raw and hungry in his voice.

She didn't want the kiss to end, didn't want to let him go. But she straightened, her thoughts bouncing back to the things he'd said. "Let me think about you meeting my uncle. Okay?"

He kissed the tip of her nose, trailed more across her cheeks. "Sure, beautiful."

Resting her head on his shoulder, she traced the lines of one of his tattoos. Inside the outline of an arrowhead were two black daggers crossed behind a skull with Latin inked beneath it, *De Oppresso Liber*.

To free the oppressed.

"I get how hard it was for you in Delta Force, losing your friends, having to kill people, the constant pressure, but you never told me why you stayed for twelve years."

He put his arm around her. "Just because it was tough doesn't mean it wasn't worth it. I believed in the mission, protecting our country, and the army gave me a family that had my back no matter what. That I could count on to pick me up if I fell, to hump me out if I got shot. Honestly, getting booted was harder than the grind of the high-ops tempo."

"Why?"

"Because I lost my battle brothers and my sense of purpose in one fell swoop. But I, uh… I know there's a new place for me out there, where I belong," he said, staring at the ocean, his voice somber.

She gave him a hard, quick kiss, wanting to erase his sadness.

"Promise me something," he said.

"Sure. What?"

"I hate the way we met, how the universe brought us together with you getting mugged, but I don't regret finding you, being with you." He cupped her jaw, brushing his thumb across her cheek. "This feels right. You and me. I want to keep doing this with you, see what's on the horizon for us, together. For as long as you want. Promise me you'll remember that."

She frowned, not understanding what possessed him to say that.

He must've read the concern in her face because he rubbed between her eyes with the pad of his thumb, smoothing away her worry lines. "Every relationship has highs and lows. When we hit a low point, I don't want to lose you. So, promise you'll remember."

"Okay. I promise."

Dutch kissed her nose. "Let's have dessert."

THEY FINISHED EATING, packed everything up and headed for the parking lot. Refusing to let her carry anything, except her tote bag, he managed the surfboard, blanket and cooler on his own.

After he got everything loaded into the bed of his truck, he walked her to her car.

"Hey," he said, and she stopped in front of her door and looked at him. Dutch wiped her lip and licked the chocolate frosting off his thumb. The gesture was intimate and assuming and she loved it. Dutch reached for her. "Come here," he said, roping his arms around her. He released a satisfied sigh as if he'd been aching to hold her. "When am I going to see you again?"

Sliding her hands up his bare chest, she appreciated that he was in magnificent shape, tip-top condition as one could get.

She was tempted to tell him *tonight*, but she was scared. Of how good his muscular body felt beneath her palms. Of how he stared at her with a mix of affection and attraction that made her knees a little weak. Of how the air, charged with desire, stimulated her skin, quickened her pulse. Of how his arousal pressed against her lower belly made her want to explore every inch of him.

"If you come by later, I think we might have sex," she admitted, her reservations lost in the enthralling deep brown depths of his potent stare.

"Would that be good or bad?"

"Both, I think." She chuckled. "It wouldn't be taking things slowly, but the more I'm around you, the more I feel my boundaries slipping away." Nerves fluttered in her belly and she chewed on her bottom lip.

"I don't want you to worry about stuff like that. Here's my promise to you. The possibility of sex is off the table until I meet your uncle."

Was he serious?

On her first date with Chad, he'd taken her to dinner at a Michelin-starred restaurant, they'd had dessert upstairs, drinks on the rooftop. Then he'd taken her home and swept her up in an aggressive tide of sexual energy, where she'd gone with the flow of it rather than drown.

Looking back on it, every time she'd slept with him had been more about survival than passion and she wanted to kick herself for being so easily manipulated. So weak.

One bad decision, one poor choice, and she was paying for it months later.

"Why?" she asked incredulously.

"Intimacy should be earned, and you should be treasured." He stroked her cheek and gave her a tender, slow kiss.

Dutch touched her the right way, with gentleness and respect, and said the perfect thing. Maybe he was too good to be true. This could quite possibly be the most brilliant use of reverse psychology.

Deny her sex to make her want it. But she still fell a little harder, faster, deeper for him.

"Well, that settles it, you're meeting my uncle on Wednesday," she said, and they both laughed. That was another remarkable thing about him. No guy had ever made her smile so much or laugh until her cheeks ached. "I want to see you later."

Spending time with him was the best kind of escape from her troubles.

"Then you will. I'll bring takeout. Thai or sushi?"

"Thai. Surprise me with your favorites." She hit the key fob, unlocking her door. "Spice isn't a problem."

"I'm not shocked you can handle the heat."

"How about seven?" She grabbed the door handle. "Is that enough time for you to miss me?"

He smiled and, cupping her face in his hands, kissed her. She lit up warm and bright as if she'd swallowed the sun.

"I don't need hours to miss you, beautiful. Before you make it out of the parking lot, I'll want you back in my arms."

"You're setting the bar pretty high for other men."

"Good. You should have high standards. Never settle for anything less than what you deserve."

She opened her door, slid in and tossed her bag in the passenger's seat. Turning the key in the ignition, she waved to him.

Dutch lifted his hand and stepped back while she put the car in Reverse.

After cranking the wheel, she threw the gear in Drive. Something buzzed past her head. She swatted it away.

A bee landed on her dash.

Isabel stiffened. Her gaze locked on the yellow jacket.

She was severely allergic to bee venom. A sting would send her into anaphylactic shock within minutes. How did it get in the car?

Don't freak out.

Rolling down the window, she prayed it would fly out as she drove slowly through the lot. Too bad she didn't have a magazine in her bag to help shoo it from the car. But the little insect stayed on the dash, unfazed by the breeze.

A second bee flew past her face, landing on the steering wheel. Dread slid down her throat and dropped in her belly hard and cold.

She pressed back against her seat, putting as much distance as possible between herself and the tiny flying killers, but the car cabin seemed to shrink around her.

A terrifying thought popped into her head. *Chad.* Did he put a couple of bees in her car?

Just as quickly, she dismissed the irrational idea. The planning, the logistics it would've taken, not to mention, he would've had to have known that she'd be here.

That was beyond crazy.

Hitting the button to roll down the passenger window, she cursed the perfume oil she'd rubbed on her skin and hair. It'd only attract them. *Way to go to smell sexy.*

Another bee buzzed up between her legs. Then another and another and another, coming from the foot well underneath her.

Dear Lord in heaven.

Panic exploded across her nerves, her heart clutching. Bees swarmed near her head, hissed across her arms. The whirring drone filled her ears.

Isabel screamed, swatting at the yellow jackets. Impossible for her to duck and dodge, there was no place to run. She felt trapped in the car.

One buzzed up her leg. The creepy-crawly sensation inched past her calf, featherlight over her knee. *Oh, God.* Glancing down, she watched in horror as two bees disappeared under her cover-up and a third landed on her chest.

No, no. Fire nipped her. A pinprick of agony, a hot match to her skin.

When a bee stung, it released a chemical that attracted others. She jerked her legs reflexively, waving wildly to swat at the rest, and slammed down on the accelerator.

"Isabel!" Dutch called.

A telephone pole rushed forward to meet her. Isabel's heart flew up into her throat. The car smashed into wood, the crunch of metal ringing in her ears.

An airbag inflated, knocking her back.

Pain bloomed in her skull, punching behind her eyes. She coughed on dust particles saturating the air.

Dazed, she registered the familiar itch spreading over her skin, deep in her flesh. She'd been stung, more than once.

God, it hurt like hell. Pure agony.

She fumbled with her seat belt, groped for the door handle and fell out of the car onto the hard concrete. Kicking the frame, she pushed her legs free and crawled to get away from the bees.

Her body's autoimmune response was happening fast—skin itching so badly it burned, face swelling, her tongue growing thick and heavy, throat closing, lungs squeezing—too fast.

Dutch scooped her up into his arms. "Isabel?" His face was pinched in fear.

"Bees," she said, wheezing. "Allergic. Epi—Bag…"

He carried her several feet from the car, set her down and took off.

A woman stepped up beside her and lowered to her knees. She held up a cell phone over Isabel's face like she was recording.

Was she videotaping this?

"Are you all right?" The woman hit a button and the phone beeped. "Oh, my God! Your face. You're breaking out in hives all over." She lifted her cell and dialed 911. "We need an ambulance. Topanga Beach parking lot. Hurry."

Isabel's lips tingled, growing numb. It was getting harder to breathe, her airways shrinking to the size of straws. Tears leaked from her inflamed eyes.

Dark spots clouded her vision, distending, swallowing the sky.

Dutch's face came into view and then oblivion.

Chapter Ten

Isabel's swelling had gone down somewhat. Her face was no longer so distorted that she was unrecognizable. But with the oxygen mask, puffy cheeks and swollen eyes, she looked fragile, wounded, not quite like herself.

The doctor estimated that six bees had stung her, on her feet, legs, arms and chest. Every spot was surrounded by inflamed skin and punctuated with an angry red mark.

According to the doctor, if she hadn't had an EpiPen in her bag, she would've died.

Dutch sat in a chair next to her bed, holding her hand. He'd never been so terrified in his life when she crashed her car and came crawling out, barely able to breathe, her face blown up worse than a prize fighter's.

His fear had nothing to do with his job, though it should've, considering how many people were counting on him. His only concern had been Isabel's well-being and safety.

There'd been so many bees in her car when he went to find her EpiPen. Not enough to constitute a hive, but more than two couldn't be discounted as a fluke or some bad stroke of luck.

"Hi," Isabel said, her voice faint and brittle, eyes finally open.

"Hey, beautiful. I was so worried about you."

"Liar."

Dutch was taken aback. "Honey, the only other time I've been more worried about someone was when a battle brother was bleeding out in my arms."

"Not that. I know I don't look beautiful right now."

He kissed the back of her hand. "The most beautiful part about you is on the inside. It's your heart. Your spirit. To me, you'll always be gorgeous." A tear slipped from her eye, and he brushed it away. "How are you feeling?"

"Like I went to war and lost."

He gave a rueful laugh. "I used your fingerprint to unlock your phone and called Brenda. She's on the way. I hope you don't mind."

"She'll make a fuss."

"You need to be fussed over. Believe me. Do you want me to call your uncle, too?"

That would be one way to meet him. An unfortunate incident where Dutch had helped would ingratiate him, but it wasn't one he preferred. Dutch wouldn't be able to look at himself in the mirror if he played a card that low.

Whether or not her uncle was called had to be Isabel's decision.

"No." She shook her head. "He'll take over, hire a nurse. Maybe have me brought to San Diego by helicopter. I'd rather be at home."

"Whatever you want."

The door opened and Brenda rushed into the room. "I came as soon as I could." Her friend went to the opposite side of the bed and gasped. "Oh, sweetie. You look awful. How did this happen? You're usually so careful."

"I think…" Isabel touched her throat like it hurt to swallow. "I think Chad did this to me," she said, and Brenda recoiled. "I have no idea *how* he would've done it. Known where I was. Gotten into my car." Isabel's eyes found his. "It sounds crazy, far-fetched, I know, but please believe me. This was him."

Dutch ran through the possibility in his head and it didn't seem far-fetched at all. "Maybe he's having you followed. I mean, he had to know you were at the grill somehow when he showed up like that. Did he ever have access to your car keys?"

"Plenty of times."

"It's possible to clone a key fob. But I can't make sense of the bees. He would've had to have direct access to a hive and equipment to contain the bees without getting stung himself, which would mean this was planned. Well thought out. Not some impulsive act of jealousy."

"Do you think he was trying to kill you?" Brenda asked.

Isabel shook her head. "He knows I carry an EpiPen with me everywhere. I never leave the house without one."

Brenda took her other hand. "Then why would he do this?"

Chad went through all this trouble for what? To hurt her? To put so much fear in her that she never looked at another man?

"If he did this," Dutch said, "then that means he's dyed-in-the-wool nuts, Isabel. A bona fide psychopath."

"That's Chad Ellis," Brenda said. "You can't begin to imagine the depths of depravity in his dark soul."

But Dutch didn't have to imagine. He knew. He'd read the file.

"We need to have your car checked," Dutch said. "Dusted for prints."

"You won't find anything," Isabel said. "He's too careful."

That wasn't going to stop Dutch from trying. Everyone made mistakes. Sooner or later Chad would slip up and Dutch would be ready to dole out retribution.

Dr. Kiser came in and stopped at the foot of the bed. "You're looking better." She flashed a curt smile. "The meds are working."

"I'm tired," Isabel said, "and I hurt all over."

"That's natural, but you're out of danger. I'm going to send you home with a prescription for prednisone. It's a corticosteroid that will help with the inflammation and itching, and two days' worth of hydrocodone for the pain. Apply a topical analgesic to the spots where you were stung, calamine lotion or Benadryl gel. Get plenty of rest, drink lots of fluids and you'll be fine. Due to the severity of your reaction, I'd recommend immunotherapy. Otherwise, if you were to get stung by a bee again, your immune system could have a more severe response even faster. Do you have any questions?"

"Can I take off this mask?"

"Yes, of course." The doctor stepped around the bed and helped Isabel remove it. "I'll get your discharge paperwork started. It should take about an hour or so."

"Thank you," Isabel said before the doctor left.

"Let me run home and change." Dutch gestured to his T-shirt and swim trunks. "I'll come right back, take you home and stick around until you and McQueen are good for the night."

"I don't want to impose on you," Isabel said. "I'm sure you've got better things to do."

Dutch gave her hand a light squeeze. "You're not an imposition. I've been looking for an excuse to spend more time with you and now I've got it." He looked at Brenda. "Will you stay with her until I get back?"

He didn't want to risk leaving her alone on the off chance that Ellis decided to show up. It was highly unlikely he'd try anything with Brenda in the room as a witness.

"I'll be right here, glued to her side."

He kissed the back of Isabel's hand and stood. "I'll be back as soon as I can." He went to the door.

"He wants to take care of you *and* your dog," Brenda whispered, but he heard it.

Didn't occur to him that making sure McQueen was fed and walked was something special. It was necessary.

In the hall, he took out his cell phone. He called Allison, not having the tolerance to deal with Draper, and gave her the rundown on the way to his truck.

"It's good that Isabel is going to be okay and the dinner on Wednesday with her uncle is fortuitous. But do you really think that Ellis is responsible for the bees in her car?"

"I think it's possible. Underestimating him would be a mistake. We need to have her car searched and dusted for prints. And she needs a different RFID chip in a new key fob."

"That'll take a couple of days."

"Fine. She's got the time. I'll be with her to make sure Ellis doesn't hurt her again."

"Dutch, no matter what, you can't go after this guy like a vigilante. There's a process and we have to follow it."

"I hear you." But he wasn't making any promises.

His patience was threadbare where Ellis was concerned. If they found a shred of evidence connecting him to this bee-stinging incident, even circumstantial, Dutch was going to unleash holy hell on that man.

STROLLING HIS BROTHER'S YARD, eight acres in an exclusive gated enclave in Calabasas, Chad passed the beehive he'd had set up four months ago. The story for his sister-in-law had been that he wanted them to have fresh honey. Nothing tasted better and the kids loved the novelty of the idea although they never ventured to the far side of the property. As for Chad's brother, it didn't matter to Brett and no questions had been asked.

That was the type of courtesy between the Ellis brothers. The less one knew, the less one was complicit.

His cell phone rang. Chad checked the caller ID, hoping it was Isabel needing him after her ordeal. He longed to hear her voice, begging for his help.

Olga. His gut tightened.

With a sigh, he released his disappointment. "Yes," he said into the phone.

"I emailed you the video."

"Will I be entertained?"

Olga muttered a string of curses. That was out of character for her, Chad thought.

"I'm following the guy home," she said, her voice sharp and agitated. "If you want his address and full name, send my payment for the rest of the week now. Then I'm done, after what you did to her."

He didn't care for Olga's tone. Or the implication, no matter how spot-on.

"I didn't do anything. I've been at my brother's place all day." Other than the one hour he'd snuck out and used the gardener's car while Brett covered, telling his family they were in the office discussing business and not to be disturbed.

"Whatever," Olga snapped. "If you didn't do it personally, then you hired someone to do it. Either way, you're responsible. She almost died. I won't be an accessory to that. Understand?"

"But you already are, and you know it." Leaving the

garden, he walked across the patio adjacent to the pool, where his niece and nephew were frolicking in the water. "That's why you're charging me such an exorbitant rate."

Some restraining orders stated "neither you nor your agent may" blah, blah, but not his. He was within his legal boundaries to hire a private investigator. But Olga knew this wasn't a situation where he was looking for proof that his girlfriend was cheating or gathering evidence regarding parenting or employability.

Olga spoon-fed his fixation on Isabel every day with updates and pictures and now a video. All the while in the loop that there was a restraining order against him. Chad hadn't even told Brett about the injunction, but he wanted a PI with loose morals who was willing to turn a blind eye for the right price.

The nerve of her to grow a conscience and get sanctimonious after pocketing his cash for the past six months.

"Send the money or I won't give you any more information about her new *boyfriend*," Olga said, deliberately taunting him. "For the record, Mr. Ellis. You disgust me."

The line went dead.

Clenching his jaw, Chad sat and reclined back in a chaise beside his brother, facing the pool. He accessed his banking app and wired the final payment to Olga.

Mindy, his sister-in-law, waltzed out of the house and handed him and Brett each a Tom Collins. Then she pranced away in her heels and bikini, flaunting her flawless figure that some cosmetic surgeon had given her.

Why couldn't Isabel be more like Mindy. Not the plastic body with implants. He liked Isabel all natural, preferred her a bit heavier before she'd started working out. Now she could wear anything she wanted. But Isabel needed to fall in line and meet expectations. Not give him a hard time. It'd only taken Brett two months to break in Mindy and within less than a year they were married and settled in wedded…contentment.

Bliss would be a bit of a stretch. Mindy either didn't know or simply didn't say anything about Brett's philandering and she'd learned to handle his temper, squirreling the children away in their rooms while she took her punishment if she dared violate one of Brett's rules.

They balanced everything, made it work for their family because they loved each other. For better or worse. Until death do them part.

That's all he wanted with Isabel. Why couldn't she see that?

He brought up the message Olga had sent him earlier and played the video.

Watching it, he sipped his drink. The low-class man with garish tattoos had his arms around Isabel, standing next to her car, as they spoke and kissed. Too bad there wasn't audio on their conversation.

It made little difference. From the lovey-dovey looks of them, Isabel deserved what she was about to get.

She climbed into her car, pulled out of the spot and rolled her window down. The angle and distance was lousy. He couldn't see the horror on her face, the panic in her eyes that she surely must've felt.

Damn it.

Then her car crashed into a telephone pole.

That was pleasantly unexpected. As Isabel was crawling from her Maserati, debilitated, face grotesquely swollen, Olga was on the move, drawing closer. The man left Isabel and ran toward her car. To fetch her EpiPen no doubt.

Honestly, Chad was a little shocked by the speed of her reaction to the bee venom. She'd been stung once when she was a child. After doing research, he'd learned that allergic reactions could be more severe in adults and in subsequent exposures.

On the screen, Olga lowered beside Isabel, the frame of the video zooming in on her face that had turned into a hideous mask. Not only was her face painfully swollen but her cheeks were drooping at the same time and her eyes were a glassy mix of agony and fear.

Holy— That was the money shot.

Chad chuckled at Isabel's monstrous image, the sound of her wheezing sending a thrill through him.

You brought this on yourself, babe.

Never should've gone out with that man. Chad bet lover boy would stay away from her until she was looking her best, which should take a day or two.

"Do I want to know what you're watching?" Brett asked.

"No."

"I should fire up the grill. Mindy has everything prepped and ready to go." He stood, grabbing his drink. "Burgers and chicken kabobs for the kids. Steaks and baked potatoes for us. I think Mindy is skipping lunch since I spoke to her about her weight. You're staying, right?"

The video ended and Chad muttered a curse under his breath over how short it'd been. "Steak sounds perfect."

"Hey, when are you and Isabel getting back together? Mindy misses her."

Of course she did. Isabel was the only friend Brett allowed Mindy to have at the house.

Starting the video over again from the beginning, Chad said, "I'm working on it."

Chapter Eleven

Lucky. That was how Isabel felt. Dutch had taken care of her and McQueen for the past two days. First thing in the morning, he was there with her coconut-milk latte and take-out breakfast from a café, then he took her dog for a walk.

They'd watched the top five Steve McQueen movies along with her favorite films, snuggled together with no pressure for anything more than comfort and affection. He paid exquisite attention to her, giving his whole self and not asking for anything in return. Dinners had been delivered and after he took her dog for one final jaunt outside, he'd hold her, kiss her and leave.

Part of her didn't want her recovery to end.

She was back in her regular routine finally, but behind on everything. Work, jogging, Krav Maga lessons. Wednesday had rushed up on her and she was supposed to have dinner with her uncle in two hours and still hadn't told Dutch one way or the other if he was going, too.

Before her near-death allergic reaction, she'd been ready to invite Dutch, but now that he'd earned his place at the dinner table beside her, she could barely contain her excitement.

Isabel dialed her uncle as she grabbed her workout

bag from the trunk of the loaner vehicle the car repair shop let her use and walked inside the Krav Maga school.

"Isabel, *mi hija*, I hope you're not calling to cancel."

"No. I wouldn't dream of it," she said, relieved her face no longer showed any sign of swelling. "It's just, I'd like to bring someone to dinner. A guy I'm seeing. I know how much you hate surprises."

"You haven't mentioned you're dating anyone."

"It's new, but he's special. I'd love for you to meet him."

"Not tonight," her uncle said. "I have business I want to discuss with you at dinner."

"How about we talk privately and then he joins us for dessert?"

"We'll discuss it when I see you later. The car will be at the gallery at seven."

Isabel groaned into the phone, wanting her uncle to hear every decibel of her frustration.

"Don't pout. It's unbecoming. I hate to disappoint you, truly, but I need some one-on-one time with you. That's it. *Te amo.*"

Isabel hung up without saying *I love you* back.

It was no wonder she'd gotten caught up with Chad and went along with his controlling behavior. She'd grown accustomed to similar treatment from her uncle, who was just as imperious. The same won't-take-no attitude. It was his way or consequences.

Thank heavens she'd met someone different like Dutch.

Isabel threw her phone in the gym bag and zipped it.

"You really pushed us today, John. Thanks," a male voice said, sending a hot rush of adrenaline shooting through her system.

Isabel looked up and stared at Chad. A class had just

finished, and he was walking out with the instructor, John. The two of them were smiling and chatting. They were chummy.

What the hell?

A torrent of emotions flooded her.

Fear that he stood a few feet away, that she'd have to face him. That he'd never stop stalking her, terrorizing her.

Flustered. Out of all the self-defense schools between Malibu and Santa Monica he was at this one. But it couldn't be some bizarre coincidence. When it came to Chad, it never was. He was a planner, acted with deliberate, dark purpose. Controlled every facet of his life.

Isabel's heart hammered, her hands growing clammy. All she wanted was to crawl into a hole and disappear, but this was going too far. A violation she wouldn't tolerate.

Fury roared through her, burning through the stupefaction that held her paralyzed. Only outrage remained. Outrage at his gall. At the narcissistic audacity it took for him to enroll at her school.

She stormed up to them, gave John a befuddled glance and glared at Chad. "What are you doing here?"

A ghost of a smile played across his lips for a second, maybe two. "For the sake of clarity, you came within fifty feet of me and initiated conversation," Chad said.

"What's going on?" John asked.

"This is *him*." Isabel pointed at Chad. "The one I told you about. He attacked me behind the gallery and popped up at the restaurant."

"Chad attacked you?" John asked with the skeptical tone she was used to hearing when it came to her ex.

"Yes!" Her voice drew attention from everyone in the hall.

"*Attacked* is a strong, ugly and untruthful word, Isabel. You called me that day. Remember?"

"I did, but—"

"You missed me, wanted to rekindle things and asked me to come to the gallery."

He was twisting the truth, spinning it into vicious lies. The same way he'd done in court, bolstering his position while tearing hers down.

Painful pressure welled in her chest, squeezing her heart. "That's not true." Her voice trembled.

To stop her hand from shaking she clenched her fingers around the strap of her gym bag.

Chad stood taller with a smug expression, his presence taking up the space, sucking up the oxygen. "You can't defame my character like this. It's not fair."

Fair? "I know it was you," Isabel said. Her pulse raced. Her breath was tight in her lungs. "The bees in my car. You wanted to hurt me. You wanted to scare me. You're a sick piece of work."

"What are you talking about?" Chad asked. "Bees?" His features twisted in an expression of utter confusion that looked so real she half believed him. "Do you hear yourself? I think you need to talk to someone about your delusions. If this is another ploy to get attention, you should see a professional." He sounded calm, rational, looked like the sane one.

Anger bled from her as anxiety seeped through, sending her head spinning. "You put bees in my car, knowing I'm deathly allergic. Admit it!"

"Isabel, I love you." He took a step closer.

A terrible rush of energy flooded her system with no outlet, no conduit. It was like her body was in full-blown flight-or-fight mode, but she was frozen, stuck.

"Whether or not we're together, I only want what's best for you," Chad said, his voice so sympathetic he should've been struck by lightning. "Why would I put bees in your car? How? Unless you have proof, you can't go around tarnishing my reputation with such outlandish claims."

Proof. Dutch had asked a friend in the police department to have her car dusted for prints. Only hers and Dutch's were found, along with a jewelry box from Tiffany's that oddly enough had no prints on it at all.

"Stay away from me, do you hear me?" Everyone stared at Isabel like she was a raving crackpot.

Even John. But at least he moved up beside her in a physical show of support. "Chad, your membership is canceled, effective immediately."

"Hold on a minute." Chad raised his palms as though he were the victim. "You can't do that."

"I just did. We'll send you a refund in the mail. Abraham." John turned to the big, buff instructor. "Escort Mr. Ellis out and let everyone at the front desk know that he's no longer to be given access to the premises."

Abraham gestured for Chad to start walking.

"If you were stung by a bee, I'm glad you're all right," Chad said, his tone deceptively sweet—almost innocent. He had unbelievable gall. "You're looking good, Isabel. Call me if you ever need anything. I'm here for you."

"Stop talking to her." John stepped between them. "Leave. Now."

Abraham shepherded Chad to the front.

At the door, Chad glanced back at her, flashed a Hollywood smile—dazzling, polished, perfected—and brushed imaginary dust from his shoulder, radiating arrogance and superiority.

Her stomach roiled.

Chad pushed through the door, whistling as if he didn't have a care in the world, and got into his car.

Isabel deflated with relief that he was gone, but she

was too far in the deep swell of a panic attack to stave it off. Digging in her bag, she grabbed her bottle of Ativan. She fumbled to remove the lid.

"I'm so sorry," John said, helping her to the water fountain.

She threw the pill in her mouth and washed it down with a swig of water. Shivering, she gripped the edge of the fountain and tried to breathe.

"I had no idea *that* was him," John said. "Chad has been so friendly, helpful in class. A great student. A fast learner. I can't believe I went bowling with him."

A sinking feeling slid down her throat like cold sludge, pooling in her belly. "How long has he been coming?"

"Well," John said, scratching his head. "He started around the same time as you. Maybe a week or two after."

She put away her meds. "Then we're at the same level, know the same moves."

John's gaze dropped. "No, Isabel. He's been coming twice as often as you. Four days a week. He's far more advanced. Just earned his orange belt."

Isabel was at the most basic level. White belt. She might be ready to test for yellow next month. But Chad had made it to orange?

Dread bubbled inside her. "What does he know that I don't?"

"A heck of a lot." John rattled off a mind-boggling list of moves, from choke holds, kicks and punches to body-defense postures. "He's getting really good at disarming an attacker."

"Get me ready," Isabel said. "Prepare me to defend against what he knows."

A grave look fell across John's face, and she wanted to vomit. "That'll take months, not days." He clasped her shoulder. "You don't want to engage in a physical confrontation with him. If you see him again, don't talk to him, don't go near him. Call 911."

THE LINES HAD blurred for Dutch. Over the past two days, he'd gone from marshal on a mission to legit boyfriend. *Damn*. What was he thinking?

But that was the problem. He hadn't been thinking or even trying to say the right thing. It was so easy with Isabel, talking to her, spending hours cuddled up in their little bubble while she recuperated, like they were two pieces of a puzzle fitting together. Caring about her was as natural as breathing. Every night when he left her condo something in his chest had ached and didn't subside until he saw her again.

He pushed through the door of the second-floor satellite hub.

"There's something I found out while you were off getting closer to the asset," Allison said as a greeting, cutting straight to it. "I dug deeper into Chad Ellis. Nothing concrete came up, but a woman did file a complaint with the police against him two years ago."

"Stalking and harassment?" Dutch asked.

"No. Virginia Campbell claimed that Ellis was behind the disappearance of her sister Patricia. Police investigated and couldn't find anything. Patricia had dated Ellis for a few months and broken up with him. Ellis dropped off the radar and Patricia started seeing someone new. Then she started getting strange phone calls and weird gifts in the mail. But when Patricia disappeared, her new boyfriend was the top suspect. Not Ellis. She was never found. It's a cold case now."

The news only exacerbated Dutch's concerns. Ellis was slippery and careful. Methodical. The more Dutch thought about it, the more he believed the guy was behind

Isabel's allergic reaction though they didn't have a shred of evidence to prove it. He hadn't pushed her to share the nightmare of what she'd been through in her relationship with Ellis. Survivors of trauma tended to keep their secrets, ashamed to share. No matter what happened with his assignment, Dutch wasn't going to abandon Isabel.

One way or another, something would have to be done about Ellis.

"We heard from the FBI," Draper said. "Their undercover agent passed along another message. The auction is going to happen this Sunday. The data is onsite at Vargas's compound, possibly in his biometric fingerprint safe."

"Can't they intercede?" Dutch asked, wanting to be done with this. To sit Isabel down and come clean. "Arrest Vargas for being in possession of classified data?"

Draper finished his coffee and crumpled the paper cup. "Since the information falls under the caveat of *Law Enforcement Sensitive* and not Top Secret, the most Vargas would get is two years since it'd be his first criminal offense. The FBI is putting together a RICO case. It could take down the entire organization and enable them to seize his assets. What they're going after is much bigger. This is as far as they'll go to help us."

Groaning his frustration, Dutch swallowed a curse.

"What's the status with dinner tonight and meeting her uncle?" Allison asked. "Are you in?"

"Dinner with Vargas is a no go."

Allison sighed, lowering her head in defeat.

"Damn it." Draper chucked his coffee cup in the trash. "Vargas comes to town for one night to have dinner with his niece and you can't manage to get yourself invited? Do you understand the mission objective?"

Dutch gritted his teeth at the rhetorical question and Draper's rude tone.

Allison looked up. "You just spent two cozy days at her apartment with her. I need to ask. Have you slept together?"

Rocking back on his heels, Dutch hadn't anticipated the question. "How is that relevant?"

"I'll take that as a no," Allison said. "And it's quite relevant. The deeper you get in with her, the easier it'll be to get access to her uncle."

"Chen is right," Draper said. "Women get emotionally invested once sex is involved. You've got to up the ante."

Allison narrowed her eyes at Draper. "That's a sexist stereotype. You know that, right?"

"But it's true," Draper said, doubling down.

"No, it isn't." Standing, Allison put her hands on her hips. "Women can have casual sex with no emotional investment. Trust me." Allison shifted her gaze to Dutch. "Isabel likes you. She's already invested, but you need to deepen the connection."

"Look." Dutch crossed his arms. "She wanted me to go to dinner, but her uncle didn't want me there."

"Then she didn't fight hard enough for you," Allison said.

Draper nodded in agreement. "Call her and have her press the issue."

"It doesn't feel right." Dutch shook his head. "She's on her way to meet her uncle now."

"Get her to tell you the name of the restaurant," Draper said. "Show up. Bring her flowers. Make it a grand gesture."

"You want me, the new guy, to pop up uninvited to dinner when she already has a stalker?" Yeah, that wasn't going to happen.

Allison raised a palm at Draper to back off. "We're desperate, here. Vargas knows where we live, the names of our kids, where they go to school. It's bad enough he has such sensitive information, but he's going to sell it to only God knows who. You've got to press a little harder. Please."

Turning his back to them, he scrubbed a hand over his face.

Maybe he could see Isabel after dinner and persuade her to arrange breakfast with him and her uncle before Vargas went back to San Diego. "Okay. I'll try."

Dutch took out his cell phone and sent her a text.

THE WAY TO find someone's weakness didn't always mean following a short, straight line. The trail to find Horatio "Dutch" Haas's was long and curved.

Prior military. Special Forces. La-di-da.

But Chad was getting closer. Or the new private investigator he'd hired to follow Haas instead of Isabel was. So far it didn't look like he was shagging Isabel, but with all the time Haas had been spending at her place, it would happen sooner rather than later.

Sitting in his car at the most recent address the PI had given him, Chad stared at Haas's motorcycle. The bike was parked in the rear of a supposedly vacant building that was conveniently located right across the street from Isabel's art gallery.

"What are you up to?" he asked under his breath.

Grinning, Chad couldn't wait to figure out the answer because it wasn't going to be anything good and might just be exactly what he needed to drive a wedge between Haas and Isabel.

Chapter Twelve

Isabel's phone chimed at an incoming message. She slipped the cell out of her purse and swiped the screen to check it.

Dutch: Can I swing by after dinner? Go for a walk with you and McQueen.

She smiled and texted back.

Yes.

Uncle Emilio cleared his throat across the table from her, drawing her gaze. "Please, Isa. Shut that thing off while you're with me," he said, frowning.

Not only did her uncle find the use of personal devices during meals rude, but he was paranoid about some hacker eavesdropping through it to steal his corporate secrets. He was so cautious that when they met for dinners, it was always in private. Tonight, he'd arranged for the entire rooftop of a glamorous French bistro with spectacular views of the skyline to be theirs. A bodyguard stood at either end—Rodrigo, who she'd known for years, and Max. She'd only encountered him a few times, but he'd risen in position quickly and flirted with her whenever her uncle wasn't within earshot. A third guard she didn't recognize, named Lucas, stood at the entrance to the stairs.

She powered down the phone and put it back in her purse. "Sorry."

"As I was saying, I'm planning to hold an exclusive silent auction at my compound for select pieces. I want you to organize everything and oversee the event from here. Handle the invitations, decor. Ensure the art is displayed properly with a floor plan and description of setup for Rodrigo. See to the menu with one of my vetted caterers, the music. Et cetera, et cetera."

"Don't you want me to come down and be there for the event?"

"No, that's not necessary. I don't want to intrude on your life. I know how you hate that."

Guilt poked at her. Her uncle had his faults. He was domineering and ran the family with a tight grip, but he only wanted her happiness. "I want to help you in any way. For how many people and when?" She took another bite of her smoked octopus with vadouvan and fennel citrus salad, humming her continued delight at the explosion of flavors on her tongue.

"An intimate gathering. Fifty guests. Sunday."

"You're joking. I can't organize an event that would be up to your standards in four days."

"I never joke, and I have the utmost confidence in your abilities. You could do this blindfolded, and I need someone I trust implicitly to see to things."

"Will your guests be able to attend on such short notice?"

"I have an exceptional item of great value that I'll be selling. One-of-a-kind. They'll clear their schedules for me. Have no fear. And you'll make the event happen for me. Yes?"

It wasn't really a question, even though he made it sound like one. "Yes."

Their waitress came out onto the rooftop and served the second course. *Loup de mer*, a Mediterranean sea bass, with white asparagus and couscous with squid ink paired with a glass of Sancerre. She tasted the wine, a sip to be polite and avoid an interrogation. The last time they had dinner, and she didn't drink, he'd accused her of being pregnant.

"So, what's the young man's name?" her uncle asked after the waitress left. "The one you want me to meet."

"Horatio Haas, but he goes by Dutch."

"Hmm. What does he do?"

Debating whether to tell him the truth, she tried the fish. Buttery, silky, delicious. The wine complemented it perfectly with a hint of honeysuckle and flint. "He's between jobs right now."

A lie, once discovered, would only anger her uncle. She'd learned that the hard way as a teenager after her father died and she went through a rebellious phase. Better to be honest and mitigate the cons rather than incur his wrath.

Uncle Emilio shook his head. "I assume you pay for everything?"

"No. He hasn't let me pay for anything."

"Yet." He wagged a finger at her. "Give it time."

"*Tio*, he's the greatest guy. Truly. He makes me happy." She could envision a real future with Dutch. He had nothing to hide, was trustworthy, reliable. Unbelievably hot.

"What's so great about him?" Her uncle cocked his head to the side, waiting.

Mentally, she ran through the long list, deciding which

thing would win over her uncle and sway him to give Dutch a chance. "I was stung by a bee the other day," she said, omitting the part about slimy Chad. "My allergic reaction was fast. It was bad—I'm not going to lie."

"*Dios mío*, Isa, why didn't you tell me?" He put his fork down. "I would've had you flown home to San Diego and ensured you were properly cared for while you recovered."

Where he would've smothered her to death with love. "That's precisely why I didn't want you to know. My home is here. In Malibu with my dog." With Brenda. With Dutch.

He tsked. "I would've brought the dog, too."

"My point is that Dutch kept a level head. Got my EpiPen and saved my life. He even took care of me for two days, walked McQueen, brought me food, breakfast in bed every morning."

He cleared his throat. "How generous of him."

"Not that it's any of your business, but I haven't slept with him." *Yet.* That would get his attention and should earn Dutch some brownie points.

Raising an eyebrow, her uncle shot her a dubious look that was also cautionary, warning her not to lie.

"Honestly," she said. "He's a good person, a gentleman, and wants to meet you. If you scare him off, I promise the next guy you meet will be on my wedding day."

Uncle Emilio laughed. "All right, my dear. I'll meet your new beau. On one condition." He raised a finger for emphasis.

"What's that?"

He smiled at her, the look tender and kind. "If I disapprove of this young man, you will stay away from him. Heed what I say as any daughter would."

Isabel sat back in her chair. "I'm entitled to date

whomever I please. I respect your opinion, but I'll follow my own judgment." Or when it came to men, Brenda's. Her bestie had steered her toward Dutch and she'd never been happier with a match.

She wished her uncle was still dating Lori Carpenter. Although Lori had been young, about the same age as Isabel, when Uncle Emilio had been with her, his attitude toward everything had been more laissez-faire, less regulated. Lori had been the best distraction for him.

To this day, Isabel had no idea why they'd broken up a year ago.

He wiped his mouth with a napkin. "Would you show your father such disrespect? Talk to him like this, if he were the one sitting here?"

"Yes. Because I'm twenty-eight. I'm not a child." She thought of her cousin out in New York, Uncle Emilio's son, and her indignation ballooned. "Miguel is two years older than me and you'd never tell him whom he should and shouldn't marry, much less date."

"You think you are your own person, free to do as you please." His tone softened and sharpened at the same time, drawing her to lean in to catch his every word. "But you are part of a larger whole. This family." He slapped the table, and Isabel flinched at the sound, straightening in her seat. "Miguel wanted to become a hotshot corporate attorney, but instead he picked up the mantle I passed to him and will carry on the Vargas legacy. It's not what he wanted, but he's thriving. Because he understands the importance of family. Of being part of a whole. The same way my brother and I understood the need for sacrifice. I wouldn't tell Miguel who to date or not to sleep with because I don't care. But when he gets serious enough about someone to introduce her to me, or chooses a wife,

I will have a say. He'll listen to me. He'll show respect. Just as you will now. Do you understand?"

Stunned to silence, Isabel nodded.

"I'm only looking out for your best interest," he said.

Chad's words rang in her ears. *I only want what's best for you.*

A lump formed in her throat at the similarity.

Her uncle took a deep breath, lightening his expression and his voice. "Your father would want me to. He was more than my brother. He was my mentor. My best friend. Losing him devastated me. When I buried him, I swore to raise you as he would've. I love you as my own. Don't dishonor his memory by disregarding what I say."

Always the expert at manipulating emotion to get what he wanted. Isabel wasn't surprised by her uncle's redirection. Expected it even. She'd spent fourteen years paying close attention, learning to do the very same thing herself when necessary.

She strategized while the third course was served. The waitress set down the plates in front of them and removed the stainless steel dome covers.

A delightful scent of lemon and herbs hit her.

"Veal medallions with brown butter and herbs de Provence," the waitress said.

Isabel reeled back. "None for me, thank you."

"What's wrong?" Her uncle cut into the meat and ate a piece. "Give it a try. It's delicious."

"I may wear leather and eat meat, but I draw the line at calves kept in small cages."

The waitress removed her plate and left.

Uncle Emilio chuckled. "If you object to eating baby animals, perhaps you should become a vegetarian. Do you think the broiler-sized chickens you buy are fully grown? Try eight weeks. Any idea the conditions they're kept in? Filthy and cramped." He took another bite. "Pigs are slaughtered at four months old. The same as calves for veal. Consider that the next time you're enjoying a piece of bacon."

Grimacing, Isabel tossed her napkin on the table. Maybe she *would* become a vegetarian.

Isabel had a choice. She could upset her uncle by confessing she'd lost her appetite or redirect the conversation to get what she wanted. "There's something I haven't told you. How I met Dutch. I was locking up the art gallery and someone mugged me."

His face went blank as he stiffened. "Oh, Isabel." He held out a hand to her.

Isabel placed her palm on her uncle's. "The guy grabbed my purse." She left out the part about the knife. "The Chanel bag that Daddy gave me." She tightened her fingers around his hand. "Dutch stopped him, brought him down like a superhero and got it back."

He lifted their joined hands and kissed her fingers. "You should've told me. This is why you need a bodyguard."

She cringed on the inside, not wanting her admission to backfire. "Dutch saved me twice. He treats me with respect. Dignity. Makes me feel like I should be treasured. No other man has ever done that."

"Not even the last one, who owns all those businesses."

Lowering her gaze, she swallowed past a flash of irritation. "No. Actually, that bigwig business owner turned out to be a real jerk."

"If a man ever disrespects you, puts his hands on you, I want you to tell me."

"Why? So you can sue him and punish me by shoving a bodyguard down my throat?"

He pursed his lips in obvious annoyance. "I would

make the man rue the day he crossed the line with you, and yes, give you a bodyguard."

No, thank you. She didn't want help with strings attached. "Well, there's no need for you to worry about Dutch crossing the line. He's incredible. Though, you might not approve of him." He would never fit the image of what her uncle wanted for her. "But I do. I want him to meet you because I respect and love you. *Please*, don't ruin this for me. Okay?"

"I see this man is important to you. I'll meet him tonight."

A smile she couldn't contain broke on her face. "Really?"

Her uncle nodded. "I do what I can to make you happy. Tell him to come to my club at eleven-thirty as my guest."

"Thank you, *tío*." Lifting out of her chair, she leaned across the table and kissed his cheek. "I must warn you that he speaks his mind and can be blunt, but we'll be there."

"You misunderstand." He released her hand and picked up his wineglass. "I wish to meet him alone. Without you."

That was strange. "Why?"

He gave her a placating grin, ratcheting up Isabel's anxiety. "Because I said so." His tone brooked no argument.

Chapter Thirteen

The call from Isabel canceling their plans had been un-expected, but worth it. Dutch was set to meet Vargas.

He pulled up to the valet in front of the Enigma night-club in the heart of LA.

"Hey, man," one of the twentysomethings wearing an orange vest said, approaching him. "Insurance won't let us take it, but you can park right there." He pointed to a parking spot in the valet area.

Dutch gave the kid forty bucks, twenty for valet and another Jackson as a tip to make sure they looked after his bike as if it were their own. "Not a scratch on it."

The guy nodded enthusiastically. "Sure thing. No one will get close to it."

Dutch rode over and backed into the spot sandwiched between a Mercedes and a Tesla. He took off his helmet and raked a hand through his hair.

Isabel let him know about the club's dress code. But Dutch had deliberately dressed down, jeans and a V-neck tee. He got that Dante Emilio Vargas had an apprecia-tion for the finer things in life and would judge a book by its cover, but there was no disguising that Dutch came from middle-class means. No hiding the way he carried himself, how he spoke, like a man born and bred on the streets.

Silk threads and putting on airs wouldn't win over Vargas anyway. Men such as her uncle respected two things. Power and strength.

At the core, neither had anything to do with money.

Besides, Dutch didn't know how to be anything other than himself, something that worked in his favor with Isabel. Other than the omission of why he'd stepped into her life—and granted, that was pretty big—he didn't have to pretend with her.

He strode past the long line to get in that wrapped around the corner and went up to the bouncer at the door. "I'm Dutch Haas. Here to see Dante Vargas."

The burly dude dressed in all black checked him out from head to toe with a wary look, but Dutch knew the vibe he gave off and was used to the split-second assessment people made about him based on his appearance.

The bouncer lifted a tablet and swiped through a list of names. After a few seconds, he glanced up. "You can go on in." He opened a door that was set off to the side of the main entrance.

Loud, throbbing electronic music and colored strobe lights washed over Dutch as he stepped inside with his helmet tucked under his arm. On his left, the general public entering through the main door paid a cover charge and had to walk through a metal detector.

Weaving through the throng of gyrating bodies, he went to the bar. The line was long, but he waited, in no rush, not wanting to seem overly eager to Vargas and needing to be certain what was in his drink. He ordered, got his drink and tipped well. Then he made his way to the stairwell, leading to the VIP area.

Instead of a waitress serving as a gatekeeper to the exclusive section upstairs, there was a bodyguard.

Dutch spotted the telltale bulge in his jacket. The man was armed.

"I'm Haas," Dutch said. "Here to see Mr. Vargas."

"Not with *that* you aren't." The bodyguard gestured to his helmet.

"Man, this is a Schuberth." The name was synonymous with top-of-the-line. Sure, his helmet was sleek and looked cool, but it was a piece of serious gear. The outer shell was made from three layers of patented fiber called S.T.R.O.N.G. and the interior padding had special hygienic material to prevent pathogens from building up while ensuring comfort, and it had a sophisticated ventilation system and noise dampening inserts for the quietest ride possible. "It's worth two grand. Where I go, it goes. Besides, I'm here as a guest. Just ask Mr. Vargas if I can bring it with me?"

The guy touched his earpiece and spoke in Spanish, which Dutch understood, into the mic that extended to his mouth, even relaying the helmet brand.

Looking around as if bored, Dutch knew exactly what the response would be. Vargas, the kingpin of Southern California, wasn't going to be worried about his niece's date carrying a helmet. Not when he was surrounded by loyal, armed men.

"All right," the guard said. "The helmet is fine, but I've still got to pat you down."

Extending his arms and spreading his legs, Dutch assumed the position, letting the man do his job. First, the guard ran a wand over Dutch's body, scanning for listening devices. Even if he had one hidden on him, with the loud, pumping music, he'd have to be right next to Vargas for any equipment to clearly pick up both sides of the conversation.

Satisfied that he wasn't wired, the guard moved on to

the pat down, going across his arms, over his torso, up and down his legs, getting a little too close to his groin.

"Watch it, buddy," Dutch said.

"Not my concern." Pursing his lips in a tight line, the guard unhooked the velvet rope and then hiked his thumb toward the steps, giving him the okay to go up.

Dutch ascended the industrial metal staircase only to be greeted by another guard at the top of the landing.

"The helmet," the second one with a manicured beard said. He had the build of a middleweight boxer, tall and lean, but wiry.

"This again?" Dutch asked. "I was given permission to take it with me."

"Well, I didn't give permission."

"Max!" Rodrigo called from the swanky seating area. According to the dossier, Rodrigo was Vargas's right-hand man and second in command. Beside him, Vargas sat like he ruled the world as young women in skimpy dresses danced around the VIP room. "Let him through."

"See. What did I tell you?" Dutch said.

Max narrowed his eyes and took a step forward, blocking him.

"You want to dance?" Dutch asked, referring to a tango with fists. He clutched the rim of his helmet so tight his knuckles strained.

"Maximiliano!" Rodrigo said again. "It's okay. He's Isabel's new admirer."

Clenching his jaw and his fists, Max hesitated before finally letting him through.

What was his problem? Did he have a crush on Isabel and wanted her for himself?

Dutch brushed past Max, deliberately making contact without being aggressive enough to start a fight. This was his element, his culture, and he knew exactly how to behave to survive. To thrive in it.

There was another set of stairs leading to a third floor, where there appeared to be only one room. An office?

He walked by two more armed guards and dancing women, up to the sofa.

Rodrigo rose. "Welcome." He ushered Dutch into the seating area and backed away as if to give them privacy.

Dutch nodded to him and strode closer to the man he came to see. "Mr. Vargas, it's a pleasure to meet you." He put his helmet and drink on the coffee table and held out his hand. "I'm—"

"Horatio Haas." Vargas shook his hand, and Dutch could tell the mob boss was assessing everything—Dutch's clothing, facial expression, exposed tattoos, the firmness of the handshake—and motioned for him to sit in the leather club chair on the other side of a round glass coffee table.

"Everyone calls me Dutch." He sat, not sure what he hated more, being called Horatio or having his back to the iron railing that overlooked the dance floor. At least he had a clear line of sight of the stairs and all the guards, and the other VIP tables were vacant and not a concern.

Dutch gave the appearance of relaxing in the plush chair while staying ready to spring into action, his senses dialed into the environment. All the women threw him easy smiles, from the ones lounging on the sofa to others dancing. They were beautiful. Blonde, brunette, red-head, curvaceous, slim, you name it and that type was there.

The women gyrating to the music and shaking their assets were a shiny lure, meant to bait him. To test him.

"Call me Emilio," Isabel's uncle said. "What are you drinking?"

Under normal circumstances, Dutch would've gotten a beer, but he had to set the right tone for the conversation. "Scotch. Macallan."

Surprise lit Vargas's cold, shrewd eyes. "I'm a Scotch man myself."

Dutch was aware.

To get her uncle's attention and keep it, Dutch had to defy expectations.

"Do you know why I asked to see you without my niece present?" Vargas asked.

How would the typical dude answer? Act as if he didn't know and perhaps, he wouldn't. Or soften the response to avoid coming across as brash.

Dutch decided to speak his mind. Unfiltered. "To size me up without the distraction of Isabel's interest in me, and if you deemed me unworthy, then try to scare me off." It wasn't a question. It was a statement. Dutch was certain that was the reason.

Vargas stilled, his gaze not faltering for a second from Dutch's. "Try? You don't think I'd do an adequate job of scaring you." His tone was teasing.

Her uncle wasn't what Dutch had imagined. Without a doubt, he was vile filth, but the cultured packaging, the detached, refined demeanor, the imposing air about him was impressive. Now Dutch understood how Isabel could've failed to see through his charismatic thrall.

"I don't scare easily." Dutch took his first swig of the Scotch. Peaty, hot, not bad at all. He noticed Max speaking into his mic and covering his ear as if trying to listen.

Max pivoted and hustled to Rodrigo. "There's a problem with the *delivery*."

Delivery being drugs. Every business that Vargas owned or paid for, including Isabel's art gallery, was used to either deal drugs or launder money.

"I'll go handle it," Rodrigo said. "But I want you to come with me." He waved the other two guards over. "You come with us." He pointed to the taller, stocky one. "Stay here and keep an eye on things."

The trio hurried down the stairs while the stout guard went to the landing and stood as sentry in Max's place.

"My niece tells me that you're between jobs right now," Vargas said, crossing his legs.

"Actually, I'm on terminal leave from the army. So, if you're wondering whether I collect a paycheck, the answer is yes."

"For how much longer? A week? Two?"

"Three, sir."

"What are your plans when that runs out?"

"I've been working since I was sixteen and I've always had a steady stream of income. Plus, I've got a decent amount saved. But I won't need to dip into it. Once my background check is completed, I'll start a position at a private security company." Dutch finished his drink and noticed Vargas's glass was empty. "Why don't I get us another round?"

"I'll have Macallan as well, but since you're buying, make it the twenty-five-year-old."

Dutch got up, thankful for the reprieve and time to think. He headed to the bar against the far wall in the area and ordered. "Macallan 25. Two."

The waitress poured a generous amount of liquor into the tumblers. "That'll be four hundred dollars."

Dutch coughed, choking on the price. The most he'd ever spent on booze was for a keg and that had cost a fourth of the amount. He couldn't whip out a credit card since there hadn't been time to make a fake one for him, so he slapped down the last of the petty cash he'd been given.

The bartender threw him a disgruntled look. The crappy tip was less than 10 percent.

"All you did was pour," he said.

She cocked a brow. "Without spitting in the glass first. I'll be sure to remember you next time."

Dutch picked up the rock glasses and walked back to the seating area, strategizing, his wits reined in tight.

Vargas shooed away a brunette who was in his lap and waved for Dutch to sit beside him.

Dutch handed him the drink as he lowered into the seat. They clinked glasses, and he took a sip. The smooth, silky heat slid down his throat.

That was what old and expensive tasted like.

"May I be frank with you?" Vargas asked.

"By all means. Cutting the crap will save us both time and energy. I'm nothing if not efficient."

Vargas chuckled. "I appreciate your directness. My niece warned me that you'd speak freely, and I see that she was right. What do you know of the Vargas name in this area?"

Dutch shrugged. "Your niece owns an art gallery and you're a big venture capitalist."

"Where are you from? I can't pinpoint your accent over the music."

"I was born in New York City. Spent some time out in Chicago—"

"I'm going to cut to the chase… *Dutch*. To put it simply, we are royalty. My niece is a princess. Whereas you are a peasant. You *aren't* good enough for her and have nothing of consequence to offer."

Dutch sat up, setting his drink down. "What about companionship?"

"Isabel has a full life. She's active in the community and has plenty of friends."

"Not male friends who she feels safe around," Dutch said, and Vargas straightened, his brows drawing together. "She's leery of men."

"As well she should. Guys tend to think with the little head between their legs, only interested in what they can get from a beautiful woman like Isabel. A night or two of pleasure. A bit of fun."

Swallowing a groan, Dutch couldn't believe how arrogant the man was, making such premature judgments based on nothing but his appearance. Vargas was the worst kind, valuing money and influence over kindness and decency.

"If all I wanted from your niece was a night of pleasure, I could've had that and moved on. Instead, I've shown her the utmost respect, which is what she deserves," Dutch said, staying focused on Vargas as well as his surroundings. "I'm here tonight not because you wanted to meet me, but because I insisted on meeting you. Isabel is leery in the way a woman is when she's been hurt by a man. Physically."

Vargas uncrossed his legs and slammed his drink down on the table, spilling two-hundred-dollar scotch like it was well liquor. "What are you saying?"

From the corner of his eye, Dutch noticed the stocky guard distracted by a voluptuous woman in a glittering gold dress dancing beside him, flaunting her curves.

Then Dutch saw it. Someone trotting up the steps, hurried—cloaked in darkness. The person wore a funnel-neck hoodie. The thin material would appear stylish when pulled down, but raised, it'd obscure someone's profile.

Too late, the guard turned and drew his gun.

The person threw something—overhand for added power and velocity. The blade struck perfectly, lodged in the bodyguard's right eye. Staggering back, the guard dropped his gun to bring his hands to the knife and fell to his knees.

Fast, so fast, the killer reached the top of the landing and raced toward the seating area while digging into a pocket. Drawing another knife, he held it by the blade. White. Synthetic. Maybe plastic or some polymer that a metal detector would miss.

The hit man threw the knife at Vargas.

Chapter Fourteen

On pure instinct, Dutch grabbed Vargas and hauled him to the floor.

The sharp knife sliced into the back of the sofa where Vargas had been sitting, spraying feathers in the air.

"Stay down," Dutch said. Then he whirled on his knees and leaped up, tackling the killer to the floor.

Dutch grabbed his helmet from the table—the only improvised weapon within reach. He slammed the sturdy piece of gear into the man's face, throttling him over and over until he stopped moving.

From the corner of his eye, Dutch caught movement. Rodrigo and Max were racing up the stairs. Two more lieutenants were behind them.

What in the hell was happening?

"Don Emilio!" Max rushed to Vargas's side, got him up off the floor and ushered him toward the stairs.

Dutch followed them closely to the office off the landing on the third floor. Two guards brought up the rear, weapons drawn.

"Are you all right?" Max asked. "Were you injured?"

"I'm fine." Vargas waved him away. "Dutch saved my life. If it weren't for him, I'd be dead."

The realization chilled Dutch to the bone as all eyes in the room shifted to him. He'd saved the life of a cartel boss, a man the world would be better off without. A man whose death might've put the US Marshals in a better position if they already had the stolen hard drive.

Damn it.

"It was nothing," Dutch said. "Instinct kicked in. That's all."

"You have excellent instincts. And it wasn't nothing." Vargas straightened his shirt and smoothed down his jacket. "It had happened so fast. One minute, everything had been under control. The next... How could anyone have gotten that close to me? What was the problem with the delivery?"

"Miscommunication," Rodrigo said. "Some heated words were exchanged, but I handled it before it turned into something major."

"A distraction." Vargas wagged a finger. "To lure you away. To give someone an opportunity to get to me."

Rodrigo turned to the guards. "I want one of you posted at the door. The other, go make sure the mess downstairs gets cleaned up. Clean this up *pronto*."

The two men nodded and left, closing the door. Max turned his hard gaze to Dutch like he was an interloper instead of the guy who'd just saved his boss's life.

Vargas poured two glasses of Scotch from his personal en suite bar and handed one to Dutch. "Here."

Dutch took a sip of the amber liquid. It was just as full-bodied as the Macallan, but deeper, richer. Or maybe the adrenaline surge sharpened everything, including his taste buds. "Smooth."

"Isle of Jura. A thirty-year-old." Vargas poured more in Dutch's glass. "What did you do in the army?"

"I was Special Ops. Delta Force."

"Ah," Vargas said in a tone that implied he'd grossly underestimated Dutch. "That explains those finely honed instincts of yours." He sat behind the desk and gestured for Dutch to take the seat opposite him. "Why did you get out of the service?"

"I was kicked out."

Vargas raised his eyebrows in curiosity. "What did you do?"

"I killed a man." Dutch took another sip, not rushing to explain his cover story. Not giving any hint of shame. Not an iota of regret. "It was self-defense, but he outranked me and had a lot of powerful buddies. Fortunately, I had a stellar record and a few friends of my own. The army gave me the boot, but with a general instead of dishonorable discharge. To hell with them."

"Isa tells me that you stopped a man from mugging her. The thought of such an assault on my niece turns my stomach, makes me want to tear someone to pieces."

Dutch understood the sentiment far too well. "To be honest, sir, she saved herself. Kicked the guy's butt. All I did was pick up her purse, shoes and get a piece of glass out of her foot."

Vargas chuckled. "Sounds like her. The women in my family are headstrong, independent. Fiery. As my brother's only child, I have a responsibility to her. I love Isa as a daughter. When I say that the Vargas legacy is the same as the Five Families in New York or the Chicago syndicate, do you understand what I mean?"

It meant he was the top dog, the mobster who controlled this region.

Dutch straightened. "Yes."

"I'm going through a bit of a turf war at the moment," Vargas continued. He pulled something out of his suit-jacket pocket and tossed it onto the desk.

It was a playing card. Ace of spades.

"First they sent me the king of spades. Then that one.

The death card. It's from the Guzman cartel and means they're coming for me. But I have something in the works to fix this problem." He leaned forward, putting his forearms on his desk. "Isabel doesn't know any of this. Her father wanted her sheltered from our affairs. She was sent to the very best all-girl boarding schools until she went to college. Scripps."

Once again, an all-girls school, just outside of LA.

"I wish to honor her father's desire to keep her in the dark," Vargas said. "But I worry about her up here by herself. She refuses to move back to San Diego and won't let me give her any bodyguards. I believe she thinks they'd spy on her for me."

"Would they?" Dutch asked.

Vargas waved his hands out. *"Por su puesto."* *Of course.* "I have the best of intentions." He sat back and crossed his legs. "I believe there is a place for you in the fold, where your skills could be of use to me. I would like to offer you a job."

"Doing what? I hope it's not spying on your niece because the answer would be no."

"You have integrity. I respect that." Vargas drained his glass. "I want you to protect Isabel. That's why I'm trusting you with this information. You need to understand what we're dealing with if you are to keep her safe."

"But Don Emilio," Max said. "You can't trust an outsider with her safety."

"Are you questioning my judgment?" Vargas said in Spanish.

Rodrigo stepped forward. "He would never. Neither would I, but we don't know him."

"Isabel knows him." This time Vargas spoke in English. "Likes him. Trusts him. She's rejected everyone else I've proposed, including you two." He cast them both a look that screamed *don't dare say another word*. Neither man spoke again as Vargas shifted his gaze back to Dutch. "It's no secret to my enemies that I love Isabel dearly. That could make her a target to some. I need to insulate her from danger. Immediately, with this attack tonight. I think you're the man to help me do that without frightening her. I doubt she'd have any objections to your presence and as you've stated, your loyalty is to her."

Dutch nodded, slowly, considering the surprising offer. "What does it pay?"

"Ten grand a month."

"Just to keep her safe?" Dutch whistled. "Heck, I'd do it for free." And he would.

"A man has to eat. Does he not?"

Dutch lowered his gaze and clucked his tongue. "Not all of us want to dine on white truffles and Strottarga Bianco."

"You know of the finer things," Vargas said.

What Dutch knew about them had come from reading an article after Googling *expensive indulgences of the stupid rich*.

"But you don't need it." Vargas studied him a minute. "I can see why Isabel is fond of you."

"I can't formally say yes to your offer until I know Isabel won't object to me working for you."

"And if she does?" Vargas asked.

"Then I'll still be there for her, to keep her safe as best I can."

"I will tell Isabel that I approve of you and I'll have a new helmet sent. A Schuberth, yes?"

"Yeah," he said, noticing that Vargas hadn't asked for his address.

"It was good to meet you, Dutch."

"Likewise, sir." He stood and shook Vargas's hand.

"Take my card," Vargas said, offering him one. "It has my private number in case you need to speak with me about my niece."

Dutch pocketed the card. On the way out, he met Max's glare and caught the suspicion in Rodrigo's eyes.

He closed the door and headed down the stairs, hoping that the USMS had taken the time to cement his cover story online and in hard records, making it ironclad, because Vargas was about to run a full-scope background check on him.

If one wasn't already underway.

The cell phone woke Isabel. After tossing and turning for hours, fretting over Dutch's meeting with her uncle, she'd finally managed to fall asleep.

She glanced at the caller ID, hoping it was Dutch with good news.

Uncle Emilio. And it was two in the morning.

"*Tío,*" she said, surprise brushing away the dredges of sleep. "Is everything all right?"

"Yes, my dear. I met Dutch. I wanted to let you know that I like him."

"You do?" The instant the words left her mouth she regretted sounding so shocked.

"I give my approval and won't interfere."

Isabel pressed her hand to her forehead. Was she dreaming? She must be delirious from lack of sleep. "That's wonderful."

What was the catch? Uncle Emilio wouldn't make it this easy unless there was one.

"But I have one condition," he said.

Here it comes. Isabel was half-tempted to hang up the phone. She was grown and independently wealthy thanks to the money her father had left her. She'd trade it all, the lavish lifestyle and the trappings that came with it, the eight figures sitting in her bank account, for a normal life, where she was safe and not subjected to the tight reins of her uncle. To live without anything hanging over her.

Sometimes freedom seemed more necessary than maintaining familial ties. But she loved her uncle Emilio and her cousin Miguel. They were the only family she had left. She had been raised to respect her elders, to seek their praise and validation. Also, dealing with the nightmare of Chad Ellis was quite enough. She didn't want to add her uncle to her list of problems.

"Why am I not surprised there are strings?" she asked.

"Watch your tone with me," he snapped in that stern way of his. "Dutch told me about his Special Forces background, something you neglected to mention. I offered him a job, but he was hesitant to take it."

"A job doing what?"

"Protecting you."

Isabel bolted upright in the bed unsure she'd heard him correctly. McQueen shifted on top of the covers near her feet.

"When he discusses the matter with you," he said, "I want you to take away his reservations."

"I don't understand."

"Do this and you get the relationship you want with a man I approve of and I'll know that you're safe. If I can ensure that you're protected and it happens to be by someone who makes you happy, then we both win. Yes?"

Her first instinct was to rail against the idea. It took extreme effort for her not to scream into the phone. She didn't want Dutch taking her uncle's money, beholden to do his bidding. The audacity to even propose such a thing to her boyfriend was unreal.

Churning it over in her head, she began to see the

flip side. If she agreed, then she'd get to have Dutch around more often and keep her uncle off her back. She wanted both.

"Don't ask him to spy on me," she said. "It would muddy the waters between us."

"Your young man already told me in no uncertain terms that he would do no such thing."

Dutch stood up to her uncle.

She smiled, her cheeks heating, a dizzying sense of warmth seeping through her down to the bone. "I can't promise anything," she said. "He's his own man and will make his own decision, but I'll talk to him and let him know that I'm not opposed to the idea."

"Excellent. I'm running a background check on him, just a formality of course. I feel certain he will be able to handle any threat to you. Despite what you might believe, your happiness is important to me. Good night, *mi hija*. I love you."

"I love you, too." Isabel hung up, wondering what exactly had happened at the club for Dutch to have made such a profound impression on her uncle.

Going back to sleep was impossible. Part of her was ecstatic and eager to see Dutch, but there was a niggle of worry in the back of her mind that wouldn't let her rest.

The sun took its time cracking over the horizon. As she sipped a cup of tea, watching daylight break through the sky, she got a text.

Dutch: We need to talk. Game for an early lunch?

Without hesitation, she messaged him back.

Let's make it dinner. My place. I'll cook.

She decided right then that her uncle's call last night was a good sign and not an omen that there was something wrong with Dutch.

Isabel went through her routine for the day, started the heavy lifting on planning her uncle's event, putting an emergency rush on the invitations, and had all but set aside her qualms until she updated Brenda.

"After one meeting, your uncle approved of Dutch instead of running him off with a shotgun?"

"I know, right?" Isabel went back to humming as she hung up the last new painting.

"What did Dutch have to do? Raid a corporation? Kill somebody?"

The melody died in Isabel's throat. What a bizarre response. "Why on earth would you say that?" she asked, turning to face her friend.

Brenda opened her mouth as if to speak, then pressed her lips together and walked to the front desk.

Isabel followed her. "Why would you think killing someone would impress my uncle?"

"It was a poor joke," Brenda said, avoiding eye contact while she shuffled paperwork around. "Sweetie, I know how much you love Uncle Emilio and because I love you, I'll never say anything bad about him."

"Bad like what?" The worst thing her uncle was guilty of was eating veal. Which admittedly was bad, but Brenda didn't know about that.

Brenda huffed. "Nothing. I'm sorry." She met her eyes and smiled. "I have a surprise. I was going to wait until later, but drumroll." Brenda tapped imaginary drums in the air. "I told my hot yoga teacher how you were mugged and asked if he could start teaching a morning class or something and he offered to give me private lessons on Sundays. Just the two of us, where he can re-

ally help deepen my poses and give me a good stretch."
She winked.

Isabel gasped with delight. "You've been trying to get
him one-on-one for months."

"I know. He really made me work for it, too. I mean,
you had to get robbed at knifepoint for Pete's sake." She
walked back around the desk like she no longer needed
it as a barrier. "I propose you skedaddle and go see your
hottie early for *dinner*," she said, using air quotes with
the last word.

Dinner and dessert with lots of icing and several cher-
ries. Isabel's heart fluttered with anticipation, but guilt
was quick on its heels. "I've already missed two days this
week, leaving you to handle everything. I'd be a horrible
friend if I skipped out early tonight, especially when I
asked you not to change your schedule for me."

"Pish, posh. Make it up to me by sharing a few juicy
tidbits." She waggled her eyebrows.

"Okay. You really are the best friend I could ask for."

Brenda nodded with a smug smile.

Isabel called for her car, wrapped up the rest of what
she was doing, grabbed her purse from the office and
went to the grocery store.

Inside, she headed straight for the fish department and
waited in line for her turn.

A young man wearing Dickies work pants and a black
shirt buttoned only at the top with a white tank top underneath, sneakers and a black-and-white bandana on his
head came up to the front of the large case where the
fish was displayed and looked around.

"How can I help you?" the fishmonger asked her after
he was done with the last customer.

"I'm cooking seafood *fra diavolo* for two. Can you
wrap up a mix of what's freshest?"

"I've got some nice lobster tails, scallops and these beauties." The fishmonger held up a handful of the plumpest shrimp she'd ever seen.

"Perfect."

"Want me to prep it for you, remove the shells and devein the shrimp?"

That was why this was her favorite grocery store. "Yes, that'd be lovely."

"Finish shopping, ma'am, and it'll be here on the counter for you."

"Thank you." Isabel strode off and grabbed linguini and a can of tomatoes. She turned to find the rest of the ingredients and spotted the same guy in a black shirt and Dickies strolling past her aisle.

He glanced at her for one heartbeat too long, but he kept going. A creeping tension sent a shiver up her spine when she realized he wasn't pushing a cart and didn't have a basket.

Her first impulse was to call Dutch, but she was in a well-lit public place and could handle herself. She didn't need anyone's help.

Get a grip, Isabel. You of all people know better than to stereotype that guy. The whole world isn't out to get you. Only Chad.

She mentally checked off what else she needed and hurried to get the items. As she picked out a couple of salad dressings Dutch might like, the guy with the bandana showed up again. He didn't look at her. Standing in front of the ketchup, he took a bottle from the shelf and turned it over, as if he was reading the ingredients.

"It's nothing," she said to herself, but she couldn't shake the feeling that something was off about the guy.

She went to the produce section. Looking over the herbs, she threw a bundle of parsley in her basket. The main dessert would hopefully be in the bedroom, but they'd cap off dinner with something light. Maybe a fruit salad.

Breezing past the stands, she tossed a ripe variety in her basket. She stopped in front of the cantaloupe, deciding if she wanted to dice one up or simply buy it chopped and prepackaged.

Another customer waltzed up beside her, bumping her basket. A hand with tattoos inked on the back grabbed a cantaloupe. "Do you know how to pick a good melon?" he asked.

She glanced over at the man. The one who looked like a gangbanger and kept popping up in the same parts of the store. He had two teardrop tattoos below the corner of his eye.

"No. Sorry." Spinning on her heel, she walked away. Forget the melon.

"Hey. Your stuff is ready," he called to her.

She pivoted and looked back at him. "What did you say?"

"Your seafood." He hiked a thumb toward the fish department. "It's on the counter waiting for you."

All the spit dried in her mouth, but she managed to say, "Thank you."

It was odd, yes, but he was only being friendly, and she was being ridiculous, right? No need to be rude, as well.

She passed another man who didn't have a basket or a cart and because he was dressed in business attire, she didn't question *his* motives for being in the store.

Isabel grabbed the seafood bundle from the counter in the fish department, tossed it into her basket and went to a register. She loaded her stuff on the conveyor belt, itching to get out of the store. As she bent over to place the empty basket on the floor, she stilled.

At the bottom of the basket was a playing card. She picked it up and turned it over.

Queen of spades.

But it hadn't been in there earlier when she'd first taken a basket. She was certain.

She dropped the card in the basket and shoved it under the conveyor belt.

Isabel paid, opting for paper bags, and hurried to her car. Hitting the new key fob, the lights flashed on her Maserati, and the doors unlocked. She opened the trunk and set her bags inside. Before closing it, she unzipped her purse and grasped the handle of her fully charged Pacifier.

Better safe than sorry.

Trying to slow her breaths that started coming too quickly, she scanned her surroundings.

No sign of the man.

She slipped inside her car, locked the doors and started the engine. Putting on her seat belt, she noticed something on her windshield, trapped under her wipers.

The queen of spades.

Her whole body went cold, but every nerve pulsed with energy. Isabel looked around outside, twisting in her seat. There was no one near her car, but was anyone watching her? Waiting for a reaction to seeing the card? How did the same queen of spades get on her windshield without her noticing anyone?

She flipped on the wipers. The wind snatched the card, carrying it on a breeze across the parking lot.

A shadow moved up alongside her window. She almost jumped out of her skin, her heart throbbing in her throat.

An older woman got inside a sedan parked beside hers and pulled off.

Isabel took a deep breath, calming herself down. She

threw her car in gear and drove to the doggie day care center, going well over the speed limit, not running red lights, but gunning it when any turned yellow.

Once McQueen was in the car she felt better, knowing she had immediate backup in case she needed it. He wouldn't let anyone get near her if he sensed danger. Too bad she couldn't take him with her everywhere.

On the way home, she checked her mirrors constantly, making sure she wasn't being followed. Not that she had any training in picking up a tail, but she'd notice if the same car stayed glued behind her.

Nothing unusual stuck out and by the time she pulled into her garage, her nerves had settled somewhat.

Entering her building, she waved hello to the concierge, who worked from eight to six at the front desk. "Good evening, Bill," she said with a shopping bag in either hand.

"Evening, Isabel. You got a package. I ran it upstairs for you, put it in front of your door."

"You're a saint," she said, wondering what it could be since she hadn't ordered anything. "Thank you."

"Need help with those groceries?"

"No, I've got it." She hit the button for the elevator. Normally she took the stairs, but tonight, she wanted to get inside her condo as soon as possible.

The chime dinged and the doors opened. She got in the lift with McQueen. The ride up was quick.

At her front door, McQueen ran up to the package and sniffed it. She put her key in the door and unlocked it. Inside, she shut off her alarm and set her groceries down, relieved to be home.

She put everything away, took out her phone and called Dutch. "Hi."

"Hey, beautiful." His deep, smoky voice brought another layer of comfort.

"Brenda is closing up tonight," she said, retrieving the package, with the phone sandwiched between her ear and shoulder. "I already swung by the grocery, where something weird happened."

"Weird how?"

She shrugged to herself. "I'm not really sure, but I'll tell you about it later." She locked the door and put the box on the counter. "I've had the busiest day, running around like crazy because my uncle wants me to organize an art auction for him down in San Diego."

"Really? When's the auction?"

"Sunday. Fifty guests. I can't believe it's such short notice. Talk about pressure." She sighed, hoping to pull everything together, not wanting to disappoint her uncle. "I'm set to cook dinner tonight, though. How quickly can you get here?"

The package was covered in brown shipping wrap and her name was typed on a label on the top, but there was no return address. Today was full of weird stuff. Was Mercury retrograde? A full moon or something?

"I just stepped out of the shower," he said, conjuring delicious images in her mind. "I'll throw on clothes and head over."

"I was thinking, why don't you bring your toothbrush and spend the night?" Smiling, she pulled at the taped-down flaps along the side and unwrapped it. "That's strange."

"What?"

"I got a package. It's a foam box."

"Foam?" Sternness spiked the word.

"Yes, an insulated cooler," she said, taking off the lid. "Wait. Don't open it."

A rancid smell hit her as she peered inside. A strangled scream escaped her lips. The cell phone slipped from her hand, crashing to the floor. She gagged, her stomach convulsing.

McQueen started barking.

Sickened and terrified, she heard Dutch yelling to her from the phone on the floor. But her mind went blank. She squeezed her eyes shut, staggering back from the box in horrified revulsion, spun toward the sink and retched.

In her entire life, she'd never seen anything more gruesome.

Chapter Fifteen

Twelve minutes. That's how long it had taken Dutch to reach Isabel and it had felt like a small eternity.

Staring at the obscene foulness in the box, a cold fist clenched his stomach.

Dear God, Almighty. Dutch had seen a lot of awful, sick things in his time in the army, but this still got to him.

Looking away from the mutilated pig's head, he put the lid on the box. He was outraged someone had sent that to her. The only reason he was able to muster a facade of calm was for Isabel's sake.

Dutch went to her in the living room. He sat on the coffee table in front of her, so close that his legs brushed the outside of hers, and he held her hands.

Her fingers were ice-cold and her face pale.

McQueen didn't know what to do. The dog vacillated between barking at the box on the counter and whining beside his owner.

Making sure Isabel was okay was Dutch's only concern after he'd called the police. His protective instincts had reached an all-time high. After grabbing the throw from the back of the sofa, he wrapped it around her shivering body.

She was in shock.

He put a mug of water with a chamomile tea bag in the microwave and poured her a small cup of pomegranate juice. "Here, drink this. It'll help." Once her blood sugar came up, she'd start to feel a little better.

She took the glass with both hands and sipped it. Her face twisted like she might be sick.

"Chug it, all at once." It was only four ounces and she needed to drink it.

A shudder rippled through her, making the glass shake in her hand, but then she did as he told her. After she swallowed, he noticed a slight lessening of tension in her muscles.

The microwave beeped. He took the glass from her, got the tea and shoved the warm mug in her hands.

"Why would Chad do this? Send me…that."

First the bees, almost killing Isabel, and now sending her such a disgusting thing. He was a sadistic monster.

Dutch clenched his fists, aching with the need to pound them into Chad's face.

"The stench." Fresh tears welled in her eyes. "I can still smell it. I need air. Please, I want to get out of here."

A loud rap at the door drew their gazes. "Police. We received a call."

Dutch got up, let the two officers in and showed them the contents of the box. They both gasped, their faces tightening with disgust as they reeled back.

"Damn," Officer Gibbs said.

Officer Lewis took out a pad and pen. "Ma'am, we're going to need to get your statement," she said, gently.

Dutch folded his arms, furious energy buzzing through him. "How long will it take?"

"It might take a while," Officer Lewis said. "We're also going to need you both to come down to the station to get your fingerprints to check them against what we find on the box."

"Can you take her statement at the station? The sooner we change the scenery, the better."

The female officer nodded. "Sure."

Dutch strode into the living room and hunkered down in front of Isabel. "After the police station, do you want to come back here? Or do you want to stay with me tonight?"

"With you," she said weakly.

He helped her up from the sofa and into the bedroom, where she packed a bag.

"Ma'am?" one of the officers called from the kitchen. "There's no postmark on the wrapping. It wasn't mailed. Did you see who dropped it off?"

"No." Isabel drifted through the room, stuffing some things in an overnight bag. "Bill, the concierge downstairs might've. He brought the box up to my apartment."

"We'll need his statement and prints, too," Officer Lewis said.

Since Isabel was in no condition to get behind the wheel, Dutch drove her and McQueen in his truck. At the station, he stopped out front.

"Go inside with McQueen," Dutch said. "I'll be back as soon as I can."

She stiffened. "Where are you going?"

Taking her hand in his, he said, "I need to make this stop."

Her eyes widened with understanding and she shook her head. "Don't go. He's dangerous."

"Not as dangerous as I can be." Ellis had no idea who he was messing with and it was time he learned. "It's okay," he reassured her in a gentle tone. "I won't be gone long."

Worry didn't leave Isabel's eyes, but she nodded. "Be careful. He got his orange belt in Krav Maga," she said as if that made Chad a lethal weapon. "I don't want him to hurt you."

If anyone was going to get hurt, it'd be Chad. By the time Dutch was finished, Chad would wish he had a second degree black belt. "Don't set foot outside the station. Don't go anywhere without me."

She nodded again, opened the door and slipped out of the car. McQueen followed. Once she disappeared inside, Dutch sped off.

The wings of cold, black rage beat through him and thanks to the file from Agent Rogers, he knew exactly where to find Chad Ellis.

IN HIS BRENTWOOD OFFICE, Chad sat behind his desk, working at his computer. Business was doing better than ever at the funeral parlor as well as with biohazard remediation, thanks to the rise in crime. If he could send every murderer in the area a thank-you note, he would.

Shouting from the front of the building had him swiveling around in his chair to see what all the ruckus was about.

Horatio "Dutch" Haas was charging down the hallway, headed straight for Chad's office.

Chad hit the intercom button for his secretary. She was fifty-something, loyal as the day was long and had been with him from the beginning. Jill sat as a gatekeeper at a desk in front of his office.

"Don't try to stop him," Chad said. "Round up the boys—have them hurry on over. Then grab your phone and record everything. No audio."

"Okay," Jill said. Her gaze bounced up to Haas as she

hung up and called the lounge, where his workers hung out between cleaning assignments.

At least five men were in the building, not that he needed or wanted them to intervene. He was stacking the deck of witnesses in his favor.

Dutch kicked open his office door, splintering the frame.

What melodramatic machismo. Chad suppressed an eye roll and stifled a chuckle. Playing the part of the victim meant he needed to appear frightened and intimidated on the video.

"How dare you," Chad said. "Who do you think you are barging in here like this?"

"You sick bastard!" Dutch stalked up to the desk, planted his palms on the surface and leaned over, bringing them eye level. "Did it make you feel like a big man to send a butchered pig's head to Isabel? You're a twisted monster."

"What?"

Rage boiled in Dutch's face as he swept everything off Chad's desk onto the floor. He stormed around, grabbed Chad by the lapels of his suit jacket, snatched him out of the chair and slammed him against the wall.

"Are you going to look me in the eye and deny sending it to Isabel?"

Hell, yeah. Not because he didn't do it, even though he hadn't, but deny, deny, deny was the second rule he lived by.

Rule number one—don't get caught.

Glancing over Dutch's shoulder, he saw Jill filming everything and the guys who worked for him gathering around the front of the office.

Chad raised his palms and pinched his features into

those of a man terrified for his life. "I don't know what you're talking about. I didn't send her anything."

But he wished like hell he had. Damn, that was a good one. Why hadn't he thought of it?

"You're a lying sack of garbage." Dutch lifted his fist. "I ought to—"

"What?" Chad asked, maintaining his frightened expression for the camera and witnesses, but lowering his voice, taunting Haas. "Hit me? Go ahead. Beat me. Kick my teeth in. Make it hurt. Don't stop until you turn me into meatloaf. You know you want to."

Reason dawned in Dutch's eyes, breaking through the cloud of wrath. He looked over his shoulder at the crowd of employees and then back at Chad. Releasing him, Dutch stepped back.

Apparently, Dutch wasn't a mindless Neanderthal who'd be easily baited. Too bad.

Chad would love nothing more than to have this riff-raff charged with assault and thrown in jail. Guess that meant Chad would have to work a little harder to push his buttons. "When Isabel and I came close to reconnecting a few months ago," he whispered, "behind her art gallery—"

"You mean when you attacked her?"

"She wanted me to be there. She wanted me to touch her."

"You're delusional." Dutch stared at him, his narrowed eyes darkening. His jaw flexed with barely contained anger. "If you go near her again," he said, dropping his voice to a whisper as well, "I'll kill you."

Isabel was his weakness. Chad's minx had gotten under Dutch's skin, slinked her way into his heart. "Tell my Isabel she should keep better company. Or she might get stung by something worse than a bee."

Swift fury gleamed in Dutch's eyes as he cocked his fist back and launched it.

The first punch smashed into Chad's face, jarring his head. The second struck the wall when Chad ducked, his reflexes honed from training kicking in, and maneuvered to the side.

One blow was enough to do the trick. Blood poured from his nose. The pain made his head buzz. Covering his face, he hid his smile and swallowed laughter along with his own blood. He had six witnesses, a video and soon a medical report as evidence. "Kiss your freedom goodbye. I'm going to have you brought up on charges."

"Knock yourself out trying." Without a lick of worry in his expression, Dutch turned for the door.

Chad growled, "Maybe she needs to take a restraining order out on you since you've been watching her." He rattled off the address to the vacant building where Dutch's motorcycle had been parked.

Dutch froze. Then he pivoted. Fear, gut-wrenching fear was plastered on his face.

Chad was so thrilled he gave a mental cheer that would've rocked a stadium. He'd found the right thread. Now he needed to pull it until this thing between Dutch and Isabel unraveled.

"Stay away from her," Dutch warned while pointing a threatening finger, and then he charged out of the building.

Chad looked at Jill. "Call the police. Tell them I've just been assaulted."

Chapter Sixteen

With a bag of ice on his bruised knuckles, Dutch sat on the sofa in the temporary one-bedroom apartment the USMS had loaned him. He stared at the new Schuberth that had been delivered, his mind spinning while Isabel was in the shower.

Everything had turned into a disaster.

An epic disaster of career-ending proportions.

Will Draper had had a conniption when Dutch was forced to call him and explain what happened at Chad Ellis's place of business. His boss had to intercede with the cops before a warrant was issued for Dutch's arrest.

Dutch had never heard such foul language from a superior, not even in the army. His ears were still burning. He was worried Draper was going to have a stroke on the phone.

The fact that Dutch was a deputy marshal had become a ticking time bomb bound to explode. The satellite hub had to be shut down. Draper and Allison would have to work out of the LA field office, putting Dutch's backup at a distance. Ellis was close to learning the truth and once he did, he wouldn't hesitate to rub it in Isabel's face.

Even worse, at the police station, the cops had found an ace of spades card underneath the pig's head. A warning to Vargas that the Guzman cartel was coming for

Isabel. Chad hadn't sent that monstrosity after all and Dutch had gone off the rails over the one thing that sicko wasn't actually guilty of.

Dutch petted McQueen who was on the leather couch with his head in Dutch's lap.

He had to tell Isabel the truth. She needed to know that she was in danger, not only from Chad Ellis, but also the Guzman cartel because of her uncle Emilio.

Guilt coiled and tightened through him, leaving him queasy. He'd give anything to have a clean slate with Isabel, a fresh start, where she wouldn't hate him.

Going into this assignment he hadn't given any consideration to how he would exit.

Falling for her had been unforeseen, an impossibility he hadn't planned for. With Isabel, Dutch found everything he wanted, something he hadn't even realized had been missing in his life. The prospect of walking away from her, disappearing with no explanation, shredded him. He wouldn't be able to look in the mirror much less live with himself.

It all snowballed in his head into one gigantic problem with no easy solution.

Isabel opened the bedroom door and came out wearing a silky peach robe that complemented her olive complexion, her hair in a high, loose knot, the long line of her leg peeking out of the slit. The sight of her walking toward him, looking so fresh and clean, was a sucker punch to the gut. She was beautiful, full of sweetness, had such courage and absolute strength. It took hope for her to open her heart to him after everything she'd been through.

God, he didn't want to put her through more hell.

Dutch set his bag of ice on the end table and shooed

McQueen off the sofa to make room for her. The dog jumped down and lay across his feet.

Isabel sat and leaned into him. Roping an arm around her, he brought her against his body. She rested her head on his shoulder, putting her palm on his chest.

She smelled good, that particular scent he now knew as hers enveloped him. Inhaling deeply, he breathed her in. *Vetiver.* They'd have fun together in Indonesia. He longed to show her the thousand islands off greater Jakarta one day. Swimming. Exploring the coves.

There were a million things he wanted to share with her.

Pipe dream or possibility?

Tightening his hold on her, he needed to believe there was a way for them.

"Are you hungry?" he asked. It was after nine and they should've eaten hours ago. Not that he had much of an appetite. "I can whip something up."

"No, thanks. I don't want to eat." She tipped her head back, running her nose across his neck. "I don't need food right now. I need..."

"What is it, sweetheart?" He rubbed her arm, up and down, soothing, slow strokes.

"There's been so much ugliness. I need to forget the fear and horror for a little while." Angling her face up, she pressed her palm to his cheek and turned his mouth toward hers. Their lips a hairbreadth apart. "Help me forget, Dutch. I don't want to think. I just want to feel something good." She drew him closer.

Not holding back, he kissed her. Not a soft, flirty peck. No, this was greedy and reckless.

In a heartbeat it turned hotter, full of edgy desire. She lay back, pulling him on top of her. He felt every lush curve of her body as he slid against her. Loosening the tie on her robe, she let it fall open. He found her damp and bare, making him instantly hard.

Only Isabel had this way of luring him in and driving him wild like no one else.

He should pull back, pump the brakes, but she took his hand, guiding it to cup her breast. Velvety-soft skin. The touch sparked across his nerve endings, setting off something primal in him. He flicked his thumb over her nipple, and she moaned, arching beneath him, spreading her legs to better accommodate him between her thighs.

Need pulsed inside him, swelled, growing urgent.

"I want you." She unbuckled his belt, groped his straining erection through his jeans.

As she unzipped his pants, he stayed her hand.

"I can't." He wanted nothing more than to make love to her and show her how deeply he felt. That everything burning inside him for her was genuine, that when he was with her, he had a sense of peace, rightness he'd never had. But not like this, with lies between them.

"Are you married?" Her mouth went to his neck. She pressed a trail of sizzling kisses up his throat to his jaw, stoking his desire for her.

"No."

"Do you have children hidden away that you haven't told me about?"

He shook his head. "No."

"An STD?"

"God, no. Nothing like that."

Her hand dove down, where she palmed him through the denim. He wanted her so much that it hurt.

"Then I don't care." Her warm breath fanned his lips. "Whatever it is doesn't matter."

"You wanted to take things slowly. This is too fast," he said, not believing what was coming out of his mouth.

Not once had he ever turned down sex and especially not with a gorgeous woman he yearned to have.

"I know we've only been together a week, but I feel closer to you than any other man I've ever been with. When we're together, I feel safe and happy. Special."

"You are special."

Everything between them fell into place right from the start, tumblers in a lock clicking into position. Her presence, her affection, her warmth, lessened the emptiness that gnawed at him.

She had a good heart and wasn't weak. This woman had grit. She was fierce and smart and trusting. An irresistible mix of qualities that were hard to find and it made him even hotter for her.

He'd never considered having a long-term girlfriend, or commitments outside the military and the USMS, but he wanted to give himself to Isabel, have a future with her.

"This may sound crazy," she said, raw vulnerability all over her face, "but I think I'm falling in love with you."

His heart ached because he was falling in love, too. For the first time in his life.

If he told her the truth about who he was, he'd jeopardize everything. But if he slept with her without her knowing, she'd never forgive him, and he'd lose her forever.

Dutch squeezed his eyes shut, the importance of the mission weighing on him heavy as wet sandbags, knowing what was at risk if he failed—the lives of fellow marshals, their spouses, their children.

There was no debate. He had no choice. Right or wrong, what he had to do next was clear.

"I told you I love you," she said. And he hadn't said it back. Not that he owed her such a huge declaration.

Isabel drew in a shuddering breath, wondering if her admission was too much for him. Ill-timed? Too soon? Was she supposed to wait for him to say something so big first?

She'd had a handful of lovers, but none that she'd *loved*, and she wanted to share herself with someone who filled her heart.

Dutch opened his eyes, his gaze locked with hers, and she knew. Without him needing to say it, she saw it crystal clear, the same affection, the same passion, an absolute soul-deep connection glittering back at her.

She let out the breath she'd been holding. Her heart stuttered and swelled with relief. She brushed her mouth across his, but there was no answering pressure.

"Isabel," he said, and she put her hand to his chest, feeling the hard muscles bunch under his T-shirt, the hammering beat of his heart beneath. "I'm undercover."

"Huh?" That hadn't been what she'd expected to hear, and it made no sense. "What—what are you talking about?"

"I'm a US marshal. Undercover." His body flexed with tension. A dark sadness, pain, filled his eyes. "I was sent to get close to you. To recover something important that your uncle stole. To save lives." The words cut through her, leaving her raw, exposed.

She gathered her robe closed, covering herself as she pushed upright and tied the sash tight. Too stunned and confused to speak, she cradled her head in her hands. She tried breaking down what he'd said into tiny digestible pieces, but before she had a chance, he kept talking.

"Your uncle isn't who you think he is." Dutch sat up beside her. "He's not a legitimate businessman. He's the head of the *Los Chacales* cartel," he said, the name ringing bells in her head—big, clanging warning bells. "At least, he's in charge on the West Coast. His son, Miguel, handles things on the East Coast since your uncle put him in power."

A chill so cold that it burned raced over her skin.

Dutch put his hand on her thigh.

She flinched, jumping to her feet. "Don't touch me. Stay away from me."

"Your uncle Emilio peddles drugs and death," Dutch said, low and calm while a storm of emotion brewed inside her. "He's a man of violence with brutal tendencies. He's also a growing threat to national security."

"That's not true!" She stumbled back. "Why are you saying these horrible things?"

Dutch strode across the room to a briefcase. He entered a code, unlocking it, and pulled out a thick file. Sitting back on the sofa, he set it on the coffee table and opened it somewhere in the middle. "Do you know this woman?"

Isabel stepped closer and peered over at a picture of a young woman she recognized and stilled. Icy fingers closed around her heart and squeezed. "Yes. She's my uncle's ex-girlfriend."

"Your uncle uses every legitimate business that he owns, including your art gallery, to wash his money or sell drugs. Lori Carpenter," he said, pointing to the picture, "worked at a capital-management firm, where your uncle laundered hundreds of millions of dollars. After he started dating her, he put Lori in charge of his account. She saw all the dirty blood money coming in and ran to the FBI. He went to a lot of trouble to try to kill her. Silence her. But she survived, just barely. Turned state's evidence and testified."

A ringing started in her ears. She put her fingers to her temples.

Seven days. She'd only known Dutch seven days and as it turned out she didn't know him at all. The concrete number gave her something to focus on. A meter by which to gauge what he was saying. No reason to believe him. No reason to believe her own judgment that screamed what he'd said might be true. "Then why isn't my uncle in jail?"

"He's clever, insulated himself with layers of protection. The Justice Department couldn't go after him directly, so they went after the capital-investment company and shut down the major money-laundering arm of *Los Chacales*."

"I would've heard about it in the news, Lori testifying in such a big case."

"The DOJ tried to protect Lori's identity by keeping her name out of the press and had a closed-door trial. But in your uncle's attempt to kill Lori, the US Marshals building in San Diego was attacked. That was on the news."

It had been all over the television and in the paper for days. The USMS building under siege.

That had been Uncle Emilio?

"Your uncle came into possession of sensitive information that was stolen from the US Marshals Service. He has the personal data of every individual in WITSEC here in California, as well as that of our marshals and their dependents. Your uncle is planning to auction the hard drive with information this weekend to the highest criminal bidder."

Putting her hand to her mouth to muffle a gasp, Isabel turned away from him. The ringing in her head wouldn't stop. Like something was there, some horrible realization, only it was too terrible, and she couldn't wrap her head around it.

To do so would bring her whole world crashing down.

"I have to retrieve the hard drive before the auction," Dutch said. "It can't be sold."

The auction. The bizarre, short-notice auction.

An exceptional item of great value. One-of-a kind. They'll clear their schedules.

And she was organizing it.

Isabel was so furious she was sickened to her stomach. She was angry at Dutch. At her uncle. At every single person on the planet. But still she couldn't accept this because then everything in her life would be a fabrication of one shade or another.

"I can't believe I introduced you to him!" she said, storming around the living room. McQueen got up at Isabel's raised voice as if waiting for instructions. "Put myself on the line. For what? So you could create these lies? Drive a wedge between us? Why are you doing this?"

"When I met him at the club, there was an assassination attempt on him."

Isabel swiveled around, faced him, her arms falling to her sides, the breath knocked from her lungs.

"He's in a turf war with the Guzman cartel." Dutch stood and stepped closer to her.

McQueen moved between them, the dog's back to Isabel, his eyes locked on Dutch.

"But I saved his life," he said. "On pure instinct. Then he confided in me. Asked me to be your bodyguard because he's worried that you'll be in danger and he's right. The queen of spades, the ace of spades, those were from the Guzman cartel. It was a message for your uncle. They're going to try to kill you to hurt him. They sent him a similar message before the attack in the club."

Isabel reeled, her thoughts a jumbled mess. How could she have been so easily duped by every person in her life?

Was Brenda the only one she could trust?

Isabel staggered away to the window that overlooked the building's parking lot. Half a mile in the distance was the ocean. Black and murky and endless. It mirrored the tumult of emotion raging inside her.

"Think about what I'm saying, Isabel. His lifestyle. The armed bodyguards." Dutch sighed, coming up slowly beside her. "The reason you were sent to boarding school was to create distance, to blind you from the truth."

She didn't want to acknowledge the legitimacy of his claims. She closed her eyes and pressed harder against her temples.

Dutch is a US marshal undercover.

"You lied to me!" The surge of pain eviscerated her. The stab of betrayal sliced deeper, past bone, down to marrow, hitting her soul. "Manipulated me."

"I'm sorry. I had to."

"I'm so stupid." She thought back to their conversations, the things they had in common, the ways that they'd clicked. "I thought this was real." But it had all been a web of lies. Layered fabrications to lure her in. To get to her uncle.

Dutch inched closer to her. "The fact that we didn't meet by accident was a lie, but everything else between us was real," he said, as if reading her mind.

It felt like another violation.

When he'd touched her, she'd never been so warm, so light, so happy. Like they were meant to be.

What rubbish!

Every fairy-tale book about the princess falling in love with some version of Prince Charming, or in her case a charming bad boy, and living happily-ever-after should be banned. Better yet, burned, so no little girls grew up with such nonsense poisoning their minds.

"Who are you?" she asked, facing him. "What's your real name?"

He looked at her, his eyes sad, his brow creased. She stared at him, studying him, trying to read his expression. But maybe she was a fool who knew nothing and had never had a thread of connection with him.

"My name *is* Horatio 'Dutch' Haas. They didn't have time to create an alias. I swear to God, you know me. About my father's heart attack, about my sister. How kids picked on me. My crush on that cheerleader. Finding the public salsa dancing to put a smile on your face. I've told you things, truths from my soul, that no one else in the world knows. Because I wanted you to *see* me. And the more you liked what you saw, the tattoos, my lack of finesse, my bluntness, my rough edges, the deeper I fell for you."

Tears prickled her eyes. The upsurge of belief in her was swiftly blunted by a daunting sense of betrayal.

"We came so close to making love, sweetheart. That would've been the easier thing to do. Sleep with you and maintain my cover. Instead I told you the truth."

Isabel slapped him hard. The sting in her palm and the flush in Dutch's cheek made the tears fall from her eyes. "Am I supposed to thank you for that?"

McQueen barked at Dutch. The dog stalked closer, teeth bared, growling.

Dutch raised his palms and softened his tone. "I told you all of this because I love you. You deserve the truth. I want to be with you. I can see a future for us, traveling, taking McQueen to the dog park, cuddled up on the sofa watching movies."

She'd wanted that too and so much more. She had been ridiculous enough to imagine what it'd be like to start a family with him. After he'd taken care of her and McQueen, she'd been certain he'd make a good father.

"You don't need to keep lying to me." Tears streamed down her face.

"Everything is on the line," Dutch said. "If we don't get that hard drive back, then good, hardworking, innocent people are going to die. But I risked it all for you. Because I couldn't live with the alternative." He grimaced, the wavy lines in his forehead deeper than before.

They stared at each other. The intensity of his eyes drew her in, made her want to believe him. But she'd been a naive fool lapping up the lies from those around her long enough.

How on earth could she trust him?

Her chest heaved as silence hung between them. He cupped her shoulders, bringing her against him into a hug and—

Boom!

An explosion shattered the quiet, rocking the night and driving them apart. Outside in the parking area, a fireball blazed, triggering every car alarm in the lot.

She leaned on the window, putting her hands to the glass in shock. A motorcycle had been blown to bits and the frame was on fire. The bike that was beside his truck.

Dutch's bike.

"Chad didn't send you the box, but I'm a hundred percent certain he's responsible for that." Dutch hitched his chin at the inferno outside. "I really hate that guy."

At least they were on the same page about something.

WATCHING THE FIRE rage in the parking lot, the aftermath of his homemade bomb, Chad stood in the darkness. A man who loved Isabel to the point that he'd do anything for her. Lie. Cheat. Commit arson. Murder.

And he would. He'd kill Horatio Haas given the chance.

How many women could say they had that?

Such devotion. Commitment. His passion could be overwhelming, sure, might even frighten her, but it was a singular love.

Why was Isabel so ungrateful?

If she didn't come to her senses and see the light, Chad would be forced to do the unthinkable.

He'd have to cleanse her.

Consume her soul so that they'd always be one and then lay her body to rest.

Chapter Seventeen

After Dutch had taken her cell phone to keep her from making any rash calls, Isabel had locked herself in the bedroom with McQueen while he dealt with the police and fire department. She'd spent all night looking through the file he'd given her, every page, every line. Twice. Then a third time, letting it sink in.

One undeniable fact struck her like a lightning bolt. Uncle Emilio was the biggest drug kingpin on the West Coast.

And he was now embroiled in a turf war that endangered her life.

The truth was sobering. Painful.

Even her art gallery was a ruse. The FBI suspected he was using it to launder money.

How would Isabel know? He owned it and she used his accountant.

To think she'd bought into his story of him wanting to be a generous, loving uncle who didn't want her to touch her inheritance. So altruistic.

Dutch knocked on the door. "Are you ready to go? They're expecting us soon."

Fully dressed, Isabel rose from the bed, grabbed her handbag and the file. She opened the door, ready to go to the US Marshals office and unleash her indignation on his boss.

He stood with a badge and holstered gun hooked on his belt, offering her a cup of coffee in a travel mug. "I don't have coconut milk. I used a splash of half-and-half."

Two days with no real sleep, she would've slurped down a cup of hot sludge if it had caffeine in it. "No, thank you." Her pride refused to let her take his coffee.

"We can stop for food on the way, if you want."

She was starving. "I'm not hungry." She shoved the file at his chest, and he took it.

"Isabel." He scrubbed a hand over his face. "It'd be nice to know if you're going to help us before you meet my boss. I'd like to be prepared."

How could she not help? Her beloved uncle was the head of a notorious drug cartel and had been lying to Isabel her entire life and using her. The same way Dutch wanted to use her.

But if she could help save lives and undo a fraction of the wrong caused by Uncle Emilio, then she would. Obviously. It only outraged her more that he doubted her, so she was going to let him stew.

"It's a lot to think over," she said. "I have questions."

"What are they? I can answer them."

"For your boss. Not you. You're just following orders. It's not your fault you lied, manipulated and used me. It's your boss's, right?" She crossed her arms. "I want to look him in the eye and hear it from him. Let's go."

Without talking, they swung by doggie day care to drop off McQueen and went to the LA US Marshals Service building located downtown across from city hall. She wasn't sure what she'd been expecting, but not Dutch flashing a badge with ease, having her stun baton confis-

cated at the metal detectors, him signing her in like she
was a visitor instead of a finagled informant.

In the elevator, she asked, "Are you trying to turn me
into an informant? Is that the correct term?"

"*Asset* would be more accurate," he said in a low voice.

Finagled asset. Lovely.

The doors opened with a chime. Dutch stepped off
first and led her to a conference room where a man and
woman were seated side by side, dark suits, hands clasped
on the table.

The fit, middle-aged man with an affable face and a
dusting of gray around his temples greeted them. "Hello,
Ms. Vargas. I'm US Marshal Will Draper. Call me Will.
Please have a seat," he said, waiting until Isabel sat before
taking a chair himself. "I'm in charge of the San Diego field
office and this is one of my deputies, Allison Chen-Boyd."

"Just Chen," Allison said with a blank expression, giving off a no-nonsense vibe. She didn't look older than
early thirties and wore her dark hair in a braid. In front
of her was a tall stack of folders.

"Sorry. I forget." Will straightened his tie and folded
his hands on the table, flashing a soft smile that said *let's
be friends.* "Ms. Vargas, Deputy Haas has updated me
on the current status of things. How can we put you at
ease with assisting us?"

"You can start by explaining what gave you the right
to invade my privacy and my life. I'm a law-abiding citizen and the only thing I'm guilty of is naivete. Stupidity
for believing in those around me who I care about." She
glared at Dutch and then refocused on the marshals across
the table. "How could you send someone in to seduce me?
What about common decency? Respect? Why didn't you
bring me in, show me your file and simply ask me to help?"

"Forgive me, Ms. Vargas," Allison said, "but if you

think that approach would work with ninety-nine percent of the assets that we recruit then you are naive."

Isabel recoiled from the harsh words and even harsher tone.

"Allison, back off," Dutch said.

"No, I'm not going to back off. If you had done your damn job and kept your mouth shut, we wouldn't be here right now."

"That's right." Isabel regained her composure. "He would've slept with me and I'd be none the wiser. I would've brought him to San Diego this weekend, he would've found a way to get back your precious database, and then what? He'd disappear?" She turned to Dutch. "Leave me behind? Like collateral damage."

"I wouldn't do that to you." He put his hand on hers and she yanked it away, clasping her hands in her lap. "Everything I said last night, I meant."

"The majority of assets have to be coerced," Will said, evenly. "Blackmailed. The FBI has more expertise in this area than we do and recommended this approach and selected Haas for the assignment."

"Why him?" Isabel asked.

"Something to do with his profile," Will said, "and an algorithm that selected him as a good match for you."

Like a dating website profile? She tamped down the discomfort and nerves rising in her. "I want to see the FBI agent who thought this was a good idea."

"I'm afraid that's not going to happen, Ms. Vargas," Will said. "If you want to feel better about Haas's involvement, then you should know, he objected to the approach we took from the get-go. He even confronted the FBI agent in question. He's demonstrated nothing but the utmost concern for you and your well-being during this difficult process."

"I'm sorry if we hurt your *precious* feelings with our

methods." Allison stood, picking up one of the files in front of her, and opened it.

She started dropping pictures on the table in front of Isabel. Of dead bodies. Shot. Stabbed. One had been beheaded.

Isabel looked away, not needing the graphic images, and wrapped her arms around herself.

"That's what real collateral damage looks like, Ms. Vargas," Allison said. "Those are innocent people who got in your uncle's way."

"Stop it!" Dutch scooped up the pictures. "She's upset. But she'll help us. Isabel just needs time to cool off."

"You didn't seem so certain of her help on the phone." Allison dug through the stack of folders and pulled out a red file.

"Don't you dare show that to her," Dutch said. "It's going too far. She doesn't need to see it to help us."

Isabel swallowed past the tightening in her throat. What more could there be?

"During your heart-to-heart last night," Allison said, "you didn't tell her that her uncle is responsible for her father's death? That dear Uncle Emilio ordered the hit because there was an internal disagreement on how best to manage the cartel's operations?"

A shocking jolt ran through Isabel like a bucket of ice water had been dumped over her.

"Damn it!" Dutch said.

Allison slapped the red folder down on the table. "Open it."

Dutch sat and turned Isabel's chair toward him, taking her hands in his. "Sweetheart, now you know. There's no reason to open it. You don't need to see the pictures of your father. Of the informant who was going to testify, but your uncle got to him first. Please don't look at it."

After everything she'd already learned, *this* truth was the most gut-wrenching. Uncle Emilio's love for her, his attention, concern, generosity was bred from guilt for killing her father?

Isabel's heart sank. There was a heaviness in her chest, making it hard to catch her breath.

This isn't real. She must be trapped in a nightmare, unable to wake up. This was a movie, a sick novel. Not her life.

She looked at the red folder and shook her head, not wanting it to be true, but knowing deep down on some level that it was. She remembered the arguments and fights between her father and uncle.

Had she blocked it all out and simply gone along with the stories they'd told her?

"I asked to come here," Isabel said, growing numb inside, needing distance, "even though I'd already decided to help you because it's the right thing to do. This is what it has gotten me. The last truth I needed to know. Will you all please excuse me while I look at it?"

On her own, without any crutches.

"You don't have to and definitely not alone," Dutch said. "I'm here for you."

The sincerity gleaming in his brown eyes and radiating in his voice was heartbreaking.

"This is something I have to do," Isabel said. "Alone."

FOLLOWING DRAPER AND ALLISON into the hall, Dutch hated to leave Isabel. Her life had been torn apart and she needed comfort. Not isolation.

Draper walked away as if relieved things were settled, with no concern to the impact this was having on Isabel. Allison hung back at the end of the hall, waiting, like she knew Dutch had a bone to pick with her.

"What the hell was that in there?" Dutch asked her. "A good cop, bad cop routine? You're supposed to be the nice one."

"Did Draper ever tell you my specialty?"

Taken aback, Dutch paused for a beat, taking a breath. "No."

Allison clutched the folders to her chest. "Think of me as the closer. A witness gets nervous while waiting to testify, I put their minds at ease and bolster their confidence. An asset that we've reeled in needs the right push to seal the deal, they call me. I read the room, I read the person and do whatever is necessary."

His gaze dropped to the files in her arms. "What's in the other folders?"

"I was prepared for any angle I needed to exploit."

"You went too far. You didn't have to break her heart. She loves her uncle."

"That love was the last hurdle. If there was any doubt in your girlfriend's mind before she came here, I guarantee you there's none left now. And I'll sleep soundly tonight knowing that we've locked in our high-priority asset."

"She's a person, you know. With feelings."

"Tell that to my seven-year-old son who I'm trying to protect. You chose your fake girlfriend and her feelings over us, your fellow marshals and our families." She took a deep breath and sighed. "Getting the hard drive back is crucial. In the event you can't, destroy it." She took a small metal device that was the size of a hockey puck from her suit jacket pocket. "It's a degausser and will wipe the drive clean if it comes in contact with it for at least two minutes."

"You need to come up with an exit strategy for Isabel in case she decides to leave."

"An exit for you two together? Or separate?"

He lowered his gaze and rubbed his forehead. "I don't know yet."

"Once you figure it out, let me know. I'm heading back to San Diego today. But there's still a problem. Vargas has seen the files, which means every marshal in my office is in danger as long as he lives. I'm sure he has our personal information memorized. There's no telling how long it'll take the FBI to build their case. If you get a clear shot at Vargas, take it."

"Are you asking me to kill him?" In Delta Force, eliminating targets was a part of the job, but those days were behind him. He was no longer an assassin for Uncle Sam or anyone else.

"I'm asking you to secure sensitive information and to end this once and for all."

No tears shed. No screams of outrage.

Isabel pulled herself together and closed the red folder on the pictures of her father's bullet-riddled body and the brutally killed informant who'd witnessed his murder and had intended to testify against Emilio.

Nothing in her life made sense.

"I'm sorry Allison was so horrible," Dutch said, coming back into the conference room. "Can I get you anything?"

"I'll help you retrieve the database, but he doesn't want me to come down for the auction."

"We'll brainstorm a reason for you to be there. A problem with one of the vendors maybe."

She stood and hiked her purse strap on her shoulder. "I want to leave."

"We should talk about what you learned."

Talk? She could barely stand. Her legs shook so badly,

it'd take all her strength to walk to the car without falling over.

She glanced through the glass walls of the conference room at the marshals watching them. "Not here. Not now. Please, take me to the gallery."

Dutch nodded and got her out of the building as quickly as possible. Without pushing conversation, he sped to the I-10. He gave her silence, he gave her space, but it couldn't last forever.

"I don't think you should go to the art gallery," he said, exiting the freeway. "We should go back to the apartment, talk, sort through how you must be feeling."

"I have work to do. I need to finish organizing the auction for my…" The breath caught in her throat. "For Emilio. It's easier to do it from the office."

"We need to talk. I know this isn't easy for you."

"How will it work in San Diego? The ins and outs. What should I expect?"

"The database is on a hard drive in Emilio's safe. I need to find it."

"The safe is in his office. I know where, but it requires his fingerprint to access it."

He nodded. "We need to get the hard drive or erase it with a degausser."

"What's that?"

"It emits a high-intensity magnetic field that'll erase the data. We need to do it before the auction during a time when the guards will be distracted, then we get out."

"What happens to me? He'll know I helped you, that I was a part of it."

"You'll have a choice. I can make it look like you didn't know, leave you tied up, gagged."

For a second, when he'd said he wouldn't leave her behind, she'd believed him.

"Once the FBI is able to arrest him later," Dutch continued, "then we could be together if you wanted."

Her vision hazed. "Later when?"

"I don't know how much longer the FBI needs to build their case. It could be weeks, months. This isn't my first choice."

"Then what is?" she asked, looking at him.

The creases in his forehead were deeper, his eyes wider. "You leave with me. But that means walking away from everything. The gallery. Brenda. This lifestyle. The FBI will eventually seize all of your uncle's assets anyway."

"You're saying that no matter what, I'll lose the gallery?" The art gallery she'd poured her heart and soul into, built up from nothing and created a reputation that others envied. And lose her best friend.

She had the unsettling realization that her whole life was slipping through her fingers and she was powerless to stop it.

"Yes, you'll lose the gallery, and if they can tie the money your father left you to any RICO charges on your uncle, they'll freeze that, too," Dutch said. "We could go away together. I'll use my vacation days. We can take a long trip to give you time to decide if you still want to be with me."

She shook off the apprehension slithering through her. "And vice versa, I suppose."

"No, beautiful." He took her hand. "I love you. I want you. I've almost been fired twice in the last twenty-four hours because of it. For knocking the daylights out of Ellis and then for telling you the truth. Isabel, what we share is real. Realer than anything I've had before. Last night, I chose you over everything else because I don't want to lose you. We're just getting started."

It would've been the path of least resistance for Dutch to continue to lie, to sleep with her when she was throwing herself at him, but he hadn't. He'd turned down sex and chosen honesty.

Chosen her.

Dutch stopped in front of the gallery. "Don't you want to see what's possible for us as a couple? I do. We can find out, no matter how you want to play it in San Diego with your uncle. And if you decide that you want me to disappear, where you never see or hear from me again, it'll break my heart, but I'll respect your wishes. Just think about it. Okay?"

"You lied to me," she said, pulling her hand away. It was a hard thing to get over. Like climbing Mount Everest with no training, no gear, struggling through the change in altitude and lower oxygen pressure.

A wounded expression crossed his face. "Our chemistry is undeniable. My body reacts to yours, your touch, your kisses, hell, your voice. I love the way you taste, the way you smell. I think about you all the time. How to bring a smile to your face, to ease your troubles. And it's not just attraction. Think about those two days we spent together in your apartment. We mesh, sweetheart. You and I—it's kismet."

She looked out the window at the sign on her art gallery. *Kismet.*

There was no better word to describe how she felt about Dutch, destiny, fate, but a part of her couldn't help but wonder if he was playing her. Not that he had any reason to at this point.

Her uncle was the devil. Satan incarnate. He murdered her father. She was furious at Uncle Emilio. It didn't take a holier-than-thou angel to help.

"I don't know if I want to be with you," she said, the lie

tasting bitter. God help her, she did want him and felt like the biggest fool for it. "I need to work for a few hours."

"Let me make sure it's safe for you to go in first."

He hopped out and ran inside. She watched him speak to Brenda for a minute, and he came back.

Dutch opened the door for her.

She climbed down from the truck. "I'll call you when I'm ready to leave."

"I'm going to park around back and order us some food to be delivered. You must be starved and I'm not leaving you," he said. Isabel opened her mouth to protest, but he went on, "It's too dangerous. I stay with you. Got it?"

"Fine," she said, too tired to argue. She turned and strode inside the gallery.

"How did it go last night?" Brenda asked, rising from her seat, bright-eyed and excited.

"Not as I expected."

"Oh, really?" Brenda frowned. "I was confident he'd be good in bed and I can tell that he's really into you. He seems like he'd be a generous lover. What went wrong?"

Isabel shook her head, not wanting to get into it. Not having the strength to say it all out loud. "The timing was off. We didn't make it to the bed. Then there was Chad. He blew up Dutch's motorcycle."

"What?" Brenda rushed around to her. "Chad is a total sicko. He scares me. I bet the cops won't be able to prove that it was him."

"Probably not." She set her purse down on the reception desk. "If you have any free time, I have a ton of stuff to do for my uncle's event in San Diego and could use your help."

"Sure, whatever you need."

A knock came at the back door.

"It's Dutch," Isabel said. "I'll let him in. He's going to hang around today."

"Aww. That's sweet."

If only her friend knew the ugly, bitter truth. Sweet had nothing to do with it.

Isabel went to the back door and put her hand on the handle. "Dutch?" No such thing as too careful.

"Yeah, it's me."

She opened the door for him. Stepping inside, he shoved his badge into his pocket, but kept his gun.

"How am I supposed to explain you're armed?" she asked.

"You've got a dangerous stalker who blew up my bike. That's explanation enough."

She turned to go to her office.

"Hey," he said, taking her wrist softly and a shiver ran through her at his touch.

Slowly he put her palm to his chest over his heart and cupped her face with his other hand, holding her gaze.

She tried to dismiss the way his gentle strength made her body thrum with electricity. The natural closeness that'd built between them, getting stronger each day. But how he made her feel was impossible to ignore. Impossible to deny.

"May I kiss you?" he asked, his voice deep and husky, stirring heat low in her belly.

The sexiest part wasn't that this gorgeous hunk of a man could have his pick of women and wanted her. It wasn't the tingles flooding her thighs or her chest tightening with anticipation. It wasn't even that he seemed unaware of the effect he had on her.

The sexiest, hottest part was that he knew she was vulnerable and emotionally fragile and rather than taking a kiss when he could've easily done so, he'd asked.

Because he'd never harm her.

Even in front of his boss and Allison, he stood up for her, sought to protect her, defend her.

So what if it made her a fool. "Yes."

He pressed his mouth to hers in the barest of touch. Brushed his lips across hers with such fierce tenderness in a whisper of a kiss that sent arousal humming through her body.

"If you can forgive me, if you come with me, I'll prove to you every day how much I care about you. Not just with words, but with my actions. I swear it."

A lump formed in her throat and she didn't know what to say. "I need to think about it."

He nodded and let her go.

Isabel smoothed down her skirt and walked back to the front. She felt his eyes on her and unlike creepy Chad, she liked the idea of Dutch watching her, wanting her.

"I ordered food for the three of us from the grill," he said. "I hope that's okay."

"Sounds great to me." Brenda put a vase of fresh-cut flowers on the desk. "Very thoughtful of you."

Deep burgundy long-stem roses called Black Pearl. Isabel hadn't noticed them when she came in. "You bought flowers to dress up the place?"

"No," Brenda said, arranging them. "They were delivered this morning without a card."

"Do you think they're from Chad?" Isabel asked Dutch, turning to face him, but his gaze had veered past her to something outside. She glanced over her shoulder.

A black van rolled by. The man from the grocery store with teardrop tattoos sat in the passenger's seat. He stuck the barrel of a machine gun out the window.

Isabel froze.

Chapter Eighteen

Time stretched, slowing, moving at half speed as a black van inched down the street. A man stuck a Heckler & Koch MP5 out the window.

Dutch didn't have much time to think, to assess. They were all in serious trouble standing in front of the plate glass window with nothing to stop the rounds that were about to tear through them.

The man lifted the MP5 and let it rip, spraying the front of the gallery. Bullets shattered the plate glass, stitching in a fiery line toward them. Dutch grabbed Isabel, whirling her away from the incoming fire, as he dove to the floor.

Brenda was hit instantly and sent spinning and falling. The vase burst. Jagged shards of glass flew everywhere like tiny projectiles.

Shielding Isabel with his body, Dutch forced her to low crawl toward the back of the desk. He feared the men outside would stop the vehicle and come into the gallery to make sure they'd finished the job.

Rounds were still being sprayed on full automatic, punching into the walls, shredding paintings. He and Isabel skirted behind the desk, beating the deadly fusillade by a blink of an eye. Bullets pounded into the solid wood, thuds reverberating through his body.

"Keep your head down," Dutch said to Isabel and drew his weapon.

Flipping off his safety, he peered over the top of the desk and pulled the trigger, returning fire. Every shot he squeezed off was controlled and well aimed.

A hot slug slammed into the shooter, throwing him back into the vehicle.

The driver accelerated and the van hurtled forward with its tires squealing.

"Stay here." Dutch raced to the front, out onto the sidewalk, and watched the vehicle speed away. He scanned for any other threats.

No secondary shooters on foot. Only terrified passersby.

He ran back inside and checked on Brenda. She lay on her back, rolling left and right. A red blotch on her abdomen seeped wider, dripping blood on the hardwood. Another bullet got her in the shoulder just under her collarbone. She was alive, but not for much longer if she didn't get medical attention.

"Isabel, grab a towel, a piece of cloth, anything you can find."

Glass crunched as she scurried to her feet. Seconds later she came to him, carrying a silk scarf. She screamed, a bloodcurdling cry that he'd never forget.

"Oh, God!" A choking sob left Isabel. "Brenda!"

Dutch snatched the scarf from her, tore it and pressed the pieces to Brenda's wounds. "Put your hands here," he said to Isabel. "Apply pressure. Don't worry about hurting her. We've got to slow the bleeding."

Isabel dropped to her knees with no care about the broken glass that bit into her skin and replaced his hands with her own. Dutch took out his cell phone and dialed 911.

Before he'd finished with the emergency dispatch operator, the sound of approaching sirens split the air.

Someone else must've already called them. Help was on the way.

Brenda was still conscious, which was a good sign. Her blood wasn't a dark red like her liver had been punctured, but the bullet might've hit her stomach. It was a nasty wound.

The ambulance and police arrived at virtually the same time. EMTs rushed inside while the police cordoned off the area, driving onlookers back from the scene.

Dutch holstered his weapon and flashed his badge to the cops. After the EMTs loaded Brenda on a stretcher, he helped Isabel climb into the back of the ambulance to ride along.

"I'll give a statement and meet you at the hospital," Dutch said. He'd call Draper and have him or Allison head over to keep Isabel safe until Dutch could get there.

Isabel swallowed hard and horror was stamped on her face. She brushed her hair back with a bloody hand, nodding that she'd heard him, but her glassy eyes were focused on her best friend.

"Brenda? Brenda!" Isabel took her hand, but her friend didn't answer.

Fear speared him as Brenda's head lolled to the side. She wasn't conscious.

"Why won't she wake up?" Isabel asked, her gaze bouncing from an EMT to Dutch.

His fear spread. If Brenda didn't make it, the loss would crush Isabel.

The EMT put an oxygen mask on Brenda. "We've got to get her to the hospital now." He closed the rear doors and the ambulance pulled away.

Life wasn't cutting Isabel any slack. It had been one horrible thing after another. No matter how strong a person was, everyone had a limit. A breaking point.

Dutch didn't think Isabel could take much more before she reached hers.

Even though she was justifiably ticked off at him, he hoped she'd let him be there for her to help her get through all this. She needed someone to lean on now more than ever.

He whipped out his phone and dialed Draper, updating him quickly so Isabel would be protected at the hospital.

"Sir," a police officer said, approaching him with two others, as Dutch hung up, "we're going to need to know exactly what happened here."

The cops didn't give Dutch a chance to catch his breath before they launched in with their questions.

"Horatio Haas is definitely a US marshal," the new PI said to Chad. "First, they went to the US Marshals Service building earlier and now he's flashing a badge to every cop he speaks to about the shooting."

That explained why the police hadn't arrested him, giving Chad's attorney the runaround and flimsy excuses. But why would the Marshals be watching Isabel?

She wasn't into anything illegal and neither was her best friend, Brenda. But the Marshals had definitely been set up across the street from the gallery for a reason.

"Are you sure Isabel is okay?"

"Yes, she's fine. She got into the ambulance with the other woman."

Good. Chad didn't want anything to happen to his Isabel unless he determined that she deserved it. And even then, Chad would be the one to dispense punishment. Him and no one else.

"Find out why the Marshals are interested in Isabel."

"That means pulling my surveillance on Haas."

"Understood." On that front, the PI had served his

purpose, and Chad could track Isabel from her phone. "This is more important."

"I still have a few contacts in the FBI. They might be able to find out something, but it'll cost you."

Tell Chad something new. He was used to paying to get what he wanted. "I need to know what the Marshals have on her. The cost doesn't concern me. I want answers ASAP."

ISABEL SAT IN the waiting room, wringing her hands, while Brenda was in surgery.

The two marshals she'd met earlier sat across from her, giving her breathing room. She didn't want to see or talk to either of them right now. If they hadn't insisted that their presence was necessary to ensure her safety, she would've thrown them out.

The nightmare kept getting worse, spiraling, growing bigger, darker, consuming every good thing in her life.

Brenda. What if her best friend died because of her?

Her bloody hands were shaking so badly she didn't know what to do with them.

Dutch shoved through the double doors, carrying the purse she'd forgotten. Her eyes fluttered shut on an overwhelming wave of relief. Then it morphed slowly with each step he took toward her, changing into an indescribable need to be held. By him.

She stood, dizzy, aching from head to toe, and reached for him. He pulled her into his arms. It was all too much being thrown at her, life forcing her to drink from a firehose of crap on full blast. She was drowning. She needed his comfort and was too weak to turn it down.

The other two marshals stood and headed for the door. "Dutch, give me a call when you get a chance," his boss said.

"Sure."

Once they left, Isabel let fresh tears fall.

"This is my fault," she said. "Brenda got shot because of me. Oh, God, she could die."

"No, sweetheart." Dutch stroked her hair, his voice calm and steady. "This is your uncle's fault. His and no one else's."

The realization hit her that if Dutch hadn't been there, if that stolen database hadn't brought him into her life— even by duplicitous means—she and Brenda would both be dead. Victims of her uncle's turf war.

Her knees gave out.

Dutch caught her and helped her sit in a chair. "Give me a minute." He got up to leave.

"Don't go." She clutched his arm, something in her chest unraveling like a pulled spool of thread. "I need you to stay."

He kissed her forehead. "One minute. Two tops. I'll just be in the hall, a few feet away, and be right back." Then he hustled out of the waiting room.

True to his word, he was back in two minutes, carrying a candy bar and a cup of coffee. He pushed both into her trembling hands. "You need to eat. We've got to get your blood sugar up and some caffeine in your system. It'll help."

She shook her head. The thought of eating repulsed her.

"You need your strength. For Brenda. Eat, honey."

She bit into chocolate and caramel, not tasting it, and washed it down with a few sips of coffee. One nibble after the other, she ate the candy bar and drank the black coffee.

Her nerves were still scraped raw, but her jitters faded, and her legs felt solid again.

For hours, they sat in the small room that had muted

colors, waiting for an update on Brenda. Dutch's arms around her, enveloping her in his warm protectiveness, was the only thing holding her together.

Finally, a doctor came in, pulling off his green scrub cap. "Are you the relatives of Brenda Reaver?"

Isabel stood and Dutch was up on his feet beside her. "I'm her best friend, Isabel Vargas. Her parents live in Ohio, but I'm her emergency contact here in LA for everything. Is she going to live?"

"Your friend got lucky. One bullet broke her clavicle and the other just missed her stomach. She lost a lot of blood and we had to give her a transfusion, but she's going to pull through."

Isabel released the breath that had bunched in her lungs. "Thank God."

"You'll want to contact her parents and have them fly out. She's going to need help for the next few weeks while she recuperates."

Isabel had wanted to wait until Brenda was out of surgery to tell them their daughter would recover or…

"Okay. Can I see her now?" Isabel asked.

"The best thing you can do for her now is let her rest. Come by tomorrow."

Isabel nodded, not liking it, but understanding.

"Let's get you to the apartment so you can clean up," Dutch said. "You're covered in blood."

She didn't object when Dutch led her out of the hospital and guided her into the car.

While he ran into doggie day care to get McQueen, she called Brenda's parents. The machine at their house picked up, which wasn't surprising. For a couple in their sixties, they were active and social and were usually only home in the evenings, but Isabel didn't have their cell numbers. She left a brief message, focusing on the fact that Brenda was going to recover and that they should fly out.

Despite Dutch's assurances that this wasn't her fault, guilt plagued her.

The door opened and McQueen leapt in, tail wagging, excited to see her, but she couldn't even pet him. She was trapped in a miasma of fear and darkness. Dutch tossed a small bag of dog food into the back seat and she was grateful he'd thought of it. If not for him, poor McQueen would starve.

At the apartment building, Dutch parked away from the burned spot where his motorcycle had been torched. She drifted into the building, into the elevator, through the apartment, bedroom and found herself in the bathroom.

Kicking off her shoes, she started the shower. Her chest was tight, a crushing pressure building, coiling, winding deeper.

She stepped into the shower, fully clothed, sat under the spray and tucked her knees into her chest. Letting the hot water cascade over her, she prayed it might warm her. She was cold, so very cold, and trembling uncontrollably.

Everything she'd been through with Chad, everything she'd learned over the past twenty-four hours turned over in her mind. A sick feeling ballooned in her stomach. With a flash of panic, it dawned on her that life as she knew it was over.

The water slid from hot to lukewarm. She had lost track of time with no way to tell how long she'd been in there.

Dutch knocked on the door. It was still open. She'd never closed it. He peeked inside. The expression on his face was a heartbreaking mix of worry and affection.

He came in, pulled off his boots and socks and climbed into the shower.

He lifted her from the tile floor, peeled off her top and skirt, leaving on her underwear. Then he washed her. Lathered her hair with shampoo, ran her bath sponge over her face, scrubbed the blood from her hands, checked for embedded glass in her legs. Holding her up under the spray, he rinsed the suds from her body.

No one had ever cared for her like this. Completely. Tenderly. Asking for nothing in return. There was no reason for him to go to such trouble unless he felt something real for her.

He turned off the water, grabbed a towel and wrapped it around her. Stepping out of the shower, he looked down at his sopping-wet clothes. A grimace crossed his face as he undressed like he wished there was a better alternative than tracking water through the apartment.

Keeping on his boxer-briefs, he lifted her into his arms and carried her to the bed. Dutch laid her down and threw the bedspread over her. He sat on the floor beside her, with his back against the nightstand, and stroked her hair, over and over, driving her mind to empty.

She was tired and aching and wanted to give in to the exhaustion that clawed at her. To surrender to Dutch's soothing caresses and close her eyes, to sleep. But she couldn't.

Pain churned, rubbing coarse as sandpaper against her insides.

Her heart wanted him, and her brain longed for an escape, but her body *needed* a release. "Dutch," she said, her voice hoarse and low, "make love to me. Help me forget every horrible thing that's happened for a little while."

He took her hand and kissed it. "I don't want you to regret this later."

"I'd only regret it if the way you say you feel about me is a lie."

"It's not. I swear. But your emotions are running high. This might be a bad idea."

"I'm an adult. I know what's best for me, what I need, what I want." Tugging his hand, she urged him up from the floor.

No resistance given, he slipped into the bed. "If you change your mind at any time and want me to stop, I will. No matter how difficult that might be. Just say the word."

This was why she trusted him in that moment, sought refuge and comfort in his arms. Even though he was strong and powerful, to the point of imposing in a scary way, and could be violent when necessary, she was safe with him, wasn't afraid of him.

There was no doubt in her mind that if she asked him to stop, he would. Every woman deserved that kind of sound assurance from the person they were with, but this was the first time she had it.

"I can just hold you if you want," he said, offering her another out, and it was another first.

She cupped the back of his head and brought his mouth to hers. In an instant, he covered her with his body, the contact lighting up her nerve endings.

Raising her hips to meet his, she telegraphed her urgency. He looked into her eyes, and she saw passion and heat and a similar plea for connection, for communion, that they were both powerless to deny.

Her whole body screamed for friction, for the need to have their bodies joined, for a release that could only be found in his arms.

He removed the little remaining physical barriers between them. There was heat and need in his gaze. He ran his hands over her body and moaned as if he'd been longing for this, too. Her nipples peaked and tightened beneath his tongue, and she was amazed by how quickly her body responded to him, growing soft and pliant and wet.

Moving his hand down to the welcoming spot between her legs, he slid his fingers between her folds. He watched her face, reading her responses for what she liked and didn't. His thumb circled her tight bundle of nerves and she gasped with pleasure.

He kissed his way down her body, diving beneath the sheet, his face settling between her thighs, treating her yet again to another first.

The sensation of his tongue, his fingers and lips all converged, swelling, cresting. It was devastating in the best way possible as an orgasm tore through her. She clutched at his hair, wishing the strands were longer, the backs of her knees over his shoulders, her heels digging into his back, and screamed his name.

Once she settled, he crawled up and hugged her to him. Her breath slowly steadied, and she remembered her name.

Brushing the hair out of her face, he looked down at her. "Should we stop? Or should I grab a condom?"

An ache drilled deep into her heart. She'd never been with anyone so generous and kind. Who'd disregard their own needs for the sake of hers.

Never had she felt more connected to another. Cherished. This was what she wanted, someone who saw through the superficial and desired her despite her flaws. Someone who'd put her ahead of anything else.

If only she could get over the humiliation of being used, the betrayal that gutted her.

Hope welled inside her but didn't scare her. Quite the opposite. In a way, it was setting her free from her past and opening the door to possibilities she'd never dared entertain before.

She caressed his cheek and kissed him, hot and needy for more. For everything he had to give. At least for tonight. "Condom."

Chapter Nineteen

Dutch awoke the next morning with Isabel in his arms, her head nuzzled between his neck and shoulder, her breath warm on his cheek, their legs tangled.

By nightfall last night, they'd both been famished. He'd whipped up spaghetti carbonara with the ingredients he had handy in the fridge. They'd eaten, made love again and went back to sleep.

Without a doubt, he knew in his heart he wanted to make her happy, give her everything she needed and asked of him and more. She deserved that and nothing less. It was staggering to realize how long he'd lived without ever knowing this feeling of rightness, completeness with another person. He never wanted to be without her again.

There were no presumptions on his part. She'd needed comfort and it didn't have to mean anything more to her. She was entitled to stay angry, but he hoped she'd agree to the trip he'd promised and then they could take it from there. No pressure. No stress. Give her time to sort through everything, and when she was ready, figure out her feelings for him. He'd be patient and wait, no matter how long it took.

First, he needed to keep her safe and get them both through the next couple of days unscathed.

Isabel roused, stretching. "I feel like I've been drugged. What time is it?"

He kissed her forehead. "Late. Almost ten."

"I can't believe I slept so long."

"You were exhausted and needed the rest. I crept out around dawn and took McQueen for a quick walk."

"Thank you." She rubbed his chest and sat up. "About last night. I needed to feel better, to lose myself for a little while, and you were there for me. I appreciate it. But I haven't made a decision about us and what I want to do."

"That's understandable. I don't want you to feel rushed, but you'll need to know by the time we take the hard drive."

She nodded. "I'm going to shower and dress. I want to go to the hospital and see Brenda."

"You need to call your uncle and give us a reason to go down today."

"My uncle's turf war has given us the best excuse. I'll need to finish the preparations on-site since I can't work from the office. Come to think of it, you should speak to him. If he knows about the attempted hit on my life, he'll welcome us with open arms."

"All right." He waited until she was in the shower and dug out the card that Vargas had given him at the club. Punching in the number on his cell, he considered whether to tell her uncle about Chad Ellis. The man was a threat but sharing that with Vargas had to be Isabel's choice, not Dutch's. The last thing she would want was for him to make decisions for her.

"Who is this?" her uncle answered.

"Dutch Haas. I'm not calling with good news."

"My niece hasn't pushed back on you being her body-guard, has she?"

"No, it's not that. Unfortunately, she learned why she

needs one. The Guzman cartel made a move on her. They sent her a pig's head with an ace of spades. Then they shot up her art gallery. Her best friend, Brenda Reaver, survived, but had to go through surgery."

"Damn it," Vargas growled over the line. "Is Isabel all right?"

"More or less. Physically she's fine, but she's quite shaken up. After what's happened, she wants to come to San Diego to take her mind off things and finish the preparations for your event."

"Yes, of course. Shall I send a helicopter for you?" Vargas asked.

"No, thanks. We'll drive." Dutch rubbed his forehead. "You said you were going to handle the Guzman problem."

"And I am. I'll move up the strike I have planned to tonight. Going after Isabel won't be tolerated. Retaliation must be swift and brutal and leave no doubt in the minds of my enemies what the consequences are."

No need to ask for the particulars to know that a lot of blood was going to be shed.

"There's something you need to understand," Vargas said. "Once Isabel is finished with the final preparations tomorrow, I want the two of you sequestered in the west wing of my villa. The individuals coming in for the auction aren't the sort I want Isabel consorting with. That's the reason I didn't want her here for the event."

"Okay. I'll come up with a reason for us to stay in the west wing." They needed to be out of the villa well before the auction, not locked inside. "We'll see you later." Dutch disconnected and looked at the clock.

The auction was set to take place tomorrow evening at eight. If they got on the road by three at the latest and didn't hit too much traffic, they'd have plenty of time to get the hard drive.

Dutch got ready as quickly as possible once Isabel was out of the bathroom. They boarded McQueen at the day care facility and swung by the hospital.

Brenda was sleeping when they arrived, perfectly natural according to the nurse and the best thing to help her recovery.

They sat quietly at Brenda's bedside. He held Isabel's hand, lending his strength, doing his best not to hurry her along.

Time ticked away, one hour slipping into the next. They were losing the day.

The USMS couldn't pull this off without her, but Dutch was painfully aware that few people in her life had put her first. There was no changing the fact that she was an asset the Marshals were exploiting, but he had to find a way to balance the constraints of the mission with Isabel's needs. He wouldn't let her become collateral damage.

Brenda stirred, her head moving from side to side. Her eyes fluttered open. She looked around, wildly, disoriented.

Isabel gently took her hand that bore the needle from the IV. "The doctor said you're going to be fine. I called your parents."

Brenda's gaze settled on Isabel. Her dry lips mouthed, *You okay?*

The woman had been shot twice, spent four hours in surgery fighting for her life and had slept nearly a day. Once she finally opened her eyes, her concern wasn't for herself. It was for Isabel.

Watching the two of them broke Dutch's heart.

Isabel nodded as a tear slipped from her eye. "I'm okay. Thanks to Dutch."

Brenda flashed a weak smile. Then her eyes closed, and she slipped back into unconsciousness.

A sob broke free from Isabel. She turned to Dutch and he brought her into his arms.

"I hate him," she said in a harsh whisper, her voice brittle. "I hate Emilio so much." She wept, her body trembling with what he guessed was a mix of sorrow and loathing.

Dutch shushed her, stroking her hair. The cold, hard truth of her words made something in his chest clench.

Would Isabel be able to face her uncle, hide what she'd learned, disguise her feelings? She wasn't an actress, a professional trained in deception.

Could she still be the asset they desperately needed? Or was she about to become their biggest liability?

THEY ARRIVED AT Vargas's place well after sundown, but there was no mistaking the villa was in fact a fortified compound crawling with guards.

Dutch had done his best to prep Isabel on the ride, guiding her in how to behave around her uncle. He hoped it'd alleviate some of his worries, but he'd only reinforced his concerns.

She was too sad, too angry, too volatile—an emotional powder keg waiting for a spark.

The best thing to do was abort, but they were down to the wire. He had to roll the dice, have faith in Isabel and pray this worked out.

After the front gates opened, he drove his truck up the long path.

"I need to know why my uncle killed my father. How

could he do such a thing? Over business? They were close. They loved each other. I don't understand."

"Money and power are strong motivators. They can make people do ugly, regrettable things."

Isabel trembled, rubbing her palms on her thighs. She looked fragile, on the cusp of breaking. "I'm not sure I can do this."

With all the new information thrown at her, he could only imagine how she felt.

"You can do this. You're going to be fine." She had to be, or he was as good as dead and there was no telling what Vargas would do to Isabel.

He drove around the elegant circular driveway with a large fountain in the middle.

Rodrigo stood at the bottom of the steps that led up to the main building and greeted them. He opened Isabel's door, and helped her from the vehicle.

Dutch cut the engine and came around the front of the truck.

"Keys," Rodrigo said to him. "I'll have it parked." He gestured off to the side where several black SUVs sat in front of a four-bay garage. "We'll have your things brought up to your rooms."

Dutch tossed him his keys.

"Rooms?" Isabel asked, emphasizing the *s*.

"Your uncle would prefer if you two didn't share a room. It's old-fashioned, I know, but he won't bend on it."

Rolling her eyes, she crossed her arms. "I can't wait to give him a piece of my mind."

Great. One more thing to poke the bear, Dutch thought.

"I've got to pat you down," Rodrigo said.

Nodding, Dutch extended his arms. Since he'd expected a pat down and to have his things searched, he'd given Isabel the degausser and the forensic lifting tape to get her uncle's fingerprint. She'd stashed both in her purse.

Once Rodrigo was satisfied, he said, "Your uncle is waiting in the courtyard to have dinner."

Isabel marched off, her heels clacking against the stone steps, spiking Dutch's trepidation.

He hurried after her. When he caught up, he took her arm, encouraging her to slow down. "Don't forget the objective. Dinner is perfect. He'll have something to drink and we can pull a print from the glass. Please, try to remain calm."

A guard opened the front door. They entered a palatial foyer, chandeliers glittering. He followed Isabel past a grand staircase. They crossed a room with a wall of windows thirty feet high that faced the ocean and went out through another door.

The courtyard was breathtaking, plucked straight from an Italian villa, and had a multimillion-dollar view of the ocean. Torches blazed and candlelight gleamed, bouncing off the silverware and crystal on the table.

"Mi hija," Vargas said, standing with his arms outstretched to Isabel. "How are you?"

She went to her uncle, allowing him to kiss both her cheeks. "I'm fine." Her voice was cold and sharp, her face stern. She sat opposite him and draped her napkin across her lap.

"Mr. Vargas." Dutch shook his hand.

"Please, call me Emilio." He gestured for Dutch to sit to his right. "Your fortitude is remarkable, my dear. Dutch told me about the crazy, random drive-by shooting at your gallery. I'm sorry to hear your friend was injured. It's unfortunate such things happen in this day and age. How is Brenda doing?"

Isabel clenched her jaw. "She's going to recover, thankfully. Her parents will fly out as soon as they can."

"I'd like to pay for her medical bills as well as her parents' expenses. We have so much good fortune. It's the least I can do to help someone you're close to."

"Yes. It is the least you can do," Isabel said, her tone scolding.

Vargas narrowed his eyes, giving her a strange look.

"What's for dinner?" Dutch asked. "Isabel has low blood sugar and we're starving."

Isabel stared at her uncle, and Dutch could feel the animosity emanating from her.

A perplexed expression crossed Vargas's face, but he picked up a bell and rang it. The tinny sound grated on Dutch's nerves.

Seconds later, servants came outside in a single, orchestrated file and placed salads in front of them. Another poured chardonnay in their wineglasses.

"Let us toast." Vargas raised his glass and waited until they had all done likewise. "To you, Isabel. May you have a long, happy, healthy life, *mi hija*. And to you, Dutch, for protecting her when I could not. Thank you. I owe you a life debt. *Salud*."

They sipped the wine and set their glasses down.

Dutch dug into the salad, but Isabel pushed the food around on her plate with her fork.

Vargas stared at her, noticing her preoccupation, too. "What's wrong? I know yesterday was difficult for you, probably terrifying. But you seem off. Like you're angry with me for some reason."

Isabel glared at her uncle, saying nothing.

Tension mounted, growing so tangible it had taken on a pulsing beat in Dutch's head. *Tick. Tick.*

"It's nothing," she finally said, lowering her gaze.

"Don't lie to me." Her uncle's voice was warm and loving. "Whatever it is, tell me."

"You should try the salad," Dutch said. "Eating will help." Though he wasn't sure if anything would make this situation better.

"Dutch, please," Vargas said and then looked at Isabel. "There's obviously something troubling you. I want to know what it is."

She threw her fork down and it clattered onto the plate. "I can't do this. Pretend like everything is all right when it isn't."

Tick. Tick.

"Then don't pretend." Vargas cocked his head to the side. "What can't you do? Tell me what you mean."

"You're upset," Dutch said taking her hand, but she pulled it away into her lap. *Tick. Tick.* "It's being away from Brenda when you feel she needs you." His heart ached looking at Isabel, seeing the internal struggle evident on her face.

"Is that it?" Vargas asked. "Or is it something else? Talk to me. I love you. I'm here for you. No matter what it is, you can tell me." His tone was affectionate and coaxing, his eyes pleading.

"I'm talking about how you killed my father," Isabel said, reaching her breaking point.

Uncomfortable silence reigned for the longest moment. Dutch schooled his expression and tried to think of a way out of this situation, but nothing came to mind.

"Why would you say such a thing to me?" Vargas asked, his voice so pained, it'd make anyone who hadn't seen the evidence of a feud, the pictures of her father and a witness both gunned down, doubt the accusation.

"Don't try to change the subject." Isabel tossed her

napkin on the table. "I know you did it. How could you? Your own brother?"

Dutch's ears rang, clear and sharp and loud as the bell had earlier. Sitting at the table, he felt like he was watching a six-car pileup, helpless to stop it.

Vargas leaned back in his chair, picked up his wineglass and drank. Maybe he was stalling for time, but he appeared composed, as if he wasn't the least bit worried. "This subject is Pandora's box. If you insist on removing the lid, you'll never be able to put it back on. It'll change everything for you. I ask you, as someone who has loved you from the day you were born, to let this go."

"Why did you kill him?" Isabel pressed, ignoring the warning. "For power? For money?"

"Who told you this?" Vargas asked.

"You don't get to ask me questions. Not until you've answered mine."

"Isabel, I've only sought to protect you. Let me do so now. Drop this."

"Tell me. Why did you kill my father? I have a right to know."

"I didn't kill your father," Vargas said.

"Damn you to hell! May God strike you dead for lying to my face. I loved you, looked up to you, when all along…" Her voice trailed off as tears fell from her eyes.

Vargas sighed and clucked his tongue. "My brother and I reached an impasse, where only one of us could survive, yes, but I didn't kill your father. Because…I'm your father."

Silence. Complete and total silence.

Isabel blinked at Vargas. The shock in her eyes was palpable.

It was one of those surreal, precarious moments. Dutch

was too stunned to move, afraid the tiniest action on his part could tip the scales in the wrong direction.

"Your mother and I had an affair. It's the reason my wife left me," Vargas said, the words flowing unpolished, tripping over one another in a rush. "It's not something I'm proud of. When she got pregnant, Luis suspected the baby wasn't his. After you were born, the doctors found cancer in your mother. Metastatic. Stage four. She was gone so fast. The day we buried her, Luis sat me down, told me that you were the last piece of your mother that he had left. Then he recounted a story from the Bible. The judgment of Solomon." Vargas's eyes turned glassy and the heavy emotion in his voice was undeniable. "He told me that either you were his and all would be forgiven between us. Or he would cut you in two like the baby in the story and we could each keep half of you. He claimed you, and I let him, to protect you. It was the price for peace that he demanded I pay. But I'm your father."

"No." The clipped reply emanated disbelief. "This is just another lie," Isabel said, shaking her head. "You never answered my question. You'll never tell me the truth, will you?" She shoved her chair back and stood. "You're not even sorry that you killed him. Are you?"

"I have no regrets." Vargas got up and came around the table. "It's no lie." He wrapped her in a bear hug. "I'm your father."

She squeezed her eyes shut, lifting her hands away from him as if disgusted that they were touching. "Are you the leader of *Los Chacales*?"

He lowered his head but didn't let her go. "Yes. I never wanted you to find out. I wanted you to build a life free from the dangers of my world."

"Well, you failed. Horribly." She disentangled herself

from him. "I almost died, and my best friend is in the hospital because of you."

His head snapped up. "How do you know any of this? Who told you? Who is trying to turn you against me?"

Reflexively, she glanced at Dutch. Vargas's gaze followed hers.

Dutch sat still as stone. His ears weren't only ringing now, they were burning. His entire face was on fire, but he kept his gaze soft, almost questioning.

"The playing cards. There was an incident in a grocery store I didn't tell you about." She stepped back. "A man from the Guzman cartel followed me in a grocery store. Put a queen of spades card in my basket. He spoke to me. You wouldn't believe the things he said. Do you have any idea what that was like for me? Did you really think I'd never find out?"

Vargas raked his hair back with his hands. "I've worked very hard to keep you in the dark about my affairs."

"And it almost cost me my life."

"You're safe," Vargas said. "I'm taking care of the Guzman cartel."

"What does that mean?" she asked.

"The head of their cartel and all their top lieutenants will be dead before sunrise. Their cartel is like a hydra—many new heads will sprout, and they'll be too busy fighting among themselves for power and control to worry about me."

"I can't do this with you right now." She pressed her fingers to her temples. "I'll finish organizing your event tomorrow. Then I'm leaving."

"I know you doubt me and question whether I'm your father but give me the chance to prove it."

Isabel backed up with tears welling in her eyes. "I

need time away from you. To clear my head. To think." She turned and rushed off into the house.

Dutch slumped in his chair, his head pounding, and noticed Isabel had left her purse.

The tape was inside. A glass with Vargas's fingerprint gleamed in the candlelight.

Groaning, Vargas pressed his fists on the table. "Why didn't you warn me and tell me she knew all of that?"

"I didn't know that was going to happen," Dutch said, letting his natural shock over Isabel's admission come through. "She told me the man who left the queen of spades in her basket spoke to her, but she didn't tell me what he said. Then everything at the gallery happened."

"I've spent three decades protecting her from the truth. Damn it!" Vargas swept his hands across the table, knocking his dishes to the floor. His glass shattered. He paced back and forth in front of the table, then caught himself and regained his composure. "Go to the kitchen. They'll give you a plate to take to your room. Get some rest. The sun will rise on a new day."

And it would be their last chance to get the hard drive. If they let emotion stop them from succeeding again, a lot of innocent people were going to die.

Dutch stood. "Let's hope tomorrow is better."

"One more thing. Respect my wishes. Stay away from Isabel's room tonight."

Isabel needed him. She needed comfort, a compassionate ear to listen, now more than ever, but under the tenuous circumstances as they were, what choice did he have? "Yes, sir."

Chapter Twenty

Isabel awoke with a start, jackknifing upright in bed. She squinted against the sunlight streaming in through the windows.

The dream stayed with her, vivid, in high definition. She remembered being six or seven, Emilio buying her toys, playing with her in the yard, him making her giggle, holding her tight and singing her songs, but only when her father wasn't at the house.

She closed her eyes and heard Emilio's voice as if he was beside her. *Our little secret, mi hija. Don't tell I came to visit. Te amo.*

The fights between her father and Emilio came back to her, as well.

Isabel is my daughter, her father had said. *Don't ever forget that unless you want a war.*

A shudder slipped down her spine.

When she was fourteen, her boarding school in Palo Alto had held a father-daughter dance. Her dad was stuck in Mexico on important business. She'd thrown the worst fit over it, and had said ugly, bratty things to him. Emilio came, not wanting her to be disappointed. But at the end of the dance, her dad had shown up as a surprise. There'd been such tension radiating between them, but her father hadn't spoken to Emilio that night, not a single word exchanged. Like the calm before a Cat 5 hurricane.

Two weeks later, her father, Luis, was dead.

They hadn't fought over the cartel. They'd fought over her.

The pain that came from the memories was almost too much to bear, like someone had slammed a dagger in her heart and twisted.

Emilio wasn't lying. She was a product of infidelity, the cause of violence and revenge. Some truths were too terrible and should never be brought out into the light.

Pandora's box. He'd warned her and now she wished she never knew.

Releasing a hiss, she brought her knees up to her chest and leaned against the headboard. She wanted to leave the villa that very instant, but she had to stay and see this through. For Dutch. For the marshals who were in danger. And maybe for her own sake, too.

As she got ready for the day, she set aside her personal issues and steeled herself for what had to be done.

She went downstairs, wondering if Emilio would show his face at breakfast.

Pushing through the door that led to the courtyard, she stepped outside and had her answer.

Of course he was there. He was playing host to them and he hadn't the decency to feel any shame. Emilio sat proud as a peacock, talking to Dutch, speaking in his animated way, waving his hands.

Isabel held her head high and strode to the table. "Good morning." She kept her tone light and neutral, hiding the enormous burden weighing on her.

Dutch stood, kissed her cheek and handed her the purse she'd forgotten last night. The way she'd rushed from dinner had been clumsy and reckless. She wouldn't blame him if he was furious with her, but when she glanced at him all she saw was compassion in his eyes.

"I'm pleased you joined us, my dear," Emilio said and took a sip of his fresh-squeezed orange juice.

"I'm not here for your pleasure. I have to eat." She sat and poured herself a cup of coffee.

"Ah, so you're still cross with me." His voice was mild and amused, and it made her want to scream. "I was hoping that tomorrow we could spend the day together. Go shopping, take a walk on the beach."

As if buying her new clothes and jewelry and taking an oceanside stroll would make everything better. "Prepare for disappointment," she said. "As soon as I'm done arranging your event, Dutch and I are leaving."

That wiped the smug look from Emilio's face. "I understand you're angry and want to punish me, but not like this. We're family. I love you, Isabel. You must find a way to embrace what you've learned. Or move beyond it. But I won't let you shut me out."

Emotions raged inside her. Isabel sucked in air, filling her lungs until she couldn't take in more. She shut her eyes and gritted her teeth, struggling for some semblance of control. *Keep it together. You have to do this.* "I won't be getting over it today or anytime soon."

Rodrigo entered the courtyard, came up to Emilio and whispered in his ear.

"Where do I know that name?" Emilio asked in response.

Again, Rodrigo whispered.

This time, Emilio's gaze flew up to Isabel and then whipped to Dutch. "Excuse me. I have a phone call I must take." He stood and walked into the house with Rodrigo following him.

"I'm sorry for losing it last night," Isabel said, mortified over how distracted and distraught she'd been. A complete wreck almost ruining everything.

"Don't worry about it." Dutch unzipped her purse and fished out the special tape.

God, she needed to quit getting sidetracked.

Working quickly, he ripped off a piece of tape, carefully took Emilio's glass by the top, and pressed the adhesive to where his thumb had been minutes ago.

Dutch peeled off the tape and held the small strip up to the light. There was a clear, solid print.

They got it.

Dutch lowered his hand seconds before the door to the house opened.

Emilio waltzed out with Rodrigo and Max. And two more guards.

She clenched her napkin in her lap. "Is everything all right?"

"I received a call from your ex-boyfriend, the business owner," Emilio said. "Chad Ellis. He's concerned about you and had some very interesting things to say."

Why would Chad call her uncle… Emilio? How did he even know she was there? "You shouldn't listen to anything he says. Chad hasn't gotten over the breakup. He's having difficulty letting go. I'm sure he's just trying to stir up trouble." To make her life miserable.

"That may be," Emilio said. "But I think Dutch can help me get to the bottom of it. Dutch, would you come with me?"

It might've sounded like a question, but it was an order.

"Can this wait?" Isabel asked, tension surging through her. "I need Dutch's help with the final preparations."

"No, it can't wait." Emilio delivered the statement like

the crack of a whip. "Max will stay at your side and assist you with anything you need."

Her stomach plummeted to her toes. The plan was to show Dutch the office and let him take it from there. She wasn't a marshal or a spy or remotely capable of handling this.

Dutch flashed a cool smile. "It's okay, Isabel." He got up and leaned over toward her. As he kissed her cheek, he slipped the strip of tape with the fingerprint into her hand. Then in her ear, he said, "The degausser needs to be in contact for two minutes. Leave me behind."

Her breath hitched. *No, no, no.*

She couldn't do this without him, and she certainly wasn't leaving him.

Isabel went to grab his arm and keep him there with her, but he stood, moving out of reach.

Dutch looked at Emilio. "There must be a misunderstanding. I'm sure we can clear it up."

"I hope so."

The two guards seized Dutch by his arms.

Her pulse skyrocketed. She didn't understand what was happening, but she knew it wasn't good. Dutch was in trouble.

"This is ridiculous. Where are you taking him?" she demanded.

"It's okay," Dutch said. "Don't worry about me. Focus on why you're here."

The auction. The hard drive.

She swallowed hard, hating the sensation of being trapped in an impossible situation.

Emilio spun on his heel and stalked back to the house with Rodrigo beside him, and the other guards hauled Dutch along.

What could Chad have said to upset Emilio?

The prospects had her growing lightheaded. With someone as deranged as Chad, there was no telling.

"What's going on?" she asked Max and sipped her coffee, trying to appear casual instead of freaked out.

He clasped his hands behind his back. With his sunglasses on, she couldn't read his eyes. "Nothing to concern you. Your uncle wants you to worry about the auction."

Part of her wanted to follow them and do everything in her power to help Dutch. But she had to think strategically, not based off emotion. This was the opportunity they'd been waiting for. One where her uncle and the main guards would be focused on something away from the office.

If she had any hope of pulling this off, it'd have to be now, while they were distracted, but the one thing they hadn't accounted for was Max.

"Once you're done eating," Max said, "I'll help you in any way you require. The great room is being set up now per your instructions."

To hell with breakfast.

"I've lost my appetite." She grabbed her purse and discreetly slipped the piece of tape with the fingerprint on it into an inner compartment of her bag. "Let's go take a look at the progress."

EMILIO LED DUTCH downstairs to an empty alcove in the wine cellar. Thanks to the stone walls, it was dank and ten degrees cooler than the rest of the house.

With a flick of his hand, Emilio gestured to his guards.

Someone hit Dutch across the back of the head. The world blurred and he fell off his feet. They slapped handcuffs on Dutch and lifted him from the ground, catching the chain on a hook suspended from the ceiling.

They must've used this space for interrogation before. It made sense. There were no windows and the stone walls would act as natural soundproofing.

"Chad Ellis tells me that you're a US marshal," Vargas said. "Care to explain?"

Dutch's head pounded. "Ellis is a psychopath. He's obsessed with Isabel. He can't be trusted."

Rodrigo punched Dutch and pain flared in his jaw. The taste of salty copper hit his tongue.

Vargas held up his cell phone. On the screen was a picture of Dutch, flashing his badge to the cops. "I asked Mr. Ellis to email those to me. He was more than happy to oblige."

Good old Chad. "Bet he was." Dutch spit blood from his mouth onto the stone floor.

"He even offered to drop off glossy five-by-sevens personally, but I said that wasn't necessary."

Did he follow them down here? Dutch hadn't been looking for a tail. So stupid of him. He'd been too preoccupied with Isabel, trying to help her contain her emotions, and prepare for how things might go. He hadn't considered the possibility. "Is Ellis in San Diego?"

"I'm the one asking the questions. Why are you here?"

"Ellis is dangerous." Dutch had underestimated him and look at where that had gotten him.

Vargas gave a curt nod. Rodrigo hit Dutch in the gut and a sharp pang shot through him.

"Why are you here?" Vargas asked. "Is it to stop the auction?"

"I'm here because you hired me to protect Isabel and invited me."

"Does Isabel know what you are?" Vargas asked.

Dutch shook his head. "No. She doesn't."

"Are you the one who told her the truth about me?"

"It was the Guzman cartel," Dutch said, determined to stick with the lie.

Another fist connected with his jaw.

"Anyone worth asking in the Guzman cartel is dead," Vargas said. "But I can't take your word for it. Not until I've broken you. When I do, you'll tell me everything I want to know."

The other two guards replaced Rodrigo and took turns punching Dutch in the sides, making his ribs and lungs ache.

"You don't have to," Dutch said, coughing. "Go to extremes. I'm a straight shooter."

"Not yet, but you will be. Even if it takes hours. Days. Eventually, everyone breaks."

Vargas had a point. Everyone's body did break, literally, but the spirit was a different beast, different rules.

A blow to his kidneys sent stabbing pain in a fiery arc across his back.

"You marshals have been a vexing thorn in my side, protecting my enemies and traitors." Vargas circled him. "Helping them testify against me, trying to dismantle my business. But the people coming here tonight to buy that hard drive will gladly root you out for me. *And* they'll pay me in the process. A firestorm from hell is about to rain down on every single marshal, not only in the San Diego office, but the entire state, and there's nothing you can do to stop it."

"Smart to get others to do your dirty work. Keep your hands clean. But I still don't know what you're talking about." Dutch had to stall long enough for Isabel to complete the mission, prevent the sale and get away.

During the car ride down here, he'd talked her through a worst-case scenario. If she got off the compound and made it to the rendezvous point four miles away off Del

Mar Heights Road, where Allison and Draper were waiting, it'd be worth every bruise, broken bone and scar.

As for Dutch, he'd trained for this in the army. Delta Force had fortified him, had ingrained one thing in him above all else. SERE—survival, evasion, resistance, escape.

Chapter Twenty-One

In the great room, Isabel told the staff where to place the remainder of the furniture and discussed lighting and music and ways to drive bids higher. For two hours, she gave directions on autopilot because as it turned out, Emilio was right. She could do this blindfolded, but all she thought about was Dutch, what was happening to him, and how to get clear from Max and up to Emilio's office.

Ten polished mahogany tables were set up, displaying sculptures, paintings and pieces of antiquity such as a spectacular fossilized gem of opalescent ammonite and a sought-after Roman coin, an ides-of-March denarius minted to celebrate the assassination of Julius Caesar. The items would catch the attention of any serious collector, but there was no reason for her uncle to sell them unless he was facing bankruptcy, which he wasn't.

The tenth table didn't have any art, only a laptop.

That was for the hard drive and to show off its contents. It had to be.

"It's always nice when I get to spend time with you," Max said, glued to her side.

Moving away from him around a table, she pulled on a polite smile. "That's sweet. You know, the caterer should be here any minute. Could you check the kitchen and see if they're prepared?"

They were using a vendor to supply the food and drinks, but only Emilio's personal staff was permitted on the premises during the auction. *For security reasons.*

Max's eyes flashed up to hers as a grin spread across his face. "I'm sure they're ready. Your uncle has such high standards."

Uncle. She had no idea how to think of Emilio. The very idea of him stirred conflicting emotions, dredged up uncomfortable memories that she had blocked out. But when she thought of him alone with Dutch, doing only God knows what to him, there was only impotent rage coupled with a pervasive sense of dread.

She couldn't lose Dutch. The connection between them had been sparked by his job, by Emilio's crimes, but their bond was real. Truer than anything she'd ever experienced.

"Because of those high standards, I need you to double-check," she said, pleasantly, but firmly. "We can't have anything go wrong this evening. The event is too important."

His grin fell as he studied her a long moment. "As you wish." He bowed, with great formality—for some reason he did things with flourish around her—and headed to the kitchen.

As soon as he disappeared out of sight, Isabel grabbed her purse and hurried for the staircase. Max would only be gone for a minute, two at the most, and she needed every precious second.

She took off her heels to move quietly and faster. Holding her shoes in one hand, she padded up the steps and ran down the hall to Emilio's office.

Grabbing the knob, she prayed the door wasn't locked.

The knob turned. She ducked inside.

She caught her breath, letting the slightest bit of re-lief seep through. Her gaze darted around, finding the painting that concealed the safe. Many times, she'd been in here with Emilio while he wrapped up work on his computer and they'd had a drink together and chatted. It was in this room that he'd steered her toward running an art gallery and away from taking a low-paying job at a museum.

Mentally kicking herself for letting him use her, she hurried to the original Renoir she'd purchased on his be-half at Sotheby's. She dropped her shoes, unlatched the right-side mounting on the painting and swung it out as one would a door.

The wall safe was sixteen by twenty, had a smooth matte-black finish, a biometric scanner and a handle. She pulled out the strip of tape, turned it the right way so his print was in the correct position and pressed it to the scanner.

A white beam of light ran across the thumbprint, once, twice, three times. Her chest squeezed, her pulse throb-bing. *Come on, work.* Tension wormed in her veins.

The lock disengaged and the safe door popped open. On the bottom shelf were various documents and two envelopes. One addressed to her and the other to Miguel.

She took the one that had *For Isabel* scrawled across the front. The envelope wasn't sealed. Quickly, she opened it and took out two sheets of paper.

One was a paternity test dated twenty-four years ago, stating that with 98.9 percent certainty Emilio was her father. Seeing it in black and white was like taking a blow to the chest.

The other sheet was a handwritten letter.

To My Beloved Isabel.

If you're reading this, then I am dead.

A wellspring of emotion bubbled up inside, but Isabel closed the letter and stuffed it into her purse. Now wasn't the time. All that mattered was the hard drive and saving Dutch. Not her deep-seated issues with her uncle who was in fact her father.

On the top shelf was an internal hard drive that'd been pulled from a laptop. There were three thumb drives beside it. Those could've been copies or contained completely unrelated data.

Not willing to take any chances, she snatched all four devices. She shoved them into the zippered compartment inside her purse and pushed the button on the degausser, activating it.

Isabel hurriedly closed the safe door, locking it, and put the painting back into place. She grabbed her shoes, whirled around to get the hell out of there and gasped.

Max stood in the doorway, watching her. "What are you doing?"

"Looking for Emilio." Her heart fluttered like a caged bird's wings. "I need to speak to him about Dutch."

His gaze swung to the painting, down to the shoes in her hand and back up to her face. "What were you doing in the safe? Better still, how did you get into the safe?" He closed the door and walked toward her.

"I wasn't in the safe." She slid her hand in her bag and felt around for the Pacifier.

"I'm not sure what your uncle would do if he knew you were sneaking around in his office, rifling through his safe. But I don't think you'd like to find out."

She gripped the base of the stun baton and positioned her finger over the switch to flick it on if necessary. "I just want to find Dutch and I want to go. Please."

He came closer, so light-footed that he didn't make a sound. His hard gaze pinned her in place.

Waiting for him to be within reach, she steadied her breath, calmed her thoughts down to one. Freedom.

Freedom from the villa, from Emilio, from the Vargas name, from its cursed legacy.

Max stepped up to her. Flipping the switch on the baton, she jammed it up toward him.

But he caught her by the wrist, not going for the baton itself as a typical attacker would naturally. There was a special *grab-guard* stun strip carrying an electric current that would shock anyone attempting to take it. Unfortunately, Max wasn't typical.

"You don't want to do that," he said in a low, flat voice.

Bright electric current pulsated and crackled from the tip of the Pacifier.

"Shut it off and put it back in your purse," he said, and she did as he demanded. "Dutch is in the cellar. You should hurry."

She scrunched her face in confusion. "Why are you telling me this?"

"If you can convince your uncle to let him go, I'll have his truck ready out front for you and ensure the gate is open."

Was this a trick? Was he going to double-cross her and use this to get in tighter with Emilio? "Why are you helping me?"

He shepherded her to the door. "Because you're a good person and you need it."

A thousand questions rushed through her head. "What about the other guards? Won't you get in trouble?"

"Heads will roll, but not mine. I'm Teflon. Nothing sticks to me." He put his hand on the knob. "Your uncle loves you, Isabel. More than you know. He'd do anything for you, which gives you the power. If you want to get Dutch out alive, use that love like a weapon."

What did he mean? How was she supposed to do that?

Max cracked the door open, peered out and then ushered her into the hall and down the stairs. He gave her a nod, like they were on the same team, and they went in separate directions.

She hustled to the basement door and flew down the steps barefoot, not wanting to alert Emilio of her presence too soon.

Once she reached the stone floor, the sound of flesh beating against flesh echoed in the corridor, making her quicken her pace. Fear for Dutch flooded her.

She followed the sounds and hesitated before going around the bend. Gathering her strength, Isabel put on her shoes and took a deep breath. She rounded the corner and stopped short at the sight of Dutch. Hanging from a hook, bloody and bruised.

"Isabel," Emilio said, his face growing pale. "You shouldn't be down here. I don't want you to see this."

He rushed to her, taking her by the arm and dragging her around the corner.

"Don't touch me." She yanked free of him. "Why are you beating him?"

"He's a US marshal. Spying on me through you. Did you know?"

"Of course not."

He eyed her as if trying to gauge her credibility. The doubt in his eyes was clear. "Go back upstairs. Let me handle this and tomorrow—"

"I'm not going anywhere without him."

"I'm afraid I can't let him go, my dear."

As she straightened, their gazes locked. She wanted to curse at him. To slap him. To scream at him for every awful thing he'd ever done. But there was only one way to get through to him and that was by using her wits. She drew on her anger, her hatred, her pain and even her love for Emilio, and she knew what to do.

"If he's a marshal like you claim," she said, "then obviously they know he's here. Right? If he disappears, that's only going to cause trouble for you. Let him go and at most, one of your minions gets charged with assault, but I'll tell Dutch not to pursue it."

He considered what she'd said. "After the auction, I'll release him. All right?"

Once the auction started, Emilio would find his safe empty. It wouldn't take him long to connect the dots to her. After he discovered that she'd erased the drive, he might not hesitate to kill Dutch out of sheer anger. "I'm not waiting. If you don't uncuff him right now and let us leave, I'll never give you what you want most."

He narrowed his eyes at her. "And what's that?"

"For me to call you Father." She let that hang in the air. The impact on him was immediate and splashed all over his face, but she had to dig deeper. "I remember your secret visits when I was little, how you played with me, always found ways to make me smile, how you used to tell me that you'd give me the world if you could."

"I thought you'd forgotten." His voice was forlorn. "I tried to be there for you as much as I could."

He had. She saw that now and clashing emotions ripped through her.

Isabel put her hand on his chest over his heart, hoping he still had one. "I don't want you to give me the world. I'm asking for Dutch. You owe him a life debt and I love him." It was fast and she despised what had brought her and Dutch together, but in her heart, it made sense. Felt right. Good. She wanted to explore the possibilities with him and if she didn't, it would be her biggest regret. "Let us leave, now, or I'll never speak to you again. You'll be as good as dead to me. On my mother's grave, I swear it."

His face and posture softened. Emotion clouded his eyes as his shoulders slumped forward. "You are my pride and joy. The one true light in my life. We'll get through this, Isa."

The sounds of a scuffle came from around the corner. Isabel and Emilio rushed down the corridor and around the bend to the alcove.

Still hanging from the hook, Dutch had managed to knock one of the bodyguards out. He swung his legs up, wrapped them around Rodrigo's neck, and using him as leverage, Dutch hoisted himself off the hook. Then he rotated, bringing Rodrigo crashing down onto the stone pavers.

Spinning up from the floor, Dutch pulled Rodrigo's gun at the same time the last standing guard drew his weapon.

Both men pointed the guns at each other in a standoff.

"Please," Isabel said, clutching Emilio's arm, not wanting Dutch to get shot. Though he seemed to have the situation under control.

"Lower your weapons," Emilio said, stepping between them. First the guard complied, and then Dutch. "You're free to leave."

Dutch gave her a questioning glance. She nodded, beckoning to him so they could get out of there. He wasted no time going to her side.

She wrapped her arms around him, needing to hold him for a moment. After a hard, quick hug, she looked at Emilio. "Thank you. Father."

Emilio nodded and they turned to leave, but then he said, "Dutch, I know the Marshals can't get a warrant in time to stop the auction. But if you interfere, in any way, there will be the harshest of consequences. I will show no mercy."

The threat had been issued in no uncertain terms, chilling Isabel's blood. "Let's go."

Emilio would keep his word, but for now, they needed to get out of there. They'd have to deal with the rest later.

She grabbed Dutch's hand and fled out of the cellar. He was close behind her going up the stairs and again at her side once they cleared the front door.

There were no guards in sight to question them and Dutch's truck was parked out front running as Max had promised.

"Good work," Dutch said, gesturing to the truck.

"I had help. From Max."

They hopped into the truck, Dutch shifted into Drive and hit the gas. They sped down the path toward the open gates and out onto the road. "Either he's got a crush on you or he's the FBI agent who's been deep undercover in the organization for a while."

"FBI?" Isabel glanced back through the windshield. No one followed. The road was clear.

She sucked in a deep breath, forcing air into her lungs. Her hands were trembling. She felt wrung out and nauseated.

"Thank you for coming to get me, even though I told you not to."

"I couldn't leave you behind." She put her hand on his leg. "I was afraid I'd lose you."

"You're not going to lose me. I'll be with you for as long as you want." He covered her hand with his. "Did you get it?"

She nodded. "Three thumb drives, as well. I took them all and used the degausser. They're in my purse."

"You're amazing."

"I feel like a wreck. Like I want to cry and sleep and rage and hold you all at the same time."

"Oh, honey."

"Not that I should complain. You're the one who's been beaten to a pulp." He had a split lip, and bruises on his face that would turn purple by tomorrow.

"I don't look that bad. Just a little banged up. They didn't break anything."

How could he take this in stride? He was the amazing one.

"We're almost there," he said, referring to the rendezvous point with the other two marshals. "Draper will take you to the hotel and get you settled. Relax in a bath, order some food, maybe take a nap while I go to the office."

"We're not going to be in a safe house?"

"Technically, you're not in witness protection and I have to get off the grid since I used my real name. The steps they're taking to keep us safe are a little unorthodox."

"How long will you be?"

"It might take a few hours to finalize our exit plan."

"What about McQueen? Brenda? I have to see her."

"Call the day care and give permission for a US marshal to pick up McQueen. As for Brenda, it's too dangerous for you now to go back to LA to see her. Your uncle, I mean dad, is going to know you helped me. He'll expect you to be there."

Isabel wrapped her arms around herself and shuddered at the thought of Emilio's consequences. A part of her was glad that his auction was going to be a disaster with him surrounded by a bunch of disappointed criminals. But she'd assumed she'd get to hug her best friend again and say goodbye. Not just disappear without a word.

They pulled up alongside a sedan.

Will and Allison got out, and Dutch lowered the window.

Allison passed Dutch his service weapon. "Don't leave us in suspense."

Isabel handed her the drives, the tape and degausser.

"Good job, you two." Allison glanced at Dutch. "The other thing?" she asked, cryptically.

He shook his head.

Allison muttered a string of profanity and lowered her head. "Vargas might not be able to sell the hard drive, but I bet he pored over every bit of information on the marshals in our office. We're going to need protection for our families."

Will nodded. "I'll square it away."

"Isabel had help from someone inside. Do you have any idea who the undercover FBI agent is?" Dutch asked.

"The FBI keeps their identities close hold," Will said. "All we know is his code name. Teflon."

Max is FBI? He'd moved up fast in the ranks. Emilio and Rodrigo trusted him implicitly.

"Sir, would you mind taking Isabel to the hotel," Dutch asked, "while Allison and I finish the rest? And it might be good if you stayed with her until I get back. No guards followed us here, but I'd feel better if she had protection while I'm gone."

"No problem," Will said. "We appreciate what you've done for the US Marshals Service, Ms. Vargas."

"What's it going to be?" Allison asked. "Double the work hashing out separate plans for each of you? Or will you two lay low for a while together?"

Isabel looked at Dutch, without a doubt in her heart, and said, "Together."

Chapter Twenty-Two

The hotel was on the waterfront of the San Diego Bay and the US Marshals Service had booked them a large suite with a separate living room, which gave Isabel her privacy and a generous amount of space to unwind in the bedroom, even though Will was there for protection.

Isabel dropped down on the comfy bed, wanting to sink into it, close her eyes and fall asleep. Maybe by the time she woke, Dutch would be there, and they could make love again. She'd missed sleeping with him last night. They needed time away together without the current stressors.

She took out her cell. Five percent battery life remaining. She'd left her charger back at the villa in her overnight bag.

Going through her phone, she found the number to the hospital in LA that she'd saved and dialed it.

"Hello," the female voice was familiar, but not Brenda. Someone older.

"Mrs. Reaver, is that you?"

"Yes, may I ask who's calling?"

"It's me, Isabel."

"Oh, sweetie, Brenda's been asking for you," Mrs. Reaver said.

"She's awake?" Isabel almost cried tears of joy.

"Yes. She's been lucid since we got here this morning. They just took her to run some tests, but she'll be back any minute. She can't wait to see you. Are you coming by soon?"

Her stomach clenched with regret. "No, I can't stop by. I'm in San Diego. Can you take down the number to my hotel? My phone is about to die."

"Sure."

Isabel rattled off the number, along with which room she was in and the fake name they were registered under. "When she gets back, if she's up to it, have her call me."

"She'll be up to it. She's dying to talk to you. It shouldn't be long."

"Okay. Thank you, Mrs. Reaver."

Isabel hung up. Her phone was at one percent and as good as dead. She climbed onto the bed and turned on the television, afraid to shower or fall asleep and miss Brenda's call.

She turned to a show about decorating houses for background noise more than anything else. One program ran into the next while her thoughts whirled, spinning around the last two days, coming back to Emilio and what she'd learned.

Glancing at her purse, she picked up her bag and put it in her lap. She thought of the letter and wondered if she was strong enough to read it. Curiosity won.

She read the letter, slowly, shocked by every line that brought tears to her eyes. Emilio had poured his heart and soul and pain out onto the page. He had written poetic lines about the depths of his love for her. Apologized for everything. Took responsibility for her mother's last days being difficult, for Luis's anger, for ripping the family apart with his selfishness, for her confusing childhood, for his brother's death. In the end, he begged her forgiveness.

He'd confessed to murder in the letter, sort of.

Could it be used as evidence to put him away? Would she use it against him?

He was flawed, corrupt and was guilty of monstrous things. But he was her father and regretted everything, despite what she had thought. Emilio was suffering, too, and he loved her deeply.

With her heart bleeding, she folded the letter, put it back in her bag and zipped her purse closed.

There was a loud knock at the main door of the suite.

"Hey," Will called from the living room. "You could've let me know you ordered room service. I'm hungry, too."

But she hadn't ordered any room service. She still didn't have an appetite and after reading that letter, it would be hours before she'd eat.

It was probably the wrong room.

There was a thud and then nothing besides the sounds of the two televisions.

She shut off her TV. "Will? Is everything all right?"

Something was wrong.

Under the door, she saw a shadow move up to the bedroom.

"Will?"

The door burst open. A man loomed, wearing a hotel jacket and holding a gun with a suppressor pointed at her.

A chilling, mind-numbing fear speared her. The man with scraggly hair, a mustache and glasses seemed vaguely familiar, but she couldn't place him.

"Hello, Isabel," he said.

That voice. Chad!

Her skin prickled, her jaw coming unhinged as she pressed back against the headboard.

"If you scream, I'll kill the US marshal and anyone else who comes running to help you, and when I leave here, I'll pay Brenda a visit in the hospital. Nod if you understand."

Isabel's breath snagged in her chest, but she nodded.

As Chad walked up to her, getting closer, she noticed he wore gloves and the suppressor was homemade—two PVC pipes, one inside the other, with some sort of end cap, attached to the barrel of the gun with a...*hose clamp*?

He pressed the gun to her temple. "Get up. Put on your shoes." His voice was deadly calm.

Trembling, she did as he told her, holding on tight to her purse.

"Come on. Walk." He nudged her forward.

"Are you going to hurt me?"

"Not unless you make me."

She stepped out of the bedroom and he pushed up against the back side of her, pressing the gun against her kidneys.

"When did you get a gun?" she asked, feeling cold down to her bones.

He hadn't owned a firearm before.

"When I found out Dutch used to be in Special Forces. I have a bullet with his name on it. I'd expected to find him in here with you. Not that one."

Isabel looked down at Will. Flat on his stomach, knocked out, but alive.

"Behave. If you don't and draw attention, I'll be forced to hurt others." Chad opened the door, keeping her close to him, and they walked down the empty hallway toward the stairwell.

Fear raced through her bloodstream. "How did you find me?"

"I suppose I can tell you since it doesn't matter anymore."

Why? God, why didn't it matter anymore? Was he going to kill her?

No, he wouldn't.

Chad wanted to be with her in a sick, abusive relationship that mirrored Brett and Mindy's, where she played the doting partner, tending to his every need, subjected to his every whim. He didn't want her dead.

"I found you through your phone," he whispered in her ear, his voice dark and pure evil. "I've been tracking you," he said, "listening to your calls, reading your emails and texts. I knew you were at this hotel, but not what room until you told Brenda's mom."

Isabel's heart nose-dived. How could she be so stupid? How could he be so twisted? So insane?

They entered the stairwell. Cupping her shoulder with his free hand, he steered her up the stairs. Not down, out of the hotel and into a car.

"Where are you taking me?" She clutched her purse against her belly and used the noise of their footfalls to cover the sound of the zipper as she inched it ever so slowly, in the slightest degrees, trying to get the opening wide enough for her hand without him noticing.

"It's a surprise."

She swallowed the scream churning in her belly, rising in her throat, and reminded herself there were cameras everywhere. Someone in security would see this, find it odd, report it.

They reached the landing one floor up and he opened the door.

In the hallway, there was a family leaving their room. Two kids were fighting, a girl and a boy, maybe eight and ten respectively. The boy hit his sister and their father snatched him up by the collar and reprimanded him as the mother closed the door. The girl smiled and stuck her tongue out at her brother behind her parents' backs.

A similar incident from her past flashed in her mind with her and Miguel. Emilio had been furious that Miguel had hurt her one day and when he'd been punished, she'd remembered feeling special, untouchable.

I have a brother.

"Keep quiet unless you want kids to die," Chad whispered to her.

The family seemed a million miles away as they walked to the elevator, not noticing them at all.

Chad stopped her in front of the first door on their left. Took out a key card and inserted it. The green light flashed, the door unlocked, and he shoved her inside.

Something creaked under her feet. She looked down. There was a thick layer of plastic covering the carpet. Industrial strength.

She stepped deeper into the room. Plastic covered the surfaces in the bathroom. More plastic had been placed over the rest of the carpet, the dresser, nightstands and the bed.

A large suitcase sat near the window.

Dear God. He intended to kill her.

Don't panic.

Too late. Her mind was being sucked down a dark vortex, chased by pure terror.

"There's security footage of us together. You can't," Isabel said, her brain reeling. It was all she could do not to beg, plead, offer to do anything he wanted, if he wouldn't go through with this.

He chuffed a smug laugh behind her back. "The security guards here make fifteen dollars an hour. I just paid two of them fifteen thousand each to ensure technical difficulties of the security cameras. Nothing is recording."

She spun around. Chad had put on a plastic coat and had the gun aimed at her head.

"I'm sorry…about everything," she said, lowering her eyes, recalling the time when she'd come out of the bathroom and overhead Mindy speaking in private to Brett. "Let me make it up to you."

The gun lowered to his side, and she looked up at him. Chad stepped closer with his brow furrowed. "If you're sorry, prove it."

"Take off your clothes," she said, digging her fingers in the leather of her purse, rubbing the outline of the stun baton. "Make love to me."

Chad backed up to the edge of the plastic near the dresser. The opening of her bag wasn't wide enough yet to get the baton out and his gaze was pinned to her, watching her every breath. He pulled the plastic down and placed the gun inside the bottom drawer. Then he replaced the thick covering.

Even if she got away from him, he'd overpower her before she'd get the gun.

Keeping the plastic coat on, he reached underneath it and removed something hidden behind his back. Steel glinted in the dim light from the drawn curtains. He tossed a large hunting knife with at least a nine-inch serrated blade on the floor in the corner of the room near the suitcase.

She'd be crazy to go after it and that was probably exactly what he was counting on.

Chad slipped the strap of her purse down her arm and tossed the bag onto the bed by the pillow. Her chest rose and fell with tight, anxious breaths.

Isabel kicked off her shoes, realizing at some point

that she'd need to run, sat on the bed, scooting up, and lay back as close to her purse as she could get.

Chad pushed her down against the mattress, the eerie sound of the plastic creaking underneath her. Grasping her jaw, he kissed her aggressively, almost violently.

Worse, she had to sell him on her performance as she kissed him back. Her stomach roiled. With her right hand, she stroked his hair and her fingers found the strange strands of the wig. She groped for her purse with her left hand, gently, quietly, trying not to disturb the plastic and draw his attention to what she was doing.

Chad undid his belt and unzipped his pants, the distinct sounds slicing through her ears, echoing in her soul. He lowered his full weight on her, pinning her to the bed.

Hot bile welled in her throat. The backs of her eyes stung with tears, but she surrendered herself to the kiss. To survive, she had to.

Her fingers snagged soft leather. She reeled it closer, drawing the zipper open more.

Chad's hands wandered, up her skirt, cupping her butt, groping her breast. She shuddered in revulsion.

God, please get me out of this. Tears leaked from her eyes.

She dug her hand in her bag and rummaged for the baton.

"I missed this, Isabel. Missed us." His eyes burned with his obsession. "I just want it to go back to the way it was."

She cringed. The fear he'd cultivated in her over the past several months bloomed, like nightshade in the darkness. Invasive vines, strangling, poisoning, blocking out the sunlight and smothering every good thing.

Don't give up! Don't let him win!

Her fingers grasped the baton. She pulled it from her purse and swung with all her might.

Crack!

The shaft of the baton struck hard against the side of Chad's head, knocking him off her. Isabel kicked him, hard, with both feet, propelling him to the floor.

She launched herself up from the bed, holding the Pacifier and leaving her purse. She ran to the door, grabbed the knob and pulled.

It didn't budge. The door was stuck. For a split second she thought of Dutch.

She tried the door again. Still nothing. She looked around, frantic to get out.

There was a doorstop wedged under the door.

Plastic squeaked as Chad righted himself. Isabel bent down and wiggled the rubber stopper. Desperation sizzled in her blood. She wrenched it from under the door.

As she stood, Chad charged toward her.

No!

She yanked the door handle.

The safety latch at the top caught and the door wouldn't open.

Chad was almost on her.

Her heart was hammering so fast that she could barely breathe. She flicked the switch on the stun baton, heard the crackle of electricity and lunged at him. Chad snatched the grab guard and an electric current flooded his body. His muscles spasmed and his eyes rolled up into the back of his head. She jammed the prods into his neck. He lost his balance, crumpling to the floor. Then she held on for a couple of seconds longer to be sure he was down.

Isabel flipped the safety latch off and threw open the door. She pressed across the threshold to the stairwell.

Ran back downstairs one flight barefoot. But the stun baton slipped from her hand over the railing. It clattered along the descent several flights below.

Damn it.

She bolted onto her floor and dashed to her room. "Will?" Isabel pounded on the door. "Will!"

Was he still unconscious?

Adrenaline propelling her, she hurried for the elevator. She glanced over her shoulder, looking for Chad. The stun baton wouldn't immobilize him for long.

She slapped the button, summoning a car.

The *L* was illuminated. It was in the lobby and she was on the sixth floor. She hit it again and again, knowing it wouldn't make the elevator arrive any faster, but what choice did she have?

Number two lit up. Then three.

At the far end of the hall, the door opened to the stairwell.

Even though she already knew it was him, she pivoted to see Chad.

Isabel slapped the button repeatedly. The car was at the fourth floor.

Growling like a wild animal, Chad bulldozed down the hall with the hunting knife raised in his hand, his face taut with blind rage. The fury pumping through him was terrifying.

If he reached her, got his hands on her, he'd kill her.

Dear God, help me! He was almost to her.

Panic exploded in her chest. She hit the button again, cursing and screaming.

A chime sounded, and the elevator doors opened. Isabel stumbled inside and landed against a wall of solid muscle.

"Isabel!" Dutch's face was ashen and bruised as he

held her closer. He glanced up, drew his weapon and put her behind him. "Stop! Or I'll shoot," he warned.

But Chad kept charging, yelling obscenities, shouting hateful, violent things.

A shot rang out. The force of the bullet stopped Chad and made him stumble. Blood poured down his body from the chest wound.

Was it over? Would he just die already and let this nightmare end?

Chad lumbered forward a few quick steps, raising the knife again.

As if reading her mind, Dutch stepped out of the elevator, and fired once more. The second bullet to the head flung Chad backward to the floor.

He lay in the hall, still, his eyes open and unmoving.

The demon was dead.

Dutch turned, wrapping her in his arms.

She fell against him, collapsing in the safety of his heat and strength. It was all she could do not to break down. Relief cascaded through her as she clung to him. "Oh, Dutch."

A few guests opened their doors and peeked out. Others left their rooms, gathering in the hallway.

"Are you okay?" His arms tightened around her.

"I will be." Now that he was there.

"God, I'm sorry it took me so long."

She buried her face in his chest, took in his scent, relieved, comforted. Safe. "You were right on time."

Epilogue

Magical. Sitting beside Dutch in front of their campfire, Isabel stared up at the majestic aurora borealis. Green ribbons of light tinged pink danced high in the sky. Pure, vibrant waves of energy. It was wondrous.

The US Marshals Service had flown them on a military plane to Eielson Air Force Base near Fairbanks, Alaska. Arrangements had been made for them to embark on the last camping tour of the season to Chena Hot Springs to catch the northern lights.

Conditions had to be optimal for them to see it. The night as dark as possible, little to no cloud cover and there had to be enough solar activity. Those elements had converged perfectly, gifting them with this.

Sort of like her relationship with Dutch. It boggled her mind to think of all the factors that had to sync up at the right time, in the right way, to bring them together.

Dutch being picked for the assignment. Her needing someone like him to walk into her life. Chad spinning out of control. The auction that never happened because they'd stopped it.

Kismet.

Emilio must be livid, plotting his revenge. She'd considered showing Dutch the letter her father had written her, had contemplated using it against him, but she couldn't and had burned it.

There was no denying her father was a monster, capable of unspeakable things. But he loved her, and she loved him. In a weird way, if it weren't for him, she never would have met Dutch, the man who might end up being the love of her life.

Even more remarkable, roughing it in the Alaskan wilderness, without the danger and adrenaline and creature comforts, they were truly happy together.

"This is incredible." She rested her head on his shoulder, snuggling against him in the frigid night air, thankful for everything. From being with Dutch to her toasty goose-down puffer coat.

He wrapped his arm around her and kissed her head. "More hot chocolate, beautiful?"

"No, I'm good." She brought her denim-covered legs up to her chest, basking in this moment. The serenity. The safety. The splendor. "Thank you, for getting Allison to make this trip happen."

"She just wanted us off the grid. The farther away from civilization the better. She didn't care where."

"You know what I mean."

"I know. I love you," he said, tightening his arm around her. "Once it's safe, we'll visit Brenda. I promise."

Who knew how long it would take before she'd be able to see her friend again?

Max was working hard to build a case against Emilio. He was smart, cunning. If anyone in the FBI could do it, it was him. *Teflon.*

"I love you, too," she said.

McQueen's collar jingled as he got up and came out of their tent. With his ears up, he stood on alert, staring at the woods. Then he started barking.

Dutch fished his gun out of his backpack, stood and aimed in the direction that McQueen was looking.

"Stand down, Haas," said a man coming out of the tree line, wearing a parka and backpack. "It's me, Captain Williams."

He was their liaison from the air base.

"What are you doing out here?" Dutch asked.

"It took me two days to find this campsite." Captain Williams approached, looking winded. "You guys really picked a remote location. I couldn't even get here with a vehicle."

"What's up?" Dutch asked.

"We got a call for you two on base from Deputy Marshal Allison Chen-Boyd. Her son's been kidnapped, and she needs to speak with you."

"Oh, God." Isabel jumped to her feet.

"Do you have a satphone we can use?" Dutch asked.

"You can't," Captain Williams said. "We might even have to trek back to base. The aurora borealis occurs during solar storms. The massive bursts of charged particles create satellite disturbances and mess with our satphones."

Isabel swallowed around the cold lump in her throat. "Does she know who took her son?"

"She said that you guys would know," Captain Williams said.

"This is my fault," Isabel said. "He took Allison's son because of what I did."

Dutch grasped her shoulders. "No, sweetheart. He's mad at the Marshals. Not you."

"He gave me a letter. Confessed to murdering his brother. I should've told you, but I burned it."

"What?" Dutch sucked in a breath. "Did he explicitly state that he pulled the trigger? Did he write the words,

I killed him? I ordered a hit? Or was he vague and left some loophole?"

The exact wording had been vague, implied things that led her to draw conclusions.

"He wrote that it was his fault the family was torn apart and he was sorry. That he was responsible for Luis's anger, for his death. I know what he meant, but the verbiage wasn't explicit." Thinking back on it, he hadn't even admitted to having an affair on paper.

But she couldn't shake the sense of guilt. Maybe if she'd stayed behind in San Diego, she could've prevented this.

"He never would have left an incriminating letter anywhere that could send him to prison," Dutch said. "Besides, he has the best lawyers that money can buy at his disposal. They would've had it thrown out of court because we didn't get it with a warrant. This is not on you."

"We have to help her get her son back," Isabel said, panic bubbling in her stomach.

He nodded with a worried look.

"What is it? What aren't you telling me?"

"It took Captain Williams two days to find us. Kidnapping cases where there's ransom or demands are usually resolved within forty-eight to seventy-two hours. One way or the other."

One way was rescuing the hostage. The other?

Her heart sank. She couldn't bear to think about it.

If her father took that child, then she needed to speak to him, bargain, negotiate. She'd do whatever he wanted as long as Allison got her son back.

"I think this is out of our hands," Dutch said. "Beyond our control." He brought her into a hug. "It's going to be okay. You'll see. They kidnapped the wrong kid."

"What do you mean?"

"Allison would move heaven and earth for her son and her husband works on the FBI's Hostage Rescue Team. They're trained by Delta Force. If anyone can get him back, it's HRT."

It was a small comfort but did nothing to erase her sense of guilt or helplessness.

Dutch pulled back and met her gaze. "We did the right thing stopping the auction."

"And no good deed goes unpunished."

He shook his head. "That narrative isn't true. Good will prevail. And love might not conquer all, but it's pretty freaking powerful."

Staring into his eyes, Isabel felt the impact of those words, deep in her heart, and hope welled. They'd stopped the auction and had beaten Chad. Against the odds, they'd won together.

He put his forehead to hers, their noses touching. In his arms, she chose to believe in that different narrative. One of goodness and love, where it would all work out.

* * * * *

COMING NEXT MONTH FROM

(H) HARLEQUIN

INTRIGUE

Available December 1, 2020

#1965 TOXIN ALERT
Tactical Crime Division: Traverse City • by Tyler Anne Snell
After a deadly anthrax attack on Amish land, TCD's biological weapons expert Carly Welsh must work with rancher Noah Miller to get information from the distrustful members of the community. But even their combined courage and smarts might not be enough against the sinister forces at work.

#1966 TEXAS LAW
An O'Connor Family Mystery • by Barb Han
Sheriff Colton O'Connor never expected to see Makena Eden again. But after she darts in front of his car one night, the spark that was lit between Makena and Colton long ago reignites. With a rogue cop tracking them, will they walk away—together?

#1967 COWBOY UNDER FIRE
The Justice Seekers • by Lena Diaz
Following the death of her friend, Hayley Nash turns to former cop Dalton Lynch for help. Dalton finds working with the web expert to be an exercise in restraint—especially when it comes to keeping his hands to himself.

#1968 MOUNTAIN OF EVIDENCE
The Ranger Brigade: Rocky Mountain Manhunt
by Cindi Myers
Eve Shea's ex is missing. Although her romantic feelings for the man are long gone, her honor demands she be a part of Ranger Commander Grant Sanderlin's investigation. But as more clues emerge, is Eve's ex a victim—or a killer targeting the woman Grant is falling for?

#1969 CRIME SCENE COVER-UP
The Taylor Clan: Firehouse 13 • by Julie Miller
Mark Taylor can put out a fire, but Amy Hall is a different kind of challenge. He's determined to keep her safe—but she's just as certain that she doesn't need his protection. As they hunt down an arsonist, will they trust each other enough to surrender...before a madman burns down their world?

#1970 THE LAST RESORT
by Janice Kay Johnson
When Leah Keaton arrives at her family's mountain resort, armed insurgents capture her, but Spencer Wyatt, the group's second in command, takes her under his protection. Spencer is an undercover FBI agent, but to keep Leah safe, he's willing to risk his mission—and his life.

YOU CAN FIND MORE INFORMATION ON UPCOMING HARLEQUIN TITLES, FREE EXCERPTS AND MORE AT HARLEQUIN.COM.

HICNM1120

SPECIAL EXCERPT FROM

(H)HARLEQUIN
INTRIGUE

Sheriff Colton O'Connor is stunned when a stormy night brings him face-to-face with a woman from his past. Seeing Makena Eden again is a shock to his system... especially once he realizes she's hiding something. As the rain turns torrential, Colton has to get to the heart of what Makena is doing in his small hometown. And why her once-vibrant eyes look so incredibly haunted...

Keep reading for a sneak peek at
Texas Law, *part of An O'Connor Family Mystery,*
from USA TODAY *bestselling author Barb Han.*

Makena needed medical attention. That part was obvious. The tricky part was going to be getting her looked at. He was still trying to wrap his mind around the fact Makena Eden was sitting in his SUV.

Talk about a blast from the past and a missed opportunity. But he couldn't think about that right now when she was injured. At least she was eating. That had to be a good sign.

When she'd tried to stand, she'd gone down pretty fast and hard. She'd winced in pain and he'd scooped her up and brought her to his vehicle. He knew better than to move an injured person. In this case, however, there was no choice.

The victim was alert and cognizant of what was going on. A quick visual scan of her body revealed nothing obviously broken. No bones were sticking out. She complained about her hip and he figured there could be something there. At the very least, she needed an X-ray.

HIEXP1120

Since getting to the county hospital looked impossible at least in the short run and his apartment was close by, he decided taking her to his place might be for the best until the roads cleared. He could get her out of his uncomfortable vehicle and onto a soft couch.

Normally, he wouldn't take a stranger to his home, but this was Makena. And even though he hadn't seen her in forever, she'd been special to him at one time.

He still needed to check on the RV for Mrs. Dillon…and then it dawned on him. Was Makena the "tenant" the widow had been talking about earlier?

"Are you staying in town?" he asked, hoping to get her to volunteer the information. It was possible that she'd fallen on hard times and needed a place to hang her head for a couple of nights.

"I've been staying in a friend's RV," she said. So, she was the "tenant" Mrs. Dillon had mentioned.

It was good seeing Makena again. At five feet five inches, she had a body made for sinning underneath a thick head of black hair. He remembered how shiny and wavy her hair used to be. Even soaked with water, it didn't look much different now.

She had the most honest set of pale blue eyes—eyes the color of the sky on an early summer morning. She had the kind of eyes that he could stare into all day. It had been like that before, too.

But that was a long time ago. And despite the lightning bolt that had struck him square in the chest when she turned to face him, this relationship was purely professional.

Don't miss
Texas Law *by Barb Han,*
available December 2020 wherever
Harlequin Intrigue books and ebooks are sold.

Harlequin.com

HIEXP1120